RISING
Star

RISING *Star*

A Shooting Stars Novel

TERRI OSBURN

Montlake
Romance

Published by Montlake Romance, Seattle

www.apub.com

Amazon, the Amazon logo, and Montlake Romance are trademarks of Amazon.com, Inc., or its affiliates.

ISBN-13: 9781542046893
ISBN-10: 1542046890

Cover design by Eileen Carey

Printed in the United States of America

For Mom and Dad. Because when your twenty-two-year-old said she was moving to Nashville alone to work in the music business, you didn't flinch. Much.

Chapter 1

"I haven't seen a penis in ninety days. Hurry your little heinie up, Charley, before all the good ones are gone."

Ruby Barnett's words hung in the August heat like granny panties on a clothesline, and Charley Layton couldn't help but shake her head. After nearly three months of working with the bawdy woman, she was no longer shocked by Ruby's crass, if honest, outbursts. As a longtime radio personality, some might think that the older woman would possess a stronger filter than most, but they'd be wrong.

All the same, Charley picked up her pace as the distant sound of singing hopefuls, ever present in this part of downtown Nashville, was interrupted by an unexpected voice.

"I'll show you mine, Ruby," offered a deep tenor from behind them. "Come have a look."

Charley turned to see the incorrigible flirt Trevor Mulligan relieving himself next to his pickup truck in a far corner of the parking garage. The good old boy from Tulsa couldn't carry a tune to save his life, but he could write a hit song like nobody's business.

The voice that woke Nashvillians five days a week on Eagle 101.5 replied, "Gee, Trevor, if I'd known you were going to be so accommodating, darling, I'd have packed my magnifying glass before leaving the house."

The elevator doors slid open, and the two ladies hopped in. Trevor hustled to join them, struggling with his zipper as he shuffled along. Flashing an evil smile, Ruby pressed the button that shut the doors in his face.

"That's rule number fourteen," she said, nodding toward the closed doors. "Never tickle the first pickle that comes along. There's always a better specimen to be had. And in this case, a cleaner, less gnawed-on version."

Poor Trevor. Charley didn't know him well, having only met him twice, but he seemed like a nice enough guy. Not very selective, as Ruby vulgarly pointed out, but charming in his own way.

As for the rule thing, ranking at number fourteen meant Ruby had learned this lesson early in life. Charley's would-be mentor lived by a long list of rules and rattled off life lessons on an almost daily basis. Just this morning, she'd shared rule number thirty-seven—never say "hand-applied" and "express lube" in the same sentence.

To be fair, they'd been broadcasting live from a car wash, and Charley had only been reading the talking points she'd been given.

"Trevor isn't so bad," Charley murmured, dabbing beads of sweat from her forehead.

"If you want to wait for him outside, I'm sure he'd happily make you the same offer he made me."

"I'm not in the market for any pickle, gnawed on or not," Charley replied as the doors once again opened.

Ruby snorted. "So you keep saying. But a woman needs a man to light her fuse every now and then. If you ask me, a little birthday sex sounds like the perfect way to celebrate twenty-five years on this spinning heap of dirt."

Exiting the garage behind the saucy redhead, Charley inhaled clean air, hot and heavy as it was. "I'll celebrate twenty-five with a couple beers and some laughs with friends. That's good enough." And safer, too, she thought. Men were much too fickle—and all too likely to leave destruction in their wake.

"That wasn't cool, Ruby," said Trevor as he stepped from the stairwell. "I'm already late for the gig at Legends."

Without missing a beat, she said, "Then maybe you shouldn't have stopped to take a piss in public."

Trevor's parting gesture conveyed his opinion of Ruby's response.

"I don't think he liked your advice," Charley said, laughing.

"I'll try to recover from the slight," she replied with dripping sarcasm.

They strolled half a block down Second Avenue, serenaded from every open door they passed, to reach their destination. The line for the popular country venue stretched to the corner at Broadway, where another four blocks of honky-tonks welcomed natives and tourists alike. Eager two-steppers, perspiring beneath their cowboy hats, waited anxiously to sweat even more on the enormous Wildhorse Saloon dance floor.

As Ruby and Charley slipped through the entrance, calls of "We love you, Ruby!" and "Why are they cutting in line?" penetrated the stifling humidity. Being semi-famous to the locals did not mean tourists gave two bits who you were.

Classic Brooks & Dunn pulsed through the club as they made their way to the bar not far from the entrance. Waitresses in short shorts and well-worn cowboy boots sliced through the crowd, trays balanced skillfully above their heads. Ruby ordered two beers while Charley slipped into tourist mode, gawking at her surroundings.

A swirling design, etched to perfection in the custom floor tiles, drew the eye toward the endless expanse of glistening dance floor. The life-size porcelain equines scattered about, all done up in their most dapper western gear, brought a smile to her lips. And the two-steppers twirling in front of the empty stage, showing off their moves with style and grace, reminded her of weekends back home in Kentucky, when she'd spun away more than one Saturday night at the Barn Dance.

"I'm going backstage to check in," Ruby said, handing Charley her drink. "You coming?"

"I'll wait for Matty."

Matilda Jacobs—Matty to her friends—was stunningly beautiful, terrifyingly brilliant, and unapologetically late for everything. At twenty-nine, she'd been navigating the Nashville nightlife for seven years and had grown disturbingly cynical. That she'd agreed to wade into what she considered shallow waters for even one night signified how much she liked her new roommate.

The depth of the dating pool meant little to Charley. She had one priority—to build her career in radio. A relationship would only be a distraction she didn't need or want.

"I'm here," called Matty, platinum locks catching the lights as she squeezed between two burly patrons. "Did I miss anything?"

"Nope. Ruby and I walked in a few minutes ago." Charley had no idea how Matty had skipped the line, but assumed she'd charmed a bouncer while flashing her radio station credentials.

Sculpted brows arched. "Then I'm earlier than usual." She nodded to the bartender who'd appeared out of nowhere. "Glass of red, please."

Dimples materialized as the man grinned in response. "Coming right up."

As usual, Matty didn't notice the adulation in the young man's eyes. Though Charley considered herself pretty enough—reasonably sized nose, good natural highlights, tolerable legs—men did not fall at her feet, nor did they hop to do her bidding. Of course, Matty also had the petite thing going for her. Even in four-inch heels, she stood a solid two inches shorter than Charley's five foot eight. To win in both looks and brains should have been against some law of nature, but as her roommate, Charley knew that Matty shaved her toes and had her mustache waxed every six weeks.

Proof that true perfection did not exist.

"So where is our redheaded wrecking ball?" Matty asked.

Charley grinned. "She's backstage."

The bartender returned with her glass of wine, saying, "Here you go, darling." Matty withdrew a twenty from her clutch purse, but he waved her off. "Compliments of the gentleman down the bar."

Her perfect features contorted as she shoved the money back in her purse. "I hate this game. Now the idiot is going to come over here and try some stupid line." She said this without bothering to even glance in her benefactor's direction. Charley succumbed to curiosity and leaned to the right to find a skinny guy in a ball cap staring at her friend. He wasn't bad, but he certainly wasn't anywhere close to being in Matty's league. She couldn't help but give him points for confidence.

"He hasn't left his stool," she shared, losing her breath when the man next to Mr. Ball Cap turned around.

Black cowboy hat, intense blue-gray eyes, and a scruff-covered chin straight out of a high-fashion magazine topped a slender yet muscled frame. The slight crook in his nose was the only visible flaw, but it added character to what might otherwise have been considered a too-pretty face. As he spoke to the man beside him, full lips parted to reveal straight white teeth, and Charley couldn't look away. Interest stirred as Ruby's words floated through her mind.

A woman needs a man to light her fuse every now and then.

Charley's fuse was good and lit, and the man hadn't even made eye contact. And then he did, and her mind went blank the same moment her knees threatened to give out. She didn't smile, and neither did he. In fact, he looked away, showing no interest at all. Ball Cap gave what looked to be a passionate speech, and the Adonis turned once more. This time, he shook his head, and Charley went cold.

Screw him, she thought. He probably sucked in bed anyway.

"Dude, she's going to cut you off at the knees," Dylan Monroe assured his drummer. "That blonde wouldn't piss on you if you were on fire."

Casey Flanagan remained undeterred. "Come on, man. She's the best-looking woman in here. Go big or go home, right?"

"You'll be going home alone if you shoot for that one. Why not try for the brunette?" he asked. "She's a bit tall for my taste, but her eyes are nice."

Her lips were nice, too. And the loose waves draped around her shoulders probably smelled good. Subtle and soft, unlike the women Dylan often encountered in the clubs. The ones with teased-out hair who considered musicians collectibles instead of real people. He'd ventured down that lane long enough to grow tired of meaningless one-night stands.

Casey spun his hat around backward. Never a good sign. "I'm going in, buddy. You distract her friend."

"I'm not going to help you go down in flames," he declared, despite a sudden urge to make the brunette's acquaintance.

"You owe me, bro. We wouldn't have anything to celebrate if my girlfriend hadn't given you the scoop on Shooting Stars."

"*Ex*-girlfriend," Dylan corrected. "Now she's your hostile roommate, as well as mine. Which means she would have told me about the new label looking for acts with or without you."

A tip that had led to a new record deal and now his first single released to the world. Two realities that came with more pressure than he'd expected, though he'd done his best to keep the mounting anxiety at bay.

Dylan's eyes strayed to the dark-haired woman once more. An air of confidence shone in the set of her shoulders. Not the typical bravado of a pretty face mixed with liquid courage, but true grit. The type that would challenge a man and make him earn her time and attention. The kind of girl he'd started to believe didn't exist.

"What do you think Pamela is going to do if you bring a chick home?" Dylan asked his friend.

"A woman like that has her own place," Casey countered. "Besides, Pamela doesn't get a say in who I sleep with. Not anymore."

No matter what his friend said, Dylan knew the truth. Casey loved Pamela, and she loved him. A simple conversation would straighten out the misunderstanding that had led to their breakup, and they'd be back to boffing like bunnies in no time. Too bad neither would drop their pride long enough to listen.

"You don't want to do this," he warned half-heartedly now.

It wasn't as if Casey had never been shot down before. He was a big boy. He could take it. And Dylan would have a few minutes with the woman now eying them suspiciously. When she caught him looking, one slender brow arched high, serving as both a dare and a warning, he couldn't help but smile at the possibilities.

"You don't see that every day," he mumbled, unaware that he'd spoken aloud.

"You're telling me," Casey agreed. "I bet those lips taste like heaven. Dollars to doughnuts she smells good, too."

"Honeysuckle," Dylan guessed.

"Nah," his friend replied. "Something expensive. Something better than Pamela's wildflower stuff."

The comment broke the spell, and Dylan glanced to the man beside him. "You're already comparing her to Pam, and you haven't even met her. Why don't you give up and admit that those pictures weren't for you?"

Casey shook his head. "If she doesn't trust me, there's nothing to talk about."

Dylan rolled his eyes. "A woman finds pictures of a naked woman on her boyfriend's phone, she's going to assume he's up to no good. What else was she supposed to think?"

Green eyes turned his way. "She was supposed to ask me about them and then believe me when I told her the truth."

"But you didn't tell her the truth," he pointed out.

"She didn't give me the chance." Shaking off the topic, the drummer focused on the blonde once more. "Doesn't matter. I've got my eye on something better."

"Buddy, that woman is a ten. You're a five at best. Maybe a six if she's had enough to drink, and she doesn't look the least bit tipsy."

"You distract her friend, and I'll handle the rest," Casey said, rising off his stool. "Come on."

Dylan followed with a resigned sigh, keeping his own enthusiasm in check. After all, he could be wrong about the taller woman. In the last year alone, he'd been mistaken on two other occasions, resulting in two failed attempts at real relationships. But then, neither had intrigued him with a single look. His gut said there was something here. Something worth pursuing.

And if not, then he and Casey would crash and burn together.

"They're coming this way," Charley hissed, bracing herself for the pretty boy's disdain.

"I'll take care of this," Matty said with a frustrated huff. "They'll be on their way in seconds."

Charley had yet to witness her friend in action. This was going to be fun.

"Thanks for the drink," Matty said before the ball cap guy could spout his opening line. He'd turned the hat around, revealing a field of freckles sprinkled across his nose and cheeks. "I'm not interested in another one," she informed him. "Or anything else you have to offer."

"I haven't offered anything else," he replied with a smile. "Yet."
Charley gave him credit for taking the direct hit with grace. "What's
your name?"

Ice-blue eyes narrowed. "Matilda," she answered.

"Pretty name," Ball Cap returned. Very smooth. "I'm Casey
Flanagan."

"I don't care," Matty replied, her pink lips curled in a fake smile.
"My friend and I are here to celebrate her birthday. We aren't looking
for company."

As Matty delivered the blow-off, the sexy figure in the black hat
sauntered over to Charley.

"Hi."

She couldn't believe he'd deigned to speak to her. "Hi," she replied,
knocked off balance by his nearness. God, he smelled good.

"Happy birthday."

The timbre of his voice sent heat dancing up her cheeks. And
ignited a few embers in lower regions as well. "Thanks."

"What do you do?" Ball Cap asked Matty.

"I eat guys like you for breakfast."

Charley nearly choked. She'd given a man the brush-off a time or
two, but she would *never* be as badass as Matty Jacobs.

"Want to dance?" asked the man in the black hat. He'd clearly been
cast in the role of wingman, charged with getting Charley out of the
way.

Before she could answer, Matty's admirer said, "I'm willing to take
the risk."

The blonde smiled. "I bet you are."

In the two and a half months they'd been roommates, Charley had
never seen Matty smile at a man. Especially not like that. If Ball Cap
could achieve such a feat, he deserved his shot.

"Sure," Charley said to the cowboy. "I'll dance."

The moment she slid her hand into his, the room shifted beneath her feet. With a firm but tender grip, he led her to the dance floor, spun her into the shifting crowd as if they'd rehearsed the move a dozen times, and set them both into motion without bumping into any of the other dancers. Lucky for Charley that she'd been two-stepping since junior high, because her partner could hold his own with the pros.

"Is your friend's name really Matilda?" he asked.

Considering he had yet to ask for Charley's name, she stiffened with irritation. "Yes."

"And is it really your birthday?"

Eyes locked on his collar, she offered another one word answer. "Yes."

The song rolled into the next, but her partner showed no indication of ending their dance.

"Twenty-two?"

She met his gaze. "Twenty-five."

Full lips split into a panty-melting grin. "Good to know. I'm Dylan," he offered, changing direction so that she no longer danced backward. "What's your name?"

All too aware of how easily this man could charm her into things Charley had no business doing, she ignored his question and asked one of her own.

"How long are we going to keep this up?"

"That depends." He shrugged, causing his biceps to flex beneath her touch. "Did you have some other activity in mind?"

Ignoring the implication, and the urge to examine the rest of his muscles, she said, "We both know that you only asked me to dance to give your friend a clear shot at my roommate. There's no need to pretend you're actually interested in me."

Pulling her closer, Dylan whispered into her ear. "What makes you think I'm not interested?"

Charley shivered as his breath caressed her neck. The distraction caused her to lose her footing, but Dylan kept her upright with little effort.

"I saw you across the bar," she explained, determined to keep her senses. "You were obviously unhappy about your friend's choice of targets."

A deep chuckle rumbled through his chest, sending sensual vibrations through hers. "I was informing my friend that he was about to get his ass handed to him. Miss Matilda is out of my boy's league, as I'm sure you'd agree, but Casey was hell-bent on making a fool of himself."

Craning her neck to peer through the crowd, Charley saw Matty toss her head back in laughter. "Don't look now, but I think he's proving you wrong."

Another quick turn and Charley's back was to the bar.

"I'll be damned," Dylan mumbled.

The full smile would have been enough to turn her inside out, but the moment he tipped the hat up to reveal a twinkle in his blue eyes, Charley knew she was in trouble. Big trouble.

"You've done your duty, then," she said. "No need to keep up the charade."

The smoke-gray eyes dropped to hers, sweeping the breath from her lungs. They'd stopped moving.

"You still haven't told me your name," he said, his attention dropping to her lips.

"I'm Charley." Voice cracking, she cleared her throat and tried again. "My name is Charley."

A slow song filled the air, lazy and seductive, and Dylan shifted into a gentle sway that lit every circuit in her system.

"Nice to meet you, Charley."

Unsure how to respond, she nodded. "Nice to meet you, too, Dylan."

As if they'd signed a truce, her partner tucked her hand atop his heart and rested his chin against her hair. Unable to help herself, Charley surrendered, if for only one song, and relaxed into his arms.

Chapter 2

Dylan had held enough women to know the effect they could have on a man. Both physically and mentally. But the heady mix of bravado and distrust in his current dance partner pushed buttons he hadn't discovered before. She wasn't the blonde bombshell her friend was, but that didn't mean she wasn't beautiful.

The tattered jean shorts revealed incredible tanned legs, while the simple gray tank hugged curves Dylan would be thinking about for days. Chestnut waves framed a serious face, featuring high cheekbones and expressive brown eyes, and as they danced, she fit against him in all the right places.

Unfortunately, looks didn't always translate into brains or brass, two traits Dylan held in high esteem. Charley possessed brass for sure. Since she hadn't added the word *like* to a sentence yet and had been quick enough to suss out his wingman status, he felt pretty good about the brains situation as well.

The notes of the slow song faded into "Cotton-Eyed Joe," and he escorted his partner off the floor. The moment they reached the crowded tables, she pulled her hand from his. By the time he spun around, thinking she might have gotten caught in a stampede, she'd shifted routes and cut a quick path to her friend. Dylan shook his head. She could run, but he wasn't finished with the birthday girl.

"How are things going over here?" he asked as he reached Casey, now perched atop a stool beside Matilda.

Charley reached for her beer and downed it like a dog newly released from a hot car.

"Good," Casey replied, his eyes on the blonde. "She hasn't taken a bite out of me yet, but the night is still young."

"Mr. Flanagan here is quite the charmer," Matilda observed, twirling the red wine in her glass. "He's taken every insult I've dished out with a smile and a wink. I'm starting to think he might be bulletproof."

"Or slow," Dylan suggested, waving to the bartender for a beer and adding another for Charley. "You need to slow down," he said, sliding up beside her at the bar. "Like Casey said, the night is still young."

"I was thirsty, that's all." She set the empty bottle on the bar and pushed it forward. "Regardless," she said, turning steady brown eyes his way, "I'm not a weakling. I don't need your advice on how to drink."

From cooperative to combative in less than thirty seconds. This woman would keep him on his toes like a nervous filly. "I believe you."

Her gaze narrowed. "You do?"

"I do. I don't think you're weak at all."

"But you don't even know me."

Dylan touched the brim of his hat. "Call it instinct."

With a pinched expression, she said, "I'm not a horse, thank you very much."

Yep. She was quick.

"You have to admit, the comparison fits." He retrieved the beer set in front of him and turned to lean his back on the bar. "You're proud. Stubborn. Skittish. And itching to break out and run."

She chuckled as she reached for her beer. "You got all that out of one dance?"

"Am I wrong?" he pressed.

Sighing, Charley stared into the distance as if pondering his predictions. After several seconds of silence, her lips turned up in a grin.

"No, you aren't wrong. I'm all of those things, but I'm not *only* those things."

In that moment, he wanted to know all the other things about her, but before he could suggest they find a place to talk, Casey smacked him on the shoulder.

"We're gonna dance. Hold the stools for us."

Matilda shrugged and handed her purse to Charley. "Might as well have a little fun now that I'm out, right?"

Charley nodded. "Yes, ma'am. Go show him how it's done."

As the unlikely pair melted into the crowd, Dylan motioned for Charley to have a seat, waiting to take the other until she'd settled in.

"Did you just wait until I sat down?" she asked, a bit incredulous.

"Guilty," he responded. "My mama taught me well."

"And where is your mama?" she queried, surprising him with the sudden change of topic.

"Castor, Louisiana. Where is your mama?"

Her face sobered. "My mother is dead."

At first, Dylan thought she might be joking, but her eyes said differently.

"I'm sorry," he muttered, feeling like a jerk.

"No." She shook her head, sending chestnut waves dancing around her shoulders. "It's an innocent enough question, and I started it, anyway. After nine years, you'd think talking about it would get easier."

"I can't imagine that ever getting easier." Dylan didn't like to think about losing either of his parents. And if he did the math right, she'd only been sixteen at the time. Damn. That had to be hard.

Silence loomed as she picked at the label on her bottle.

"Your friend must be a real charmer," she finally said, changing the subject. "Matty is as jaded as they come, and she dished it out pretty hard when y'all first walked up."

Dylan nodded. "That boy doesn't have the sense God gave a gnat, but he never backs down from a challenge. Did you say Maddy?"

"Matty," she said louder, emphasizing the *t*'s. "Short for Matilda, of course. She hates it, but I think it's nice."

"Charley is nice, too," he offered. "Is it short for anything?"

"Charlotte." He studied her face for several seconds, until she said, "What?"

"You don't look like a Charlotte."

Slender brows arched. "Really? What do I look like?"

"A Charley," Dylan said, tapping his beer bottle to hers. "Charley fits you perfectly." When her brows met above her nose, he added, "Compliment, I promise."

"If you say so."

As she lifted her beer for another drink, a burly guy in a straw hat shoved his way to the bar, nearly knocking her off her stool in the process. Dylan caught her before she landed in his lap, losing his beer in the process. As glass met tile, the shatter echoed above the music, and his IPA became a puddle at his feet.

"Hey!" he yelled at the asshole who hadn't bothered to turn around. "Watch what you're doing."

A wall of a man spun their way, deep-set eyes buried beneath thick, bushy brows. The beard reached his third button, and the lack of sleeves revealed several tattoos scattered up and down his arms. None of them looked as if the artist knew what the hell he was doing. "You talking to me?"

"I don't see any other dipshits plowing into women around here."

"Dylan, don't—" Charley started.

"Are you calling me a dipshit?"

Not the brightest buckle in the bunch. "You owe this woman an apology. And you owe me a beer."

The bully grunted and turned his back on them as the bartender approached. "Jack and Coke," the big man ordered, ignoring his other obligation.

Dylan took the matter into his own hands. "Joey, get me another beer and put it on this dude's tab."

"I really don't think—" Charley tried again.

"I'm not paying for shit for you," Goliath argued.

The idiot needed a lesson in civility. "You see that?" Dylan said, pointing toward the floor. "That's my beer. I was enjoying it until you tried to knock my woman off her stool."

"Your what?" Charley squeaked.

"Look, you little pissant. I didn't do shit to you or your *little woman*. So go fuck yourself."

From the corner of his eye, Dylan saw Joey wave for a bouncer. Now to make sure the guy went out the door and not to another table.

"Didn't your mama teach you any manners?" he asked, rising to his feet. By his calculations, the oaf would either be slow enough to throw a punch that the bouncer would arrive first, or, if they were lucky, he'd land on his ass in spilled beer.

Of course, Dylan hadn't figured Charley into his math.

"Don't you talk about my—" the big guy started, taking one step before Charley cut him off.

"That's enough." A slender hand flattened on the giant's chest. "Say you're sorry for bumping into me," she ordered.

He opened his mouth as if to argue, and she crossed her arms, careful not to drop her beer or Matty's purse.

"Fine," he conceded. "I'm sorry."

She then turned to Joey. "He'll pay for Dylan's beer, but get him an extra Jack and Coke on me."

"What are you doing?" Dylan asked behind her. The look she shot him said, *Shut the hell up.*

"Now," Charley said, "if you two still want to go outside and compare dick sizes, have at it. But it won't have anything to do with me." Stepping around the puddle at her feet, she disappeared into the crowd, leaving the men gaping after her.

"That's some woman you've got there," muttered the now-docile hillbilly.

"She sure is," Dylan agreed, tapping his new beer bottle against the other man's Jack and Coke. "She sure is."

His guess had been correct. Miss Charley *was* a one-of-a-kind woman. The bit about her being *his* might have been a stretch, but if Dylan was lucky, he'd get the chance to make it the truth.

"Why do men have to be such idiots?" Charley fumed, pacing the backstage area where Ruby sat propped on a bar stool.

"They can't help themselves, darling. It's all that testosterone running through their bodies." The redhead sipped her gin and tonic. "Sounds kind of chivalrous in a way though. You say the other guy was how big?"

"Too big," she huffed, heart still racing with fear that Dylan might right now be getting his fool self killed. Charley possessed a lifetime's worth of experience dealing with a barn-size male, though even Elvis, her best friend back home, would have hesitated before taking on such a behemoth. He'd have still done it, but he at least had Marine Corps training to fall back on. "What was he thinking?" she went on, continuing her rant. *"His woman."* The nerve of that claim. And her treasonous body's reaction only made matters worse.

Charley was not some helpless damsel who wanted—or needed, for that matter—a big, strong man to fight for her honor. Her response should have proven that as clear as the drink in Ruby's hand.

"You say his name is Dylan?" Ruby asked. "Did you get his last name?"

She shook her head, still pacing the small space. "No, I didn't. And I don't care what his last name is. As if all the attention from the bottle breaking wasn't enough. No. He had to go and make some manly scene. Everyone within twenty feet was watching."

Ruby laughed. "Is that what you're all riled up about? Being the center of a scene? You do realize that your job is eventually going to require you to stand on a stage in front of twenty thousand people, right?"

Of course Charley realized that. Didn't mean she had to like it. She'd picked radio for a reason. The public could hear her, but not see her. And if they didn't like what she said, they could change the station, and she'd be no more the wiser.

"I guess I should go find Matty," she mumbled, dreading going back into the club. "She might have grown tired of her freckle-faced admirer by now and be looking for me to save her."

"You know better than that. Matty can take care of herself."

A woman with a headset and a clipboard peeked from behind a curtain. "Ruby, we're ready in two."

The emcee hopped down to her well-worn cowboy boots. "Duty calls." After setting her drink under the chair, she turned Charley's way. "I have an idea."

"About what?" Charley asked, instantly dubious. The last time Ruby got an idea, Charley found herself singing karaoke with a video jock from the Country Music Network.

"Come on." The older woman snagged Charley's hand, sending Matty's purse to the floor, and pulled her through the curtain the stagehand had just closed. "You're going out there with me."

"Are you crazy?" Charley attempted to free her hand, but Ruby held tight. "I'm not supposed to go out there with you."

Within seconds, they were hovering in the wings, surrounded by musicians ready to take the stage.

Ruby said hello to the boys, ignoring the crazy woman trying to claw her arm free.

"Ruby," she hissed. "Don't do this to me."

"You'll thank me later, kid."

The woman in the headset returned. "It's all you, Ruby."

To Charley's horror, she found herself stumbling onto the stage of the Wildhorse Saloon, blindsided by both the bright lights and the sudden roar of the crowd.

"How y'all doing out there tonight?" Ruby drawled into her microphone. "Are you ready for a great show?"

The roar grew louder, and Charley's heart threatened to beat out of her chest. Her ears began to ring, and tiny black dots invaded the edges of her vision.

"Before we get to the main attraction, I was hoping y'all would help me say happy birthday to this pretty lady right here." Ruby lifted Charley's arm above her head, eliciting more cheers from the crowd. "This here is Miss Charley Layton, and she's the newest addition to our Eagle 101.5 family. You've been listening to her from ten to three five days a week, and now I want you to give her some love on her birthday."

Charley had no idea if she was smiling because she could no longer feel her face. Ruby might as well have thrown her in front of a Dodge and slapped the word "Bambi" on her forehead, but if she looked scared, the audience either didn't notice or didn't care.

"Can I get a Wildhorse rendition of 'Happy Birthday' for our girl here?"

Oh no. She wouldn't. She couldn't. *And she did.*

With one sweep of Ruby's hand, the crowd broke out in song, and Charley used every mental trick she could think of not to puke or pass out. It wasn't as if she'd never been on a stage before, but barbecue festivals in Liberty, Kentucky, were very different from standing on the Wildhorse stage in front of nearly two thousand people. Despite her best efforts, Charley's stomach rolled. Taking two steps back, she braced for a run to the closest bathroom. But Ruby had other plans.

When the serenade finally ended, Ruby wrapped her arm around Charley's shoulders and squeezed tight. "That's one way to pop your stage cherry," she whispered into Charley's ear, miraculously not making the declaration into the microphone.

There was only so much humiliation a woman could take.

"Now let's get to the reason we're all here." Ruby released Charley to shift the microphone to her other hand, providing the escape she so desperately needed.

With a quick wave to the crowd, Charley backed off the stage and broke into a trot the moment she hit the wings. Ducking down two hallways, she paid little attention to where she was going, only to find herself standing before the VIP tables outside the backstage entrance. Most people were focused on the stage, but a publicist she'd met the week before noticed her passing by.

"Happy birthday, Charley!" the pretty brunette called.

Charley couldn't remember the woman's name. "Thanks," she said, picking up her pace. Keeping to the edge of the room, she rounded a back corner and ran straight into a wall. A wall that smelled like a field after a fresh rain and that somehow knew her name.

"Charley, are you okay?" Dylan asked, his voice heavy with concern.

She shook her head. "Get me out of here."

The cowboy took her hand. "I can do that."

Chapter 3

Dylan forced his way through the crowd, which thinned as the lights dropped and people rushed toward the stage. Holding tight to Charley's hand, he charged through the exit and led her away from the noise of the club.

"Are you okay?" he asked, after ducking into the pass-through next to McFadden's. The walkway offered pedestrians a path through the connected buildings, leading from Second over to First Avenue, and then on to Riverfront Park.

Charley nodded. "I'm better now. Just give me a second." She pressed her back to the red brick and closed her eyes, chest rising and falling as she pulled her frantic breathing under control. He held silent until color returned to her cheeks.

"Do you want to tell me what happened back there?" Dylan queried. He'd never seen a person run from the "Happy Birthday" song before. There had to be more to it.

Charley met his gaze. "I need to be someplace quiet. How far do we have to go to get that?"

Finding silence in this part of town was nearly impossible. But then he remembered the park.

"Come on." Taking her hand once more, he set a more sedate pace, keeping her beside him through the tunnel, past the shuttered storefronts. Once they reached First Avenue, he glanced both ways, waiting for traffic to clear before crossing to the park. Nissan Stadium loomed large in the distance as the sounds of the Nashville nightlife faded behind them.

"Wow," Charley whispered when they reached the grassy area. "I didn't even know this was here."

"You never noticed the river that runs through the city?"

"I mean this park, and you know it." She shook her head, chestnut locks dancing in the breeze off the water, which did little against the stifling humidity. "I've only lived here since the beginning of June. Sadly, I haven't found the time to explore much."

Dylan pointed toward the stairs up the block to their left. "Then let's explore."

They strolled in silence until reaching the stairs to the lower side-walk that ran parallel to the Cumberland River. Sensing a change in the woman beside him, he smiled her way. "Better?"

Charley exhaled. "Much. You must think I'm crazy."

He shook his head. "No, ma'am. I think you're interesting."

And a sexy distraction from the pressure of his new endeavor.

She laughed. "That sounds like a nice way to say I'm crazy."

"How about crazy in a good way?" he offered.

"I'll take that." Turning her face to the wind, she said, "This is like walking in front of a hair dryer."

"Yes, it is." Dylan removed his hat and swiped his damp forehead with his shirt sleeve. "That's the bad thing about the black hat. Holds in the heat."

"I'm sorry." Charley stopped walking. "You should be back inside where it's cool." She backed away. "I'll be fine."

Dylan tapped the hat against his leg. "I'll go if you go, but I'm not leaving you out here alone."

"I can't go back in there," she replied, stiffening.

"Then I'm good right where I am."

Brown eyes narrowed, but she didn't argue when he regained her hand and moved them along once more.

"Was it the lights," he asked, "or the noise?"

"Neither," Charley answered. "It was the attention."

Now she'd confused him. "The attention?"

Slender shoulders rose and fell with a sigh. "I don't like being the center of attention." They reached another set of stairs, and she asked, "Do you mind if we sit?"

"Don't mind at all." He waited for her to have a seat, and then he settled down beside her. "Doesn't your line of work require you to be the center of attention?"

"Nope," she replied. "That's why I love it. When I'm on the air, I can't see them and they can't see me. They really only care about the music coming through their speakers."

Dylan had never thought of radio quite that way. As a singer, he'd been in front of an audience on a regular basis since he was fifteen years old. First school talent shows and church programs, and then the bars and honky-tonks. With any luck, his new deal would launch him into arenas and amphitheaters.

Though after releasing two weeks ago, his single was still struggling to find its audience. He considered asking Charley if she'd heard anyone at the station talk about him, but he didn't want to sound as if he were angling for some kind of favor.

Plus, every second of his life these days revolved around Dylan's budding career and the fact that the livelihoods of everyone at his new label rested on his shoulders. A side effect of being the only artist signed so far.

"I'm assuming you worked in radio before you came here," he said, digging deeper.

Charley wrapped her arms around her knees. "I've been on the air since I was eighteen years old. A sidekick for the first couple years, and then on my own from twenty on."

"And you didn't ever do public events?"

She snorted. "Public events in Liberty, Kentucky, are very different from events here."

"How so?"

"For one," she started, "events back home were much smaller, naturally. But whether twenty or two hundred, I knew them all. I'd grown up with them and gone to church with them, and it was . . . different."

Made sense, he supposed.

"You had to know that taking a job in Nashville would mean doing these kinds of gigs."

Running a hand through her hair, Charley stared out over the water. "I've wanted to be a part of this world for as long as I can remember. While my friends were playing with dolls or honing their cheerleading skills, I was spinning records on Grandpa's old stereo, injecting my own childish commentary between 'Folsom Prison Blues' and 'Coal Miner's Daughter.' There's no way I'm going to let some stupid fear get in the way of doing this."

Dylan admired her determination. "Did Ruby know about your fear?"

Her silent nod made him want to storm back into the club and give Ruby Barnett a piece of his mind. "That's damn shitty."

"To be fair," Charley admitted, "I might have watered down the true depth of my anxiety. Ruby thinks I'm just a little nervous about crowds. I don't blame her for dragging me out there. She wasn't trying to be mean."

Her confession didn't alter his feelings on Miss Ruby one bit. "We all have our crosses to bear," Dylan said. "At least you're prepared to face yours head-on."

Her look of disbelief took him by surprise. "I doubt you have anything to *bear*, as you put it. You clearly don't suffer from a lack of confidence, considering you attempted to take on a Neanderthal twice your size not thirty minutes ago."

Little did she know. "I wasn't trying to fight him." Though he would have if necessary. "I was trying to get him thrown out."

"You purposely taunted him. You called him a dipshit, for heaven's sake."

"And then Joey behind the bar waved for security. The bouncer was less than ten feet away when you slapped your hand against the dude's chest, demanding that apology." Dropping his hat onto her head, Dylan added, "You looked pretty damn confident to me."

Charley tipped the Stetson out of her eyes. "Someone had to save your stupid ass. That guy would have killed you."

"Wow. That doesn't dent the ego at all."

"And what was that 'my woman' crap?" she asked. "Women aren't cars or big-screen TVs. We aren't *your* anything."

Man, he loved her spunk.

Staring into snapping brown eyes, he made a confession. "Did you ever stop to think that maybe I was trying to impress you?"

Perfect lips opened and closed as she examined his expression. "You're serious."

"Yes, ma'am."

"You really want to impress me?" she asked.

"I do."

"Then feed me."

Certain he'd misheard, Dylan said, "Do what, now?"

"I've been running all day, and I'm starving. Where can I get a killer burger without having to venture into one of these noisy clubs?"

Rising off the step, Dylan held out a hand. "I know just the place."

By the time Dylan turned onto James Robertson Parkway, Charley realized that a total stranger was currently driving her to an undisclosed location. This was how stupid women ended up the featured victim on those true-crime shows.

"Where are we going?" she asked, pulling her phone from her back pocket to text Matty.

"For a burger, as requested," he replied, flipping on his blinker and edging the truck onto an exit on the right. The sign said ELLINGTON PARKWAY.

"But where, *specifically*, are we getting this burger?" Charley tried again, attempting not to sound like a woman who knew she was about to be murdered and chopped into little pieces.

Dylan reached across the giant console between them to pat her knee. "I'm not a serial killer, Charley."

That's what they all said. "I need to let Matty know where I am," she confessed. "You know, in case you *do* kill me."

"That would be a waste of time. I would never leave your body where you told your friend you'd be."

"Spoken like a true serial killer."

"Come on, Charley. I'm kidding."

"I'm sure that's what Dahmer said."

"Fine," he said with a chuckle. "I'm taking you to the Pharmacy."

A man had only one reason to take a woman to a pharmacy on a Saturday night.

"Nope. Not happening. Take me back."

"You said you wanted a burger," Dylan countered.

Charley crossed her arms. "I did. But I'm not having sex with you to get one."

The black hat smacked the back window as he threw his head back in laughter. "You really are something. You know that?"

She was something, all right. Something he was not having sex with. Regardless of how gorgeous, sweet, and protective he was. Or how good he smelled. Though he really did smell amazing. And was probably really good in bed. Any guy this gorgeous would presumably know his way around the bedroom.

You mean the man who might tie you up and lock you in his basement? she asked herself.

Her brain had a point. No orgasm was worth dying for.

"Regardless," she said. "You can skip the pharmacy and go straight to the burgers."

"Too late," he said, making a left turn. "We're here."

Charley spotted the sign on the side of a nondescript white building. **THE PHARMACY BURGER PARLOR & BEER GARDEN**. She hadn't seen that coming.

"Who names a burger joint the Pharmacy?"

Dylan didn't justify that with an answer.

"Looks like we got lucky," he murmured, pulling into an open space on the curb before the entrance. "It's a great place to eat, but parking is a bitch since they don't have their own lot."

Great. How good could a restaurant with no parking lot be?

After cutting the engine and the lights, Dylan undid his seat belt and bolted out of the truck. Charley didn't like the look of the area and considered locking herself in and calling the police. But then her door popped open, and her escort flashed a sexy grin. "Come on," he said.

The smell of perfectly cooked meat hit Charley in the nose, causing her mouth to water. Maybe she should give the place a chance.

"That smells like heaven," she admitted, accepting his hand and sliding to the sidewalk.

Dylan held his ground, bringing their bodies into contact. "This will be the best burger you've ever had," he said, close enough for her to notice a tiny scar at the corner of his mouth. "I promise."

Charley forgot about food when his eyes dropped to her lips. "Best ever, huh?" she said, leaning into him.

"Only the best for the birthday girl," he drawled.

And right there, beneath a dim streetlight, his lips lowered to hers and the world slipped away. Rising on tiptoes, Charley slid her arms around Dylan's neck and melted against his muscled frame. One taste unfolded into an exploration that had nothing to do with geographic location. A hint of pale ale lingered on his tongue, and as his hands slid up her back, her bones turned to liquid. With a tilt of his head, Dylan deepened the connection, eliciting a desperate moan of pleasure and making her forget her resolve not to have sex with him.

Lost in sensations, neither noticed the group of revelers exiting the restaurant.

"Get a room!" someone called, as another gave a loud whistle.

Startled, Charley pulled away, thankful that Dylan held her upright, as her knees were no longer up to the task.

Struggling to catch her breath, she said, "We should probably go inside."

His hat tapped her forehead as he nodded, breathing as heavily as she was. "I'm going to need a minute."

Their proximity revealed his dilemma.

"Oh," she whispered, forcing herself to put space between them. "I don't usually kiss strangers on street corners." Which made this man all the more dangerous. In less than an hour, he'd made her forget her anti-man policy. Though, technically, it was an anti-relationship policy. Didn't mean she couldn't follow Ruby's advice and give herself a little birthday present.

"I'm glad you made an exception this time," he mumbled. "Because that was a damn good kiss."

Charley felt oddly flattered. "Thanks," she replied.

His chuckle shot straight to her core. "No," Dylan said. "Thank *you*. Now let's go eat before I forget that I'm a gentleman."

Clay Benedict, longtime record executive and owner of the newly launched Shooting Stars Records, walked into the Wildhorse Saloon for the first time in nearly a year. He'd once been a regular, scouting for new talent or showing support for a Foxfire artist who might have been head-lining the show. As the case would have it, that's exactly what was happening tonight. A rising star on the Foxfire label entertained the crowd, only Clay wasn't here for her. Because Foxfire wasn't *his* label anymore.

He did have an artist in the room, or at least Dylan was supposed to be there. Scanning the crowd, he spotted Casey Flanagan, the drummer in Dylan's band, holding court at a cocktail table with a gorgeous blonde. Most men had a type, and poor Casey, redheaded and scrawny as the day was long, had a thing for blue-eyed blondes who were typically out of his reach. As Clay made his way toward them, the woman rolled her eyes and sauntered off.

"You're a slow learner, Casey," he said, raising his voice to be heard over the show. "But you get points for persistence."

"Dylan says the same thing," replied the easygoing musician.

"Speaking of," Clay said, "where is Dylan?"

Casey waved over a passing waitress. "He took off with that blonde's roommate," he yelled. "Didn't sound like he planned to come back, either, which leaves me high and dry for a ride."

When the woman balancing a tray reached them, she said, "What are you having?"

"Jack on the rocks," Clay replied. "Thanks."

"Coming right up," she chirped and whirled off toward the bar.

"You need me to take you home? I don't plan to stay long."

Shaking his head, Casey straightened his ball cap on his head. "Lance and Easton are over at Tootsie's. Think I'll head that way. You want to join us?"

Though Clay liked the other members of the band, he saw no reason to crash the young men's outing. At forty, he didn't consider himself old, but he'd long ago passed the point of trolling the bars for a hookup.

"I'm good here. You go ahead."

"Cool, man. See you later then."

The show came to an end as Casey took his leave, and Clay pulled his phone from his pocket to check his email. He'd been waiting on specific news from his label publicist, Naomi Mallard, regarding a local radio visit for Dylan. They'd already booked a station tour that would kick off in just over a week, but many programmers took their cues from Nashville, which meant getting airtime in town could give them a far-reaching advantage.

Naomi had been out sick the day before but had assured Clay that she'd work from home to make the appearance happen. And according to the newest email in his inbox, she'd done exactly that.

"I didn't expect to see you here," chimed a familiar voice, dragging Clay's attention away from his phone.

"Tony," Clay said, not surprised to see his former partner in the house, but irritated with himself for not avoiding this encounter. "I thought I'd come see your new artist." He delivered the lie with a straight face.

The fact was, Clay had signed Mallory Tate to the label six months before he'd struck out on his own.

"She's come a long way, don't you think?" Tony Rossi beamed like a proud papa.

Since Clay hadn't watched the show, he kept his answer vague. "We always knew she had the potential."

"You mean *you* saw her potential," he corrected. "I was against signing her. As usual, you were right."

"That scenario happened in reverse often enough."

The two men had been a successful team ever since they'd divvied up a paper route when they were ten years old. Tony had taken one side, while Clay took the other, and they'd knocked out the job in half the time.

The waitress returned with Clay's drink. "Do you want to start a tab?" she asked.

"No," he said, fishing his wallet out of his inside jacket pocket. "I'm leaving after this one."

"Put it on the Foxfire bill," Tony cut in. Flashing a regretful smile, he added, "It's the least I can do . . . considering."

His friend had no idea how little he owed to Clay. In fact, the truth was quite the opposite. Which was why he'd ended their partnership in the first place.

Stuffing the wallet back where it belonged, he nodded. "Thanks. I appreciate that."

"Do you want to come over and talk to Mallory? I'm sure she'd like to see you."

Clay turned down the offer. "Like I said, I'm leaving after this drink. You should get back and celebrate with the team."

"Right." Pale green eyes dropped to the drink on the table. "It isn't the same without you, though."

Choking on his own guilt, he held silent.

"Are you ever going to tell me why you left?" Tony asked.

A sizable swig of Jack burned down Clay's throat. "The reason is still the same. I needed a change."

His childhood friend tapped the table. "A little warning would have been nice."

"It's going on a year, Tony. Let it go."

"That's obviously easier for you than for the rest of us." Straightening his tie, he brought their visit to a merciful end. "Good luck with your new artist. I hope he sells a million."

The parting shot had been a direct reminder of their earlier days, delivered with a precision honed from thirty years of friendship. As hopeful twenty-two-year-olds, they'd cut a mediocre EP and titled it *I Hope It Sells a Million*. Something only the two of them likely remembered.

More than once, Clay had considered telling Tony exactly why their connection had to end. But doing so would only allay his own guilt while shattering the best man he'd ever known. Which was why he'd come up with the lie in the first place.

Because some secrets should never see the light of day.

Chapter 4

"This place is amazing," Charley praised from behind her napkin. "Messy, but awesome. I can't believe I can get ham, bacon, *and* an egg on a burger."

"Told you," Dylan replied, pretending the way she licked her fingers wasn't driving him wild. The kiss outside had set his body on go, and it was a wonder he'd made it through the meal without dragging her across the table for another taste.

"Why did no one tell me about this place before now?" she said, popping the last bite of burger into her mouth. Her moan of pleasure didn't help his uncomfortable condition. "How's the cheeseburger?"

He pointed to his empty plate. "I offered you a taste. You should have taken it when you had the chance."

Charley scrunched up her nose. "I didn't want to be *that* person."

"What person is that?"

"You know. The one who eats off other people's plates. The food moocher." She shrugged and reached for her drink. "And this might be better than the burger. I've never heard of a Kentucky Mint soda before, but I love it."

Leaning back with his beer—root beer, that is—Dylan took pleasure in watching Charley enjoy her treat.

"You're an easy girl to please, Miss Layton. I like that in my women."

She twirled the straw in her glass. "And you're a smart-ass," Charley quipped. "I don't like that in *my men*."

Dylan raised his glass in salute. "Don't worry. It'll grow on you."

Her laughter, free and feminine, made him want her more.

"I'm curious," he said, unable to resist a little shop talk. "As a disc jockey, you must be an expert on music. Who's your favorite artist? Someone like Tim McGraw? Or Carrie Underwood?"

"While Tim is inarguably one of the most attractive men ever, he is not my favorite."

"I don't know that I'd say most attractive *ever* . . . ," he cut in.

Charley shot him a quelling glare. "Did you miss the *inarguably* part?"

"Fine," Dylan conceded. "Then who is it?"

Shoving a fry around her plate, she said, "I'm a Jack Austin fan."

"Really? I love his work."

"I've followed him ever since his debut album. Drives me nuts that he gets ignored for every award." Charley leaned forward. "His voice is authentic, you know? His whole sound is. Don't get me wrong. I love country music, but this pop-country fusion thing is getting old. Hopefully, Jack's new album due out next year will swing back the other way."

Dylan breathed a sigh of relief. "I'm with you on that. My stuff . . ."

"Crap!" she cut in, dragging her phone from her back pocket. "I need to let Matty know where I am. She must be worried sick by now." Staring at the screen, she mumbled, "Wow."

"What?" he asked, leaning forward.

"No calls or texts. I guess she's not too worried about her roommate disappearing."

"She knows where you are," Dylan explained. "When you hopped into the restroom earlier, I sent Casey a message and told him to make sure your friend knew you were okay."

Brown eyes went wide. "You thought to do that?"

Didn't seem like a big deal to him. "Sure." He considered trying once again to tell her about his music, but the moment had passed.

Charley shook her head. "You're like a cowboy in shining armor. First you got me out of the Wildhorse. Then you gave me the best birthday meal I've ever had. And somewhere in between, you made sure my friend wouldn't worry. Are you for real?"

"I should be asking if *you're* for real," he countered. "You shut down that bully at the bar with a look. You ate every bite of that burger when other women would have played dainty and eaten less than half. And you didn't smack me outside when I lost the battle not to kiss you."

Pink rolled up her cheeks, but she didn't so much as flutter an eyelash. "To be fair, I kissed you back. And if there's one thing I've never been accused of, it's being dainty."

"Dainty is highly overrated," Dylan drawled.

"I don't know," she argued. "Matty is the definition of dainty, and men fall at her feet."

"I don't fall at any woman's feet, but I've been known to kneel in the right situation."

The deepening of the blush meant she picked up his meaning right away.

Clearing her throat, she straightened her spine. "Time to change the subject." She looked up to the ceiling as if searching for a topic. "Oh, I know. Let's get back to what we were talking about by the river. You never told me what your 'cross to bear' is. I still contend that you don't have one. Prove me wrong."

Holding her skeptical gaze, Dylan debated whether to tell the truth or make something up. Certain she'd neither mock nor laugh at him, he stuck with the truth.

"I'm a songwriter," he started.

"Really?" Charley looked at him as if he'd confessed that the earth was round. "I mean, we are in Nashville after all."

"Do you want to hear this or not?"

"Sorry," she said, not the least bit contrite. "Go on. You're a songwriter . . ."

"I'm a songwriter, *but . . .* ," he added, "I never let anyone hear my songs."

Her expression shifted from cynical to confused. "What's the point in writing them if no one ever hears them?"

Excellent question. And one for which he had a perfectly logical answer. Or so he told himself.

"I've let people hear them in the past, and things didn't go well. I guess you could say I got burned, so now I keep them to myself."

"What does 'things didn't go well' mean?"

That was a detail Dylan would not be sharing.

"Nope. One secret is all you get tonight."

At that moment, the waitress approached the table. "Sorry to interrupt your good time," she said, piling up their plates, "but we're closing in ten minutes."

"Dang," Charley said, reaching for her phone. "Going home before midnight on my birthday. I'm a sad case."

"You don't have to go home if you don't want to," Dylan coaxed. "I know a place right down the street that's quiet and has free beer."

"Free beer? What kind of a bar gives out free beer?"

"I never said it was a bar."

Eyes narrowed, she said, "Is this the part where you kill me? Was this my last meal? Not that I'm complaining or anything. Just curious."

Pulling his wallet from his pocket, he fished out enough cash to pay the bill. "Have you always been this paranoid?"

"I watch a lot of true-crime shows."

Those shows did make every stranger seem like a murderer.

36

"I'm inviting you back to my place, Charley. Not to kill you," he added. "To talk and have a beer. What do you say?"

Charley rested an elbow on the table and propped her chin on her hand. "You brought me to a restaurant down the street from your house, but you have no ulterior motives? Doesn't that sound far-fetched to you?"

Testing the waters, Dylan queried, "If I did have ulterior motives, would they get me anywhere?"

She stared hard, expression unreadable. "Maybe."

He'd take that. "Then let's go."

"But I have one condition."

Dylan dropped his ass back to the chair. "And what's that?"

"If I come back to your place, I want to hear one of your songs."

Damn. She was really going to make him work for this. "That's playing dirty."

She waved her phone in the air. "I can order a car. I'm sure they'll be here within minutes."

His head told him to send her packing, but his body said to play her a damn song.

"Okay," he surrendered, rising to his feet. "One song coming up."

When Dylan said right down the street, he meant it. They could have walked to his house from the restaurant. The short row of townhouses seemed out of place, mingled with the older brick homes across the street. Dylan pulled his truck into a drive past the last townhouse and parked three spaces down from a large Dumpster.

To keep the running joke alive, and to buy herself time since she hadn't decided yet how this night would end, Charley asked, "Is that Dumpster where they'll find my body?"

"Everything but your head," he replied without missing a beat. "My place is down the sidewalk a bit."

By the time she'd unfastened her seat belt, Dylan had crossed around the front of the truck and reached her door.

When he opened it, she said, "Is this something else your mama taught you?"

"Nope." He grinned, eyes unreadable beneath the hat. "You can thank my daddy for this one."

Allowing him to lift her to the ground, she lost the ability to speak the moment her feet hit the pavement. From chest to knee, not a breath could pass between them.

"I like it when you blush like that," he whispered, making her wish she, too, had a hat to hide her features. "Lets me know we're thinking the same things."

Charley cleared her throat. "I'm here for a song, remember?"

"You *are* a song, Charley Layton."

Pressing her back to the truck, Dylan took her mouth again, but this kiss was nothing like the first. Every lick, suck, and nip fanned the flame she'd forced herself to smother during their meal. Moving on instinct, she wrapped her arms around his neck and dragged him closer, as if that were possible. When his muscled thigh pressed between hers, she ground against him, her body growing hotter by the second.

Breaking the kiss, Charley panted. "You said something about free beer?" She needed something cold, and she needed it now.

"Yes, ma'am," he answered on a ragged breath. "You good to walk?"

The question confused her at first, until she realized Dylan was the only thing holding her upright.

She nodded as she pushed against his chest. "I can make it if you can."

"That's debatable, darling. You make a man weak with those lips of yours."

A shot of power heightened her arousal, and she slid her hands down his chest. "You're doing a number on my knees, pretty boy. Don't sell yourself short."

Dylan planted a hard kiss on her lips before taking her hand. "Follow me."

To Charley's relief, all body parts did their job, and she followed Dylan down a dark, narrow sidewalk to a weathered deck several units down. With surprising speed, he unlocked the heavy French doors and pulled her inside. Before the doors clicked shut, she was up against the wall, covered by a man who smelled like heaven and made her want every naughty thing that would send her straight to hell.

She gasped when his mouth traveled along her jaw and down her neck. Shoving her hands into his hair, Charley's knuckle met the hard Stetson. Without thinking, she hurled the hat into the darkness and heard it land with a thud. Seconds later, as Dylan trailed hot, wet kisses across her collarbone, something soft and unexpected brushed across her calf, causing Charley to scream like a banshee.

"What?" Dylan yelled, stepping back but keeping a firm grip on her arms. "What's wrong?"

Charley did her best impersonation of Irish clogging as she stuttered, "Something . . . On my leg . . . There's something in here!"

Dylan flipped a switch, blinding them both and eliciting a soft meow from her attacker. As her eyes adjusted, Charley looked down to see a giant orange cat weaving between their legs.

"Good God," she breathed with a hand over her racing heart. "You have a damn tiger?"

"Jesus, Bumblebee," Dylan said, shooing the cat away from her feet. "You scared her half to death."

"You named your tiger Bumblebee?"

Smoky eyes, still dark with desire, locked with hers. "He's a tabby, Charley. He's like fifty times smaller than a tiger."

"And he's five times bigger than any cat I've ever seen," she informed him. The thing didn't even have a neck. Just a big head sitting on a barrel chest. As if confirming her fears, the cat blinked up and yawned, revealing long white teeth. "What do you feed him? Raw steak?"

Dylan ran his hands through his hair, making the short brown locks stand on end. "Only on special occasions, but most of the time it's whatever cat food is in the house." Leaning a hand on the wall above Charley's shoulder, he sighed. "Are you always this jumpy?"

The teasing grin gave her the urge to jump his bones. Instead, she defended her behavior. "Standing in a strange man's house in the dark and having something furry touch my leg tends to spook me. Call me crazy."

There was a reason she was a dog person. A dog would have barked when they walked in. Not slithered about scaring poor, innocent souls out of their boots.

"Fair enough." Rising off the wall, he looked to the feline. "You're killing my game, Bumbles." A self-deprecating smile flashed Charley's way. "I'll get the beer."

"That would be good."

When he left her to fetch the drinks, Charley's body cooled, as if her essential source of heat had abandoned her. What the heck was she doing? She'd gone home with a man she'd just met. Was standing in his . . . Charley took in her surroundings. His kitchen.

Good, she thought. *There's still time to come to my senses.*

But then her host returned with a cold bottle and a warm smile, and her senses said, *Happy birthday to us!*

"So," Charley said, eyes everywhere but on his face. "That song."

"You're going to hold me to that, huh?"

She'd like to hold him to something.

"Of course," she squeaked, her voice betraying her nerves. "That's the only reason I'm here."

His bottle tapped hers. "Right, ace. The only reason." With a nod he said, "My guitar is up in my room."

Charley stayed where she was as he strolled toward a hall leading out of the room. Before turning the corner, he glanced back. "Come on, woman. You wanted a song. You're going to get one."

Reaching for a chair at the small table before her, she sat. "I'll wait here."

"Oh no," he drawled, shaking his head. "Your condition was that I play you a song. My condition is that I play it where I decide."

"And you decide that has to be in your bedroom?"

He leaned one shoulder against the wall. "I swear that nothing will happen in that room that you don't want to happen. Do you trust me?"

The chuckle came out as a snort. "I don't trust *me* is the problem."

Dylan tipped his head. "I can't promise not to let you ravish me, but I'll do my best to defend my virtue."

Hot *and* witty. Heaven help her.

She took several seconds to ponder her next move. This *was* her birthday, after all. Why not give herself a little present? Charley glanced down to Dylan's formfitting jeans. Or a big present.

"All-righty then," she said, rising from the chair. "Let's go to your room."

Chapter 5

"I didn't figure you for a cat person," Charley said as she followed him up the steps.

"Bumblebee belongs to my roommate," he replied, reaching the landing and stepping aside to let Charley join him.

"You have a roommate?"

"Two," Dylan confessed. Two people who would be surprised to hear he'd brought a woman home. "I doubt either will be home for a while," he added, sending the message that they would not be disturbed.

"Right." She nodded. "Of course." Rubbing her hands on her thighs, she looked around. "Which room is yours?"

With a tip of his chin, he indicated the door straight ahead. "In there."

Charley sighed, as if some final decision had been made. "Shall we?" she asked.

"After you."

"You don't need to go in and . . . tidy up or anything?"

What the heck? Not all men were slobs. "I haven't polished the light fixture lately, but otherwise it's good."

That garnered a smile as she inched toward the door. "If you say so."

Dylan pushed the door open for Charley to enter, and he followed her in. Except she stopped on the threshold, resulting in her back pressing against his front.

"Tell me you have a cleaning lady," she muttered. "Because if you keep this room immaculate all by yourself, I may have to propose right now."

The idea didn't frighten him nearly as much as it should have.

"All me," he confirmed. "Have a seat."

After closing the door, he crossed to the guitars in the corner and grabbed the Gibson as Charley settled on the edge of the bed. His palms grew slick as he dropped into the chair. Common sense told him to calm the hell down. This wasn't a fancy showcase for a roomful of record execs. Something he'd experienced three times since moving to Nashville, and he'd survived every time.

But his heart continued to race. No one had heard one of his songs in three years. Not Casey. Not his manager, Mitch. Not even the head of his new record label, Clay Benedict. Three and a half years ago, when he'd signed his first deal, Dylan had insisted on recording only his own songs. After four months in the studio, and countless arguments with both the producer and the head of the label, he'd turned in his debut album. Within weeks, the collection had been deemed unfit for release, and he'd been unceremoniously dropped by both the label and his then manager.

Dylan had been devastated.

For a year, he never so much as jotted down a lyric, and then Casey had started seeing Pamela. The two had been so damned in love that watching them sent melodies floating through his brain. Lyrics came next, invading like ants on a picnic.

The result had been a tattered collection of random snippets and partial compositions scrawled in a cheap notebook, none of which would ever see the light of day.

Until now.

Charley crossed her legs and leaned back on her hands. "Here we go, then. Sing me a song."

Ignoring the inviting scene before him—for now—Dylan rattled through the choices in his head. Nothing felt good enough to share. Strumming the strings on his guitar, he bought himself time by tuning the instrument. "Are you sure you want to hear this?" he asked. "I never claimed any of my songs were good."

"A deal's a deal, buddy boy. No backing out now. Besides," she added, "I'm not here to judge. I couldn't write a song to save my dog, so there will be no stones cast from my direction."

"You have a dog?" he asked, embracing the diversion.

"Pooter lives back in Kentucky with Grandpa. And before you ask, he got the name for the exact reason you'd assume."

"Sounds fragrant." Dylan laughed. "What kind of a dog is he?"

Crossing her arms, Charley leaned forward. "A mutt. And you're stalling." Of all the women he could have picked up tonight, he had to find a ballbuster. "Play me your latest," she encouraged. "What's the last song you wrote?"

Just as Casey and Pamela had inspired his first forays back into writing, their breakup had inspired his latest effort.

Time to man up and get this over with.

"For the last couple weeks I've worked on something called 'Come Back, Girl.' It isn't finished yet, but I can play you what I have." Dylan strummed the opening chords, filling the room with a midtempo melody.

> A man can't be tied down,
> Wants no part of that ball and chain,
> Gotta keep his options open,
> Gotta keep himself in the game.

Brown eyes narrowed as she listened.

> Then one day a pretty woman
> Comes along and tries to stay,
> But a man has to tell her,
> Darling, things don't work that way.

One well-worn boot hit the floor as if Charley might storm out of the room. Dylan kept playing, certain the chorus would save his night.

> And that man will keep his freedom,
> She'll leave, taking his world.
> He'll think he's better off without her,
> He'll say good riddance, girl.

> But the truth will come too late,
> When he's lonely on the floor.
> If only he had said the words,
> I'm sorry, come back, girl.

Rose-colored lips widened into a sappy grin. "*That* is awesome. Stupid enough to be manly, but with a romantic twist." Leaning forward, she added, "Your voice is incredible, Dylan. You should be performing somewhere."

"Maybe I'll do that," he said, failing to point out that he'd been performing for nearly half his life. Charley had stuck around this long not because of what he was, but who he was. An experience novel enough to make Dylan reluctant to see it end. "You think it's worth playing on the radio?"

"Heck yeah."

"Then I guess it's worth my time to finish it."

As he put the guitar back on the stand, Charley sighed. "I envy anyone who can play like that. When I was little, I tried piano lessons, but after only a month, my teacher, Mrs. Borowitz, told my mother that I had no musical talent and she was wasting her money."

"That's a crappy thing to say about a kid. How old were you?"

"Eight," she replied. "And I was heartbroken. Mama could sing like an angel, and I wanted to be like her. We all knew well before I hit eight that my singing voice was closer to a dying rooster than an angel, but I still had dreams of playing an instrument as Mama sang. Yeah. Old Lady Borowitz put an end to that real quick."

Dylan picked the guitar back up. "Oh, hell no." Snatching a capo off his dresser, he settled on the bed next to Charley.

"What are you doing?" she asked as he scooted close enough to put half the guitar in her lap.

Sliding the capo onto the second fret, he said, "We're going to prove Old Lady Borowitz wrong."

Charley had not been prepared for what came next. The bed sagged beneath Dylan's weight as he slipped a leg around her and tucked her butt up close to his groin. At least he wasn't suffering the same condition he had outside the restaurant.

"Dylan, I can assure you this is a waste of time."

"Nonsense. You need the right teacher is all." He draped himself around her and leaned to their left. "I'll do the strumming, and you're going to handle the fret work. We'll start with something easy."

The guitar pressed against her breasts, still warm from his body heat, which was currently searing her back. "But I've never played a guitar before."

He was undeterred. "Then tonight's the night. Wrap your left hand around the neck like this," he said, showing her what he wanted. "We're going to start with a G chord, so put your middle finger up here on the top string."

She followed his direction and pressed on the string. "How hard do I have to push on it?"

"Hold it against the neck as well as you can." As she pressed the string, Dylan leaned the other way and, with a pick she hadn't noticed before, started at the top and plucked four different strings. Charley recognize the sound immediately.

"Hey, that's—"

"Not yet it isn't. Stay with me." He shifted again. "Middle finger same string but up a fret." Dylan nudged her finger into place. "Now put your ring finger down here on the G, and use your index finger to hold down these two."

So much for easy. "My fingers don't work that way."

"Come on now. You don't want Mrs. Boringwitzer to be right, do you?"

"Borowitz," Charley corrected. "And she's been right for seventeen years. I don't think one guitar lesson is going to change that."

Dylan dropped his hands to her hips. "Did you not just play the opening of a song that you recognized right away?"

She couldn't help but laugh. "You played it, not me."

"I plucked a few strings, but you did the work. Now come on. Middle finger at the top, ring finger on G, and to make it easier, drop you index finger across all of them."

Charley bit her lip with concentration and did as instructed, ignoring how the strings bit into the pads on her fingers. Four more plucks and the familiar tune vibrated to life. "That's so cool," she said, amazed to be playing an actual song. "Let's see if I can do them together now." Leaning forward to see her fingers, she moved back to the first position.

"That's right," Dylan said before doing his part. "Now shift."

The change took longer than she liked, but she did it, and Dylan plucked out the tune. "Oh my gosh, this is so cool. What's the next part?"

"You want B and D. Index here and middle finger here." His callused digits positioned hers in place. "Now we need your little finger down here on the skinny E. Can you hold that?"

No way was she letting him down now. "I can do it," Charley said with a nod. The skinny string hurt worse than the rest, but she didn't complain. Six little plucks later and she'd managed nearly the entire classic intro. "All together. All together," she insisted, bouncing on the mattress.

Laughter rolled through his chest, shaking them both. "Love the enthusiasm. Back to your G-chord then. There you go. You ready?" She nodded like a bull rider braced to leave the chute, and the tune rang out again. She made the first transition quicker, and Dylan said, "That a girl," as she slid into the third with staunch determination. One bar remained, and she'd have the entire intro learned. At least on the fret side.

"Your middle finger has a big job in this last part," he warned, locking her index and ring finger into place. "When I say now, you tap that bottom string, okay?" She tested the action, and he said, "Like that. Keep it off the string until I say so." Dylan took his place on her right again, dropping his chin onto her shoulder. "Here we go." After plucking four strings, he gave the signal, and as he strummed for a fifth time, she pressed down on the skinny string.

"That sounded off," she said, not as happy with that pass.

"But you were close. Think you can put all four together?"

Charley stretched her arms and cracked her knuckles. "Let's do this."

"Okay, maestro. When you're ready."

She locked her fingers into position and nodded again. Dylan pressed the pick to the strings, and together they played the intro to

"Friends in Low Places" by Garth Brooks. As the last note rang out, Charley turned to the man pressed close against her. "I played a song. I made music."

His hands dropped back to her hips. "Yes, you did. You're an excellent student."

Getting lost in his eyes, she murmured, "And you're a really good teacher."

Lifting the guitar off her lap, Dylan lowered it to the floor beside the bed before tucking a loose lock behind her ear.

"What do you want to do now?" he whispered, trailing his thumb across her lips. "Do you want to go home?"

Going home was the last thing she wanted to do. "I'd rather stay," she replied, turning until her legs were draped across his thigh. "Do you mind entertaining me a little longer?"

Trailing a hand down her neck, his eyes dropped to her mouth. "I wouldn't mind that at all."

Dylan wasn't too far gone to recognize the irony. For years, he'd been playing *for* girls to get them into bed. Who knew that teaching them to play for themselves was the better way to go? Letting his hand continue past her knee, he removed Charley's boots, followed by her simple white socks. Red-tipped toes curled as he dragged callused fingertips over strong calves to the inside of her thigh.

"You're like a fantasy come to life," he breathed. "You sure you want to do this?" He liked this woman and wanted more than a one-night stand. At the same time, Dylan wasn't stupid enough to turn down a willing woman.

"What was it I said earlier?" she asked, nipping at his earlobe. "No backing out now."

As she kissed her way across his jaw, Dylan let his fingers dance a little higher to press against the warm denim. "Just making sure," he said, before meeting her lips for a searing kiss that sent power surging through his body. Slender arms wrapped around his neck as Charley kissed him back, and they toppled backward onto the bed. He shifted his weight, letting her land softly on the mattress beside him, and slid his leg between hers.

Reaching for the buttons on his shirt, Charley worked them open, yanking the cotton out of his jeans to finish them off. Lips still locked on his, she flattened a hand against his bare chest, searing him like a brand.

"I know it's a cliché," she mumbled, "but I don't usually do this sort of thing."

Though he doubted she'd believe him, he replied, "Neither do I."

Desperate to touch her, he tugged the gray tank off her shoulder and spread kisses across her collarbone. A thin white strap glowed against warm, tan skin, and Dylan followed the string of satin down to the smooth mound threatening to spill into his hand. Charley arched in response, curling her fingers into the hair on his chest.

Their mouths met once more, urgent and hungry. She pushed the shirt off his shoulders, and Dylan rose up enough to free his arms and toss the thing to the floor. Charley wasted no time exploring every inch of his torso before sinking her teeth into his left nipple. The growl ripped through his chest as her nails cut across his rib cage.

"You're trying to kill me," he said, burying a hand in her hair.

Trailing her tongue across his pecs, she mumbled, "We can stop if you want."

Oh, hell no. "Not a chance."

She gave his other nipple the same little bite, and Dylan's brain shut down. Determined to return the favor, he forced the strap off her shoulder and freed her breast from the lace-tipped cup. Wrapping his mouth around the pink peak, he sucked hard, eliciting a gasp of raw pleasure that shot straight to his dick. "Off," he muttered, tugging at the hem of her shirt.

Charley leaned up enough for him to drag the thing over her head, and Dylan noticed the bra clasped in the front. A quick flick of his fingers and two beautiful breasts spilled out before him, begging for attention. "Perfect," he uttered before kissing the crevice between them.

"Oh yeah," she moaned, fingers digging into his scalp. "More of that."

Nothing got him hotter than a woman who knew what she wanted. "I aim to please," he assured, suckling her breast until she cried his name. Glancing up, he caught her heavy brown gaze. "My name sounds good on your lips, baby. Let's see if we can't do that again."

Tracing his tongue around her nipple, Dylan trailed a hand down her stomach and freed the button on her shorts. The moment his hand slid inside the denim, her hips lifted in invitation. As his mouth continued to tease, his fingers delved lower, behind a thin strip of satin to find her hot and wet. Time to drive her over the edge.

Finding her clit, he rolled it hard at the same moment he closed his teeth around her nipple.

"Holy shit," Charley cried, bucking against his touch. "Don't stop. Whatever you do, don't stop."

"Honey," he drawled, nibbling her lower lip, "we're just getting warmed up."

Chapter 6

Dylan rocked her clit again, and Charley stopped breathing. Bright lights flashed behind her eyes while her body lingered somewhere between heaven and hell.

"So slick," he mumbled against her ear. "So wet."

His talented fingers slid down her folds, and every nerve in Charley's body centered around his touch. Pressure pulsed in her core while anticipation sent her heart racing. He teased at the opening, building the tension, and she gritted her teeth to keep from begging for more.

Taking her mouth once more, Dylan's tongue danced with hers, mimicking what was to come. Her body writhed, riding his hand until she was certain she couldn't take much more. Muscles tight, she clamped her arms around his neck, whimpering with need.

Finally, when Charley feared he might never take the last step, Dylan drove two fingers in deep. The orgasm slammed through her like a lightning strike, and his name ripped from her lips to echo off the dark blue walls around them. Desperate for an anchor in the storm, she clung to his shoulders, helpless to control the tremors snaking through her extremities.

"I've got you, baby," Dylan whispered. "Relax into it."

The climax crested, and with a final shiver, Charley fell back to earth, panting heavily against his neck, certain her limbs lay scattered about the room. Part soothing, part arousing, Dylan caressed her bottom still covered in denim, and the realization dawned. She wasn't even naked yet, and he'd given her the strongest orgasm she'd ever had.

Future birthdays had a lot to live up to if they ever wanted to top this one.

"That was amazing," she said, rubbing her leg along his throbbing erection still trapped behind his Wranglers.

"Like I said earlier. Only the best for the birthday girl." With a finger beneath her chin, he tipped her face up until their eyes met. "You're pretty amazing yourself, Miss Layton."

"Thank you very much, Mr. . . ." The words fell away. Tucking her head again, she mumbled, "I can't believe I don't know your last name. What kind of a girl am I?"

The kind who enjoyed casual sex with a virtual stranger, if the last few minutes were any indication. Maybe one-night stands weren't such a bad thing.

"A beautiful, passionate one," he offered before rolling her until she lay sprawled atop his chest. "And my name is Dylan Monroe." Cupping her ass, he smiled. "If it'll get you out of those shorts, I'll tell you anything else you want to know."

Sexy. Smart. *And* seductive. She could get addicted to this boy real quick.

Which was the exact reason not to get too personal. A contradictory thought considering her bare and still swollen breasts lay pressed against his naked chest, but she had to draw the line somewhere. And right now, she was skating dangerously close to crossing every boundary in the book. The one absolute in her life was that Charley did not want a relationship.

"Only one question really matters at the moment," she said, tapping his bottom lip and keeping her tone light. "If we take this night to its logical conclusion, are you prepared to protect us both?"

Another roll and Charley found herself flat on her back, blanketed by six feet of delicious male. Without a word, Dylan opened a drawer on the stand beside the table and withdrew a blue box.

"I've got the night covered, and maybe a couple times in the morning."

There would be no morning sex, but Charley saw no reason to burst his bubble. Squirming her legs free, she danced her nails across his ribs as she pulled up her knees to hug his hips between her thighs.

"In that case, I'd like to unwrap the rest of my present." Never breaking eye contact, she reached for the top of his jeans, and Dylan lifted his weight to give her access. "I'll try not to scream this time," Charley said truthfully. She'd never been a screamer in the past, but then she'd never experienced anything close to Dylan's skills.

"And I'll do my best to make sure you do," he promised, doing a push-up to drop a kiss on her lips.

Charley worked the zipper down. "Impressive," she offered, enjoying the sight of pure muscle flexing above her. "How long have you been practicing that move?"

Dylan leaned to the side and caught her hands. "I'm not a player, Charley. I don't practice moves, and I didn't bring you here to put another notch in my bedpost."

She hadn't meant to insult him but had a hard time letting go of her assumptions. "Then why *did* you bring me here?"

Dropping onto his elbow, he brushed the hair off her forehead. "Because I like you. And because you let me."

Well, hell. "I like you, too," Charley admitted, unable to lie when he looked at her that way. A little too much for her comfort, which meant she needed him to stop looking at her as if she were the girl of his dreams. "Now, where were we?"

"Right here." He smiled, and like a scene in slow motion, Dylan kissed her, not with mindless lust, but with care and restraint. Falling into a relationship with this man would be the easiest thing in the world. And in no time, her life would be about him. About *them* and not the career she'd come here to build.

Locking her walls in place, Charley clamped down any thoughts of tomorrow and put the focus back where it belonged—on the feel of his thigh pressed between hers and the taste of his kiss.

Convinced he'd found the most alluring and unpredictable woman in town, Dylan turned his attention to finishing what they'd started. Kissing as he went, he tugged the shorts down her endless tan legs to find a delicate white thong, the last barrier between him and his destination. Before he could examine the feminine wisp of satin, Charley lifted her hips and shoved the undies down to her ankles, kicking them into the air.

"Now you," she demanded, nodding toward his jeans. The woman meant business.

"The boots have to come off first." Dropping onto the foot of the bed, he tugged off one Tony Lama and then the other, before standing to remove the denim. More than happy to give her dinner *and* a show, he watched her watch him undress. When his dick sprang free, brown eyes went wide with surprise, which quickly heated to appreciation. "You like what you see?" Dylan asked.

Charley licked her lips. "God, yes," she breathed, rising to her knees and crawling toward him. Elegant fingers traced his abs. "Perfection." The exploration traveled lower, and his lungs constricted when she took him in hand. "I'm a lucky girl tonight."

The moment she kissed the tip, his control snapped. Within seconds, he had her back on the bed and was ripping open a condom with his teeth. "Slide it on," he ordered. Charley followed his bidding without question. Sheathed, he balanced between her legs and took her mouth in a kiss that left them both burning with need. Every lunge and suck was returned with hot demand.

Bracing a hand behind her knee, he opened her wider and held his body in check, giving her the tip and nothing more.

"Dylan, don't do this to me," she begged. "Please. I want it now."

As earlier, he kept her on the edge, withholding the ultimate prize. "What do you want, baby?" A couple more inches slipped inside. "You have to tell me."

Charley dug her nails into his ass. "Deeper," she moaned, arching against him. "All of it. Now."

Losing the battle, he gave in and plunged to the hilt. Charley clenched around him, whimpering with gratitude as she met him thrust for thrust. Lost to everything but the woman clawing at his shoulders, Dylan kept a steady pace as he took her mouth in a series of bites and licks, before sinking his teeth into her shoulder. When she bucked, he drove harder and tasted the sweat on her skin. Salt and lust flooded his brain as his blood surged in one direction.

Knowing he couldn't hold off much longer, he reared up and rolled his thumb over her clit. "Come on, baby. Come with me."

Her body bowed as she cried out, panting with every roll of his hips. Gripping her thighs, he felt her tremble into oblivion as his own release ripped through his chest. Muscles locked as he gritted his teeth and buried his face in her neck. Dazed and spent, he dropped to the bed, coherent enough not to crush her. Charley's chest heaved with her efforts to breathe, and he couldn't resist the tight peak inches from his chin.

An aftershock took her hard when his lips closed over her breast, her languid curves tightening for a second more before the quiver reached her toes.

Lying in a tangle on top of the covers, Dylan couldn't make himself stop touching her. "You okay?" he asked when she grew quiet.

He felt more than saw her head nod. "I may never recover from that."

"Sure you will," he replied, kissing her temple. "A few more rounds and we might get good at this."

Even her laughter was sexy. "A few more rounds my ass." Turning in his arms, she pressed her back to his chest, and he pulled her in tight. "Let a girl recover, would you?" With a deep sigh, she closed her eyes.

Dylan gave her a squeeze. "Are you going to sleep?"

"A quick nap," she replied, voice fading fast. "You wore me out."

Accepting her need for sleep, he reached up for a pillow and tucked it beneath his head as Charley seemed content to rest on his arm. An arm that would be asleep and tingling within minutes, but it was worth the pain to have her tucked up against him. As her breathing grew more even, Dylan picked up the rhythm and drifted off himself.

Charley floated into consciousness, uncertain of where she was. The pillow didn't smell like her pillows. Easing one eye open, she slammed it shut again. Why in the world was she sleeping with the light on? The whirl of a ceiling fan penetrated her foggy brain. Charley's room didn't have a ceiling fan. Cool air danced across her skin, and she reached for the blankets only to make contact with warm skin that wasn't hers. Skin covered in a light dusting of hair that definitely was not hers.

Both eyes popped open, and she mouthed *oh my God* as reality hit. Her movements stirred the man behind her, and a heavy leg landed on her bare thigh, bringing another part of Dylan Monroe's anatomy into contact with her ass.

Lungs seized as she held her breath, praying he wouldn't wake up. Three seconds. Four seconds. Soft snores set a steady rhythm. She released her burning lungs but stayed as still as possible and assessed her situation.

Yes, she'd gone home with a man. Yes, she'd had sex with him. No, she did not regret that choice—especially considering how good the sex had been—but dammit, spending the night had not been her intention. Dylan had made repeated comments that indicated he saw their little roll in the sheets as the start of something, not the sum of it. Staying would lead to more sex, and then an awkward morning after, and Charley knew without a shadow of a doubt that she would not be able to look this man in the eye and tell him, "Have a nice life."

Which meant she had to get out now. Nip this in the bud, as Grandma had liked to say. Though this was so not the time to be thinking about Grandma, rest her soul.

First step—disengaging.

Charley slowly eased toward the edge of the bed, dragging her legs from beneath his. *Please be a heavy sleeper,* she thought, inching her way to freedom. Listening for any change in his breathing, she closed her eyes and crept a little farther until her toes cleared his calf. Dylan snorted and she froze, feigning sleep, but the snores resumed, even and subtle. Of course he'd be a considerate snorer. The man was freaking perfect.

Too perfect. Too kind and sweet and caring. The urge to stay knocked on her chest, and she cast a glance his way. Sweet baby Jesus, look at all that muscle. And those lips. No man should have lips like that. Perfectly full with a little curve in the top one, as if he'd been born with a built-in sexy grin.

No. No way. This was a complication she did not need. Clothing. That's what she needed.

Shuffling around on her hands and knees, she located her panties first and shimmied into them. Her socks and shoes were next. She shoved the anklets into her Justin boots and continued the hunt. The shorts and bra were on the floor on his side of the bed, which slowed her progress. Crawling like the coward she was, Charley snagged both items, along with her cell, and did a visual search for her tank top as she slipped on the bra.

The blasted thing was nowhere in sight. That would teach her to pay attention the next time she let a virtual stranger strip her naked. Not that she'd be partaking in this level of lunacy again anytime soon. Blast Ruby and her stupid advice. And blast Charley's libido for buying into the birthday sex idea without a solid exit strategy.

Something black caught her eye next to a chair in the corner. Dylan's shirt. That would have to do. Forced to reach between two guitars balancing on stands, she eased onto her knees and extended an arm as far as she could without touching the instruments. One wrong move and she could kiss her narrow escape goodbye.

The tip of a finger touched the cotton, but she couldn't get close enough to grab it. Sucking in, as if that might somehow make her boobs smaller, she tried again, but the lace of her bra caught the edge of a string, wringing out a low bong.

Suppressing the urge to curse aloud, she sent up a silent prayer for luck and waited for any sound from the bed. When the snoring continued, she let out a slow breath and switched to plan B. As gently as possible, she lifted a guitar off its stand and leaned it against the chair. After snatching the shirt and pulling it on, she put the guitar back and collected her boots.

Blessed freedom lay less than ten feet away. Forcing herself to move slowly, Charley crawled to the door, turned the knob with excruciating care, and slipped into the hall, using the same measured touch to close the door behind her. Back to the wall, she exhaled with relief, amazed that she'd actually done it. Looking down, she righted her clothes. The shirt fit more like a dress, so she fastened enough buttons to cover her chest and tied the rest in a knot around her hips.

A quick hand through her hair and she headed for the stairs, checking the time on her phone. Three a.m. If she hurried, she could probably get a car still out waiting for the late bar-hoppers. Entering her info, Charley realized she didn't know Dylan's address. Had she ever thought anything through less than this night? Pausing halfway down, she racked her brain for a solution.

The restaurant. The Pharmacy was right up the street. Surely a driver could find that. Keying in the location, a car popped up on the screen. Ten minutes away.

"I sure hope this is a safe neighborhood," she muttered, hurrying the rest of the way down. At the bottom step, she sat and put on her socks and boots, debating whether or not to use the bathroom before running out the door. The pressure on her bladder won out, and she did a one-eighty back toward the kitchen, hoping one of the doors they'd passed might be a powder room.

Unfortunately, what she found was a woman.

"Well, hello," the blonde said, eyes wide over a red coffee cup.

Charley went with the first thing that came to mind. "Please tell me you aren't his girlfriend."

"Depends," the woman said, setting the mug on the counter. "Which room did you come out of?"

"Top of the stairs. On the left."

The eyes went wide again. "*Not* my boyfriend. But you must be something special. I've lived here two years, and Dylan has never brought a woman home before."

He really *was* the most decent guy on the planet.

"Actually, I'm nothing special. A car is coming to get me at the restaurant up the street, but I really need to pee. Is there a bathroom down here?"

The high ponytail bounced as she nodded toward the door on Charley's right. "In there. I'm Pamela, by the way."

"Charley," she said, shuffling toward the restroom. "I'll be right out."

With quick movements, she took care of business and washed her hands before stepping back into the kitchen.

"If Dylan comes down soon, could you *not* tell him that we ran into each other?"

Perfectly penciled brows arched. "Unusual, but I suppose you have your reasons. Do you steal a shirt from all the guys you do and ditch?"

So much for female solidarity. "I couldn't find the shirt I had on last night. If you'll give me this address, I'll send it back to him."

Pamela shook her head. "That would be too easy. Better go catch your car."

A check of her phone showed the driver was only blocks away. "Right." Charley spun toward the door, but she couldn't leave without making something clear. "I know that Dylan is a good guy. That's why I have to go."

Blue eyes softened. "You'd better hurry then."

Without another word, Charley hustled to the door and made her final escape.

Chapter 7

The soothing sounds of AC/DC ripped Dylan out of a sound sleep.

"What?" he mumbled, opening his eyes only to close them again. Between the sun slicing through the window and the glaring bulbs overhead, he'd be seeing spots for hours. As Angus shredded on guitar, Dylan felt around the nightstand for his phone and knocked the clock to the floor. The first order of business once his vision cleared would be changing that damn ring tone.

Dylan leaned up on an elbow and peeked through shuttered lids to notice two important facts. He was naked. And he was alone.

"Damn," he sighed, dropping back to the bed. When the drums kicked in, he followed the sound to the chair in the corner and answered the call. "Hello?"

"About time," greeted Clay Benedict. "Where were you last night?"

Double damn. "I forgot you were coming out, man. I left early."

"So I heard. Casey didn't appreciate you ditching him for a girl."

"When I left Casey, he had his own girl on the line."

Clay chuckled. "If you mean that gorgeous blonde, she broke his heart just as I got there. He left for Tootsie's before I had my first drink."

Swiping his boxer briefs off the floor, Dylan tucked the phone against his shoulder and slid them on. "I warned him he didn't stand a chance with that one. Really sorry I cut out on you."

"Was she worth it?" the record exec asked.

Glancing to the bed, Dylan smiled. "Yeah, she was."

"Good. Write a song about it."

Clay had been nagging him to write his own stuff since their first week in the studio. Dylan had pointed out all the great songs they already had to choose from, and assured the label owner that if he ever wrote something worth cutting, Clay would be the first to know.

"I've got good news," the older man continued. "Eagle 101.5 is going to add your new single starting tomorrow, and they want you to do it live on the air."

Dylan dropped to the mattress. "Are you serious? During the morning show?" *Ruby Barnett's Country Crew*, a syndicated show, aired on hundreds of stations across the country.

"The news isn't *that* good. Aldean is already scheduled during Ruby's show, so they're giving us a late-morning slot. You'll be on the air with this new girl, Charley Layton, between eleven and twelve."

If that wasn't a sign, Dylan didn't know what was.

"I'll take it," he said. "Have you let Mitch know?" Dylan hadn't heard from his manager in a week, but news like this should have gone through him first.

"I called, but no answer," Clay replied. "Since this is tomorrow, I didn't want to hold off letting you know. This is it, Dylan. Eagle has a huge audience here in town, and what the station adds, other stations pick up. You'll be nationwide within a month."

He appreciated his boss's confidence, but Dylan preferred to stay cautiously optimistic. Too many of his friends had gotten this far only to fade into oblivion by the time they'd signed their first autograph. "Sounds good, man."

"Are you ready for your life to change?"

Smothering his inner realist, he replied, "Yes, sir. Bring it on."

"That's what I like to hear." The sound of a door opening echoed down the line, and Clay's voice tightened. "Dylan, I've got to go. Be at the station at ten forty-five in the morning. I'll meet you there."

"You've got it, boss."

The line went dead, and Dylan settled back on the bed, letting the phone drop to the mattress beside him. "See, Charley? You should have stuck around," he muttered to the ceiling fan. "We could have learned the good news together." Then again, maybe she wouldn't see this as good news at all. He'd thought they'd made a connection, but then he'd been wrong about women before.

Stretching his arms, he found something wadded up under his pillow. Lifting it above his head, he couldn't help but laugh. "If this is here, what did you wear home?"

Dylan sat up and looked around. Boots. Jeans. Empty condom wrapper.

"You little thief," he whispered, but couldn't help imagining how good she must have looked in his shirt. "Looks like we have some unfinished business, birthday girl."

"What do you want, Joanna?" Clay Benedict asked, foregoing civility. He'd considered putting Mrs. Rossi on the do-not-admit list, but to do so would only stir curiosity and make him look like more of an asshole than he already did.

The diner waitress turned debutante maintained her brittle smile. "Don't be so boorish, Clayton. You know I don't scare off that easily." She circled his office, taking in every bare inch and looking out of place in her white Chanel suit and pearls.

All of Clay's money had gone into launching Shooting Stars Records, with little left over for anything but the necessities. The staff possessed all the means to do their jobs, while he'd limited himself to a desk, a chair, and a computer. A minimalist at heart, the meager decor served Clay fine.

"Does Tony know you're here?"

"Don't be silly," she replied. "He thinks I'm at church."

Which reminded Clay that he shouldn't be working on a Sunday.

"Won't someone tell him you didn't show?"

The queen of lies and alibis said, "I put in an appearance. That will do if he asks, though I doubt he will."

Tony's failure to pay attention to his wife had resulted in the errant Mrs. Rossi falling into his best friend's bed, and it had also made their clandestine meetings so easy to pull off.

"I have work to do, Joanna. Tell me why you're here."

Stopping before his desk, she tucked an obscenely expensive clutch beneath her arm. "I want to know why you're being so stubborn, Clayton. Tony has no idea that we're lovers."

"*Were* lovers," he corrected. "Past tense."

"Only because you're being ridiculous about this."

Of course. Because no longer sleeping with his best friend's wife was such a silly notion.

"Tony suspected you were having an affair. For Christ's sake, he came to *me* concerned that you were going to leave him. He thought I might know who you were seeing, and even I'm not bastard enough to keep up that charade."

She leaned on the desk, clutch still tucked tight. "But you know that I have no intention of leaving my husband. All you had to do was assure him that I was still the good little wife, and we could have gone on as we were."

"Do you hear yourself?" Clay asked, astounded that he'd ever found this woman attractive. Hell, he couldn't even name a part of her body that hadn't been upgraded, tweaked, or lifted in the last ten years. "That's your husband you're talking about. You may not have a problem making a fool of him, but that doesn't mean I'm going to help you do it."

Her husky laughter filled the room. "You *helped* me for a year, until your conscience reared its ugly head. There's no reason we can't go back to enjoying each other, Clayton. Tony has his golf game and his poker nights, and I have my *me* time, which happens to include fucking you. We all win."

Clay shook his head. "You're a real piece of work, Joanna. Why don't you divorce him? You know he'll give you anything you want."

"Because I don't want to divorce Tony. While you two begged and borrowed to get that damn record label off the ground, I put up with roach-infested apartments, piece-of-shit cars, and collectors banging down the door. I've earned my place as Mrs. Tony Rossi, and I have no intention of giving that up. Not for you or anyone else."

"And I have no intention of touching you ever again, divorce or no divorce."

Slate-blue eyes flared with anger, but she didn't lose her composure. Instead, she rounded the desk and planted her nipped and tucked ass on the shiny brown surface, legs wide in invitation.

"We were good together, Clayton. You can't deny that."

"It doesn't take much to be good at sex, Joanna. I've told you before. You'll have to find someone else to scratch that itch." Without another word, he rose from his chair and walked to the door, holding it open. "Goodbye, Mrs. Rossi."

She lingered for several seconds, as if waiting for him to change his mind. When Clay held his ground, she finally slid to the floor.

"You still want me, Clayton. If you keep me waiting too long, I might not be willing to take you back."

"I'll muddle through."

"Remember," she purred, joining him at the door and standing close enough to leave her scent on his clothes, "if you replace me, I'll know. And I won't be happy about it."

"My personal life is none of your concern, Joanna. And I don't give a shit if you're happy or not." Putting space between them, he motioned to the exit. "Now have a nice day."

With narrowed eyes and a pout on her berry-red lips, she toyed with a button on his shirt as if debating whether or not to press her case. In the past, he'd have caved and taken her on the desk by now. But Clay wasn't that man anymore.

"Goodbye, Joanna."

The blonde tapped a finger on his lips and said, "Until next time, my dear." The warning was implicit—this conversation was not over.

"The happy little hussy finally makes an appearance."

Charley was in no mood for Matty's sarcasm. Grabbing a box of Cheerios from the top of the fridge, she dropped her phone on the kitchen table as she took a seat opposite her roommate.

"This is my first day off in two weeks. I'm allowed to sleep in."

Matty flipped a page in her magazine. "You slept late because you strolled in around four. Spill, woman. I want details."

"You know who I was with, and you know what I was doing. That's enough details for today."

"Oh, come on. Give me something."

Flipping the script, Charley said, "I'll share if you will. How was your evening with Casey?"

Her roommate waved away the question. "Please. The boy broke a cardinal rule—never talk about your ex with the chick you're trying to pick up. If I'd have heard the name Pamela one more time, I was going to scream."

The name of the woman Charley had encountered in Dylan's kitchen. Which meant Casey was the third roommate.

"I met her on my way out. She seemed nice."

"To hear Casey tell it, she's a harpy with trust issues. Which, of course, means she's a strong woman who called him on his shit. What's she look like?"

Odd question. "Petite, blonde hair, and blue eyes." Pausing with a handful of cereal, she said, "Now that I think about it, she looks like you."

"I knew it," Matty mumbled, flipping another page. "After I sent him packing, he danced with three other women. All blue-eyed blondes."

"At least he's consistent," Charley credited. "She still lives with them, so that must be awkward. I wonder why she hasn't moved out."

The magazine dropped to the table. "Why should she move out? Let him get another place. With the population growing by nearly a hundred people a day in this town, apartments aren't easy to come by."

She had a point. If Matty hadn't been looking for a roommate when Charley got hired, she wasn't sure where she'd be living right now. "Fair enough. Did Ruby ask where I was?"

"Yep. I told her you left with a hottie, and she said good for you." Feet tucked into bunny slippers landed on the chair to Charley's right, ankles crossed. "And since you were inconsiderate enough to cut out before we gave you your cake, we cut into it without you."

"You got me a cake?"

"It was your birthday, numb nuts. Of course we got you a cake." Matty pointed to the counter behind her. "Your piece is up there."

A piece? "You and Ruby ate the whole thing?" she asked, setting aside the cereal and crossing to the counter.

"Don't be silly. We shared it with the VIP table."

Charley popped open the Styrofoam container to find one small corner piece of cake covered in white frosting. No words. No flowers. Nothing to indicate what the thing had looked like. "Did you at least take a picture?"

Matty returned her attention to the magazine. "Someone did, but I can't remember who. I'll ask at work tomorrow and maybe we can find it."

Retrieving a fork from the drawer, she carried her sad little cake to the table. "Happy birthday to me," she muttered as the fork cut through the chocolate sponge.

"Hey," the blonde snapped. "You got something way better than cake last night, didn't you?"

Chewing her treat, Charley recalled the night before, and her body flushed with heat. "He *was* really good." Possibly the understatement of the decade.

"That's what I thought. Are you going to see him again?"

"Heck no," she said around another bite. "That was a birthday one-off. Over and done."

The bunny slippers hit the floor. "He's gorgeous as hell *and* really good in bed, but you don't want to see him again? Did you slam your skull too hard on his headboard or something? Woman, that's a winning combination."

"No," Charley explained, "*that* is a distraction. I'm here to build my career. I don't have time for a relationship."

"Who said anything about a relationship? Use him for sex."

Regardless of the fact he'd taken her home only hours after they'd met, Charley knew for certain that Dylan was not the "use him for sex" type. If his own claims hadn't been convincing enough, Pamela's comment that he never brought women home had confirmed her suspicions.

"Not an option," she said. "I doubt our paths will cross again, and we didn't exchange numbers."

Matty laughed. "You're on the radio, Charley. He can find you if he wants."

Dang. She hadn't thought of that. "Maybe leaving without saying goodbye ticked him off enough to make sure he doesn't come looking." *Unless he wants his shirt back,* she thought.

"You left without even saying goodbye? Who does that?"

Charley stuck the fork in her cake. "I'm new at this one-night stand stuff, okay? Things got too real, and I panicked."

"Too real?" Matty asked.

How was she supposed to explain that Dylan had turned out to be one of the good ones—which Charley considered a bad thing—and not sound like an idiot?

Setting the plate on the table, she leaned her elbows on the edge. "You told me you moved to Nashville to be with a guy, right?"

Matty stiffened. "What does my stupidity have to do with this?"

"You weren't stupid. You put your trust in the wrong guy. He said all the right things, and you gave up everything to be with him."

"I did," she muttered.

"So I don't want to do that."

Tucking the magazine under her arm, Matty rose and pushed in her chair. "Glad I could serve as a cautionary tale."

"Wait," Charley pleaded, grabbing her roommate's arm. "I'm sorry, that didn't come out right." She took a deep breath. "The fact is, my mother made the same choice that you did. She met a guy and fell in love, and suddenly none of her dreams mattered. She walked away from a college scholarship, and her lifelong goal of being a teacher, for a man."

Violet Layton, Charley's late mother, never complained or even hinted that she'd regretted her decision, but then she couldn't have known how unfairly her life would be cut short.

Matty plopped down in her chair. "What happened?" she asked.

Charley shoved both hands into her hair. "She got pregnant with me, my dad was killed in a combine accident before I was born, and then, when I was sixteen, Mama died of breast cancer. Two months before she'd been scheduled to start her online degree."

The kitchen chair scraped across linoleum as Matty scooted closer. "Oh, honey. I'm so sorry."

Willing back the tears, she shook her head. "Forget it. I'm fine." Charley swiped a knuckle beneath her nose. "The point is, a career in radio is all I've ever wanted, but I also know that for the right guy, I might do the same thing. So . . . I have to avoid the right guy. And that means not seeing Dylan Monroe ever again."

With an understanding nod, Matty said, "All right then. No more Dylan Monroe."

At that moment, Charley's phone buzzed, indicating a text message. Checking the screen, she saw a text from Elvis.

> Maynard says he hasn't heard from you in a while. Checking to make sure you're still alive down there.

When Charley rolled her eyes, Matty said, "What is it?"

"Elvis checking up on me. Sometimes I think he and Grandpa believe I've moved to the jungles of South America instead of Nashville." Setting her thumbs in motion, she typed her response.

> Still alive and kicking. Crazy busy with work. I'll call soon, promise.

"I still think it's weird that your best friend is a guy," her roommate said. "Maybe he checks on you so much because he thinks of you as more than a friend."

Charley shot her a droll look. "We've been over this. Elvis and I are more like sister and brother than friends, and he'd tell you the same. His check-ins are a combination of annoying me and concern that he thinks I'm ignoring Grandpa. If he actually thought I was in danger, he'd be pounding on our front door, prepared to rip the head off whoever or whatever had been stupid enough to attack me."

Interest twinkled in Matty's blue eyes. "Maybe we should invite him down for a weekend. I'm dying to meet this 'sibling' of yours."

Such a meeting had trouble written all over it. "Elvis is not your type," Charley mumbled as she read the returning text.

I'll tell him you'll call tomorrow.

The message served as a threat that Charley knew better than to ignore. And because she never let Elvis win one of these pissing matches, she rose from the table, phone in one hand and cake in the other.

"I'm going upstairs to make a call."

"Invite him down," Matty repeated.

Charley ignored the order as she marched toward the stairs.

Chapter 8

"All I'm saying is that he ought to be here," Casey repeated for the third time.

Dylan had sent Mitch Levine four text messages and left him two voice mails after getting the news from Clay the day before. But as he waited in the lobby of the Eagle 101.5 offices for his big moment, he had yet to hear from his manager.

"He doesn't *have* to be here. Clay can handle things."

Casey, like most drummers, couldn't sit still. "Clay shouldn't have to handle things," he said, tapping out a steady beat on his thighs. "Shit is getting real, man. Times like these are why you have a manager."

The argument was nothing new, nor was Dylan's response.

"Relax. He's gotten us this far." Though Dylan was the official act, with Casey, Lance, and Easton merely employees in the band, he still thought of them as a group. They'd been playing together for four years. They were a unit, regardless of what any contract said. "I'm sure there's a good reason he isn't here."

"If you say so." Casey increased his tapping to double time, proving he was as nervous as Dylan. Only they were nervous for different reasons.

Charley Layton knew Dylan's secret. By now, she likely also knew exactly who he was, and she might see his failure to disclose certain details as some sort of deception. If she called him out on the air about writing his own songs, Dylan couldn't be sure how he'd react. With luck, he'd get a minute alone with her before they went live.

"There's my boy," said Clay, rubbing his hands together as he entered the building. Clasping Dylan's hand, he patted him on the shoulder. "You ready for this?"

"Ready as I'll ever be," Dylan replied, grateful for the executive's support and enthusiasm.

No one had been willing to touch Dylan after his first failed album. That was the downside to the Nashville music scene. Everyone knew everything that went on. When his first deal had gone south, so had his credibility as a viable artist. Pride had kept him from turning tail and moving back home, but if the Shooting Stars offer hadn't come along when it did, Dylan would have been hard-pressed to stick it out.

"Morning, Casey," he said, glancing around. "Is Mitch here?"

"Hell no," Casey replied, earning a stiff elbow to the ribs.

"Mitch got tied up," Dylan explained. "He had a meeting he couldn't cancel."

Clay no doubt knew the statement to be a lie, but he played along.

"All right then. Let's go launch a career, shall we?"

Dylan's gut clenched, and his palms grew sweaty. The dream he'd been chasing for nearly half his life was on the verge of coming true. Or that dream was about to crash and burn—again. If he failed this time, there wasn't likely to be a third chance. And as the launching artist of Shooting Stars Records, the success of the company also rested on his shoulders. A reality never far from his mind.

"This is what we've worked for," he said, lifting his guitar off the floor. "Let's do this."

"That was a classic from Reba here on the Eagle," Charley said into the mic. "Don't forget about our Manic Monday giveaway coming up in the noon hour. One lucky caller will pick up a pair of tickets to the Country Music Hall of Fame, and all you have to do is listen to win. Eleven seventeen now. Music from our favorite singing Aussie coming up after the break."

Charley fired off the commercials and removed her headphones. After rolling her shoulders, she reached for the weather and checked the computer for the current temperature.

"You ready for your guest?" asked John Willoughby as he breezed into the booth. The program manager never simply walked into a room. He blew in like a tornado, without warning and moving fast. "He'll be playing acoustic, so we'll put vocals on mic B and the guitar on mic C."

"No one told me I had a guest today," she replied. Charley didn't like surprises, especially not live on the air.

"I put a note on the log," he said, shifting stools around and twisting the movable metal arms that held the microphones. "Dylan Monroe on air between eleven and noon."

Her heart dropped to her knees. "What did you say?"

"Dylan Monroe," John repeated. "He's the first artist launching on the Shooting Stars label. The single's been out for a while, but we're only adding it now. He's here to play it live today."

A nervous laugh escaped her lips. "I didn't get any note," she repeated, as if John would throw his hands in the air and cancel the appearance because Charley hadn't been warned ahead of time that her one-night stand would be walking into her booth.

Her boss merely shrugged. "Life is full of surprises, I guess."

The man had no freaking idea.

"Don't you usually do these things on the morning show?" Ruby was syndicated, which meant exposure nationwide instead of solely in Middle Tennessee.

"Not debut artists. If he makes it, he'll get a slot with Ruby, but for right now, he's a nobody."

Insulting both to Dylan and to Charley. The nobody singer only gets to hang with the nobody DJ. And then a meaningless exchange from Saturday night played back in her head.

Your voice is incredible, Dylan. You should be performing somewhere.
Maybe I'll do that.

What a jerk. He must have gotten a good laugh out of that one. She'd been totally honest with him, and he'd let her believe he was some shy, struggling songwriter too chickenshit to let anyone hear his work.

"That asshole," she mumbled as John whipped open the door and three men strolled into the tiny room.

Immediately, Dylan locked eyes with her, but his features were unreadable. He didn't greet her by name or act as if they knew each other. Charley glanced to her computer screen to see her last commercial was about to end.

"I'm on air in five seconds, so you all need to be quiet." Sliding on her headphones, she pulled her microphone into place and cleared her throat. Flipping a switch, she reeled off the forecast and then promo'd her surprise guest. "Stay tuned to the Eagle to hear a brand-new artist play his debut single live on the air, but first up, as promised, it's Keith Urban."

Headphones around her neck, she leaned back on her stool. As much as she wanted to call Dylan on his deception, she remained professional. "Let me know when you're ready, and we'll cut in between songs. Do you have any sort of bio? I need something to work with."

"My publicist sent that over first thing this morning," said the slightly older man in the expensive-looking suit.

"I've got it," Willoughby assured, tapping the stool across from Charley. "Dylan, have a seat right here and put the microphones wherever you need them. I'll run down to my office and get the bio."

As John dashed from the room, the suit reached a hand across the console. "Clay Benedict," he offered. "I get the impression you didn't know we were coming."

"No," she said, accepting the handshake. "I found out less than a minute before you walked in."

Charley made a point of ignoring Dylan. Being professional only went so far, and at that moment, she wanted to swing the mic stand hard enough to knock the black Stetson off his head.

"Morning, Charley," greeted Casey, who leaned against the wall, ankles crossed and wearing a smile that didn't reach his green eyes. Two fingers tapped in rapid time beneath his armpit.

Dylan remained silent, giving his full attention to removing a guitar from its case and finding a comfortable position on his stool. The same guitar that had rested on her lap two nights ago.

As if concerned that his artist was making a poor first impression, Clay Benedict stepped in. "We're grateful for this chance to play for your audience, Miss Layton. Aren't we, Dylan?"

Eyes that had haunted Charley's recent dreams remained in shadow beneath the black hat. "I'm much obliged for the air time," he muttered, his tone impersonal and aloof.

So that's how this would go? Fine by her.

"What's the name of your song, Mr. Monroe?" she asked, wondering whether he'd name the song from Saturday night.

"'Down Here Down Home,'" he replied with a strum of the guitar. "Will this pick up okay?"

Charley pressed a button on the board and said, "Play it again." Dylan did as asked, and the LEDs on the channel for microphone C lit up. "You're good."

She couldn't believe they were sitting four feet apart, acting for all the world as if they hadn't seen each other naked less than forty-eight hours ago. A memory that had also invaded her dreams and kept her awake half the night. If he felt any guilt at all for duping her, Dylan hid it well.

John buzzed back into the room and slapped a sheet of paper down in front of Charley. "This will get you started to let the listeners know a bit about our guest here, and then you can transition into the live performance." Turning to Clay Benedict, he said, "You and Casey can come listen in my office."

She hadn't expected to be alone with Dylan and nearly argued that they should all stay.

Casey patted Dylan on the back. "You got this, man."

Dylan nodded, expression stoic and focused.

Following the two older men, the drummer stopped at the door and turned back to Charley. "Make him sound good, okay?"

Charley gave a silent nod. One lie by omission didn't mean she'd ruin Dylan Monroe's budding career. While they were live, he'd receive the same treatment she'd give any other artist. But once the interview was over, all bets were off.

Once they were alone, Dylan took his first step into the minefield.

"Hi," he said with a friendly smile.

Charley ignored the greeting. "This song has two minutes left. We'll introduce you and give a little background to the listeners, and then you can play the single." Indicating a set of headphones on the console in front of him, she added, "You'll need to put those on."

He hadn't been sure what to expect, but the ice queen act took him by surprise considering the fiery passion displayed during their first meeting.

Removing his hat, Dylan tried again. "I'm sorry they sprang this on you. I'd be irritated, too."

She leveled him with a glare. "That's why you think I'm annoyed? Guess again."

Fearing she might trash him on air, Dylan kept his temper in check, but barely. "Can we discuss this after the interview?"

Ignoring his request, she reviewed his bio. Five seconds into the silent treatment, she snorted. "The album is called *Pickup Artist*. How appropriate."

"That song is about a guy who keeps getting dumped and becomes an expert at picking himself back up," he explained, not sure why he was defending himself. "A sentiment I'm familiar with in more ways than one."

Her emerald-green top slid off one smooth shoulder, revealing a tiny red mark he knew was his doing. "Leaving you to wake up alone after a one-night stand does not qualify as dumping you," she argued.

Her blunt summation of their night together hit a nerve. "So that's all it was? A one-night stand?"

"We had sex less than four hours after we met," Charley hissed in a low voice. "What did you think? A late-night meal followed by two orgasms and I'd be madly in love with you?"

"Wow," he said, strumming the guitar strings. "Thanks for the honesty."

Charley leaned forward, and his view went from bare shoulder to tempting cleavage. By his dick's reaction, her icy attitude didn't make him want her any less.

"You've got some nerve talking about honesty," she snapped. "You walked in here acting like we'd never even met."

"I didn't think you'd want to explain *how* we know each other," he said, teetering between walking out and kissing some sense into her. "Apologies for considering your feelings."

"Right," she snapped. "Because I'm the one who likes to keep secrets."

"What is that supposed to mean?"

She waved her hands in the air. "This, Dylan. Why didn't you tell me that you're a professional singer? You knew everything about me. Where I work. What I do. Even where I'm from. And you told me virtually nothing. Was that 'I'm a shy little songwriter too scared to share my work' just a line? Something you toss out there so gullible females like me will be all 'take me home and sing me a song, Dylan.'"

The guitar pick dug into his palm as his grip tightened. "I told you once that I'm not that guy. Would knowing I had a record deal have changed anything? If you thought you'd bagged a guy on the verge of money and fame, would you have stuck around until morning?"

Brown eyes snapped with fire as the last notes of the Keith Urban song faded out. Without missing a beat, Charley lifted her headphones into place and pulled the microphone forward.

"That was Keith Urban here on Eagle 101.5, fresh off a couple shows in Canada this month. I bet it's cooler up there than is it down here right now. Charley Layton getting you through another workday, and as promised, I have a special guest in the studio with me. Without further ado," she said, motioning for him to put on the headphones, "I give you Dylan Monroe. Nice to have you with us today, Dylan."

Dazed by the sudden one-eighty, he took an extra second to answer. The panic in her eyes was almost worth the brain freeze. "Thanks for having me, Charley. It's good to be here."

"So not only are we going to hear your first single today, but you're the first artist signed to the new Shooting Stars label. Does that add extra pressure for this release to be a success?"

Nothing like going for the jugular. "There's always pressure for a new artist starting out, but yeah, a little extra in this case. My label has put a lot faith in me, and I'd like to make them proud."

"Tell the listeners where you're from and how long you've been at this."

"Sure," he replied, amazed that she could sound so sweet and friendly without the hint of a smile on her face. "I hail from Louisiana, not too far from Shreveport, and I've been knocking around Nashville fighting for a break for five years."

Tapping a finger on the console, she tilted her head, looking interested for the first time. "That's a long time to fight for a dream. Have you gotten close in the past?"

"Once," he said, shifting on his stool. "But none of that matters now. I was born to do this, and thanks to Shooting Stars, I'm finally getting my chance."

Expression finally matching her tone, Charley said, "Good. I hope it works out." Staring as if seeing him for the first time, she fell silent.

Dylan raised his brows and nodded toward her microphone.

"The album," she blurted. "Tell us about the album."

"Love to," he replied. "*Pickup Artist* is a collection of eleven songs from some of the best writers in Nashville. The title track is about a guy who trusts a little too much and has to pick his heart up off the floor on a regular basis. Then there's 'Flowers Down,' about a guy who sends his girl flowers only to find them in the trash."

Charley frowned. "I'm sensing a theme here. Do women play the villain in all your songs?"

"Not all," he said. "'Working at Home' tells the tale of a guy who's landed the girl of his dreams and has the family life he's always wanted. And there's plenty of upbeat songs, like the new single, 'Down Here Down Home,' about being happy in a small town."

"Did you write that one?" she asked.

His voice faltered. "No, I don't have any cuts on the album. The talent in this town is so good, I gave them all the spotlight."

Fist propping up her chin, Charley said, "Really?"

"Yeah, really," Dylan replied, worried she might bring up the song he'd played for her.

Clay didn't know that he'd been writing songs. If she outed him on the air, he'd have some major explaining to do.

"But the single is so close to my life," he continued, "I related to it as if I'd written the song. Young kids running down back roads, having bonfires, and enjoying total freedom is pretty much the story of my teen years. I'm hoping lots of country music fans will relate as well."

"I'm sure they will," Charley said with conviction. "And that sounds like the perfect segue to me. Are you ready to play for us?"

"Yes, ma'am," Dylan responded, strumming the guitar.

Reaching for the board, Charley said, "One more tidbit for our listeners before you start. Ladies, in case you're wondering, he's as pretty as he sounds."

Maybe there was a chance for them yet.

"Not sure I've ever been called pretty," he said, "But I'll take it. And if anyone out there likes this song enough to want to see us live, we're playing a celebration show this Friday night at the Marathon Music Works here in town. Maybe you can join us, Ms. Layton."

Brown eyes narrowed, and the ice queen returned. "I'll have to check my schedule. Here now, singing his debut single, 'Down Here Down Home,' Eagle brings you Shooting Stars artist Dylan Monroe."

Chapter 9

Just because he'd made Charley like him again, and sounded amazing on the radio, did not mean she and Dylan had resolved anything. Why did he have to be such a hard-luck case? Charley was a sucker for an underdog story. Not that Dylan should have been an underdog in anything.

He had the looks, the voice, and the songwriting chops to stand with any artist on the charts, past or present. In fact, she'd have bet that next to the term *the whole package* in the dictionary would be Dylan's picture. Was the term *the whole package* even in the dictionary? Maybe not, but if it was, his face would be there.

The moment he'd finished the song, which was upbeat and catchy as all get-out, Charley thanked him for coming into the studio, encouraged listeners to request and download the song, and then fired off the Alabama tune up next in the computer.

Before she and Dylan had removed their headphones, the door flew open and the three men returned, along with Sharita from the PR team, who'd been snapping pictures through the window to the hall while Dylan played.

"Good job, everybody," praised John. "That's the way to debut a song, Dylan. The listeners will light up the phones in no time."

No comment was made about Charley's interviewing skills.

"Charley deserves the credit," Dylan replied. "Pretty sure she could tell that I was nervous, and she put me right at ease."

The boy could spin a yarn with the best of them. Four seconds before she'd cracked her microphone, she'd nearly cracked him in the jaw.

"Of course," John agreed. "Charley made you look good."

"Doing my job," she muttered, setting her headphones on the console.

Fluttering like a hummingbird on steroids, the schmoozing manager shook the record exec's hand as if he were pumping a well. "Once Dylan packs up his guitar, we'll head to the conference room to meet some of our staff and snap pictures with our newest star."

Charley was happy to avoid the photo shoot—and any further conversation with her guest, in public or in private. They'd established their positions, formed a tolerable truce, and could now retreat to their respective corners, never to cross paths again.

With three songs scheduled back-to-back, she took the opportunity to visit the ladies' room, certain that Dylan would be long gone by the time she returned. Stepping into the hall, she pivoted toward the restroom.

"Hey," Dylan called from behind her. "Can I talk to you a second?"

Charley sighed as she turned around. "There isn't much left to say at this point. You think I'm a heartless floozy, and I think you're a gifted actor who manipulates the truth to suit his needs. We're both a little wrong, but got some awesome sex out of it, so let's call it even."

His laughter took her by surprise. "You really are the most interesting woman I've ever met."

"Glad I could show you a new side to half the population. Now if you'll excuse me . . ."

"Go out with me," he said.

Sweet bread and butter, the man didn't know when to quit.

"Why would I do that?"

"Because you like me," Dylan declared with unwavering confidence and a *tell me you don't* grin. "And because I should have been up-front about my singing, and you shouldn't have cut out while I was sleeping. So let's start over. I promise to have you home and in bed by midnight. Alone," he clarified.

A big fat *no* teetered on the tip of Charley's tongue. She'd fled Dylan's bed for a reason. A very good reason. Only she couldn't quite remember that reason with him hovering all hot and sexy and smelling like an apple crisp closed in a cedar chest.

A combination that made her think of home, and then feel guilty for thinking of sex and Grandpa's farm at the same time.

"I'm not sure you can call a do-over once two people have slept together."

With a twinkle in his eye, he said, "But we haven't slept together, remember?"

Now he had her on a technicality.

"This is pointless."

"What if I said I plan to make one of your wildest dreams come true?" he asked.

Charley rolled her eyes. "You think a date with you is one of my wildest dreams?"

The self-deprecating grin chipped away at her resistance. "My ego isn't that big. Just trust me. You don't want to pass this up."

"Fine," she sighed. "Where are you taking me?"

Tipping up the black hat, Dylan said, "I'll pick you up at four on Wednesday."

This told her nothing. "You didn't answer my question."

"Can't a guy surprise a girl?"

"I don't like surprises," she said, tapping an impatient foot.

Dylan tucked his hands in his pockets. "You'll like this one."

Out of patience, Charley threw her hands in the air as she stomped off toward the bathroom. An entire song had likely played through by now.

"You're a pain in my ass, Monroe."

"I need your number," Dylan hollered with a chuckle.

She waved the request away as she picked up her pace. "Leave yours in the booth, and I'll considering getting in touch."

Twenty minutes into the meet and greet that Dylan hadn't been aware would take place, he received a text from his manager. A cryptic message out of the blue.

Come see me. I'm at the house.

Dylan didn't have time to respond, instead tucking the phone back into his pocket and smiling through another round of pictures. When he thought they'd finally reached the end, he turned to find Charley's roommate leaning against the wall. He searched the room for Casey, finding him in what looked like deep conversation with an intern who'd been introduced as Gunner a few minutes before.

"Are you waiting for a picture?" he asked Matty.

Appearing bored, she shook her head. "I'm not the selfie-with-a-celebrity type. Especially not when that celebrity is a complete unknown."

Coming from Charley, the comment would have struck him as a harmless, if blunt, observation of the truth. From Matty, the words felt more like a verbal attack.

"You're used to making the first cut, aren't you?" Dylan asked. "Insult them before they insult you?"

"You should have told her who you were," she said, ignoring his question. "Charley deserves better."

"When she disappeared from the Wildhorse, did you notice? Charley said she didn't have any texts from you asking where she'd gone."

Though he hadn't mentioned it at the time, several things that night had bothered Dylan. First, a supposed friend had put Charley in a situation knowing she'd be uncomfortable, and then the other friend didn't seem to notice either her distress or her disappearance.

Matty straightened off the wall. "Casey told me she was with you. I didn't know that you two had left the club until later, when one of the interns said she'd watched you go out the door."

"That still leaves a good half hour before Casey got my message," Dylan continued, closing the distance between them. "You didn't lay eyes on your friend for that long, yet you weren't concerned enough to even text her."

Blue eyes flashed with anger, but not before a hint of guilt slipped through. "She's a big girl, and that's a big place. I figured she was out dancing. I'm her roommate, not her babysitter."

"You and I both know how the bar scene works, especially for women, so that excuse isn't going to fly."

"I don't give a shit whether it flies or not. You're the one who took her home under false pretenses," she snapped. "So you can stick your judgmental attitude up your ass."

"Not that either of you seem to care," Casey said, joining them in the corner, "but you're drawing an audience."

Dylan managed to keep the expletive under his breath.

"We're done here anyway," Matty quipped. "Stay away from Charley."

The blonde sauntered out of the room.

"Looks like I dodged a bullet there," Casey murmured. "Hateful woman."

Shaking his head, Dylan turned to face his friend. "She hates herself more than she hates anyone else."

Casey looked flummoxed. "Did we witness the same thing?"

"Forget it." Surveying the now dwindling crowd, he pulled out his phone. "I got a text from Mitch."

"What'd he say?"

"Wants me to come see him at his house."

"We've got rehearsal at two," the drummer reminded. "He's all the way down in Franklin, and it's already after noon."

Dylan shoved the cell back in his pocket. "I can make it if I leave now. Think Clay will mind if I go?"

The redhead glanced around. "This thing is about over. I doubt he'll care."

"Did the others really hear my talk with Matty?"

"Who's Matty?" his friend asked. "You mean Matilda?"

"Charley told me she goes by Matty. Didn't you get that info Saturday night?"

"She left that part out. And no, but you two were getting louder, and Clay noticed. You've got to be on your game, man. That chick isn't worth blowing our chance over."

Antsy to hit the road, Dylan grabbed his guitar off the table. "I know how important this is, all right? I'm not going to do anything to screw it up. Tell Clay I'm leaving." Walking away, he added, "I'll see you at rehearsal."

"That man is a total asshole. You were right never to see him again."

Charley had never witnessed Matty this angry. She'd also not expected her to storm into the booth twelve seconds before the end of a song.

"Hold that thought," she said, slipping on her headphones. "Blake Shelton wrapping up another ten in a row here on Eagle 101.5. Charley

Layton with you, and still to come this hour is our Manic Monday giveaway. When you hear the sound of maniacal laughter, be the ninth caller and you could pick up those Country Music Hall of Fame passes. Twelve twenty-three now, and after the break I'll have the new one from Luke Bryan."

The second the headphones were off, Matty resumed her pacing. "How dare he call me a bad friend?"

No need to ask whom she was talking about. "Dylan called you a bad friend? Why?"

"Because I didn't frantically text you Saturday night after you left the club. You weren't gone that long before Casey told me you were with Dylan, and I assumed that meant you were with him in the club, not alone together somewhere else."

"We weren't alone in the restaurant," Charley pointed out.

"I mean," Matty hedged, ignoring the comment, "I wondered where you were before that, because you had my purse, but I found it backstage once I remembered that Ruby had dragged you into the spotlight with her."

So she'd really only been worried about her purse. Nice.

"Why do you care what Dylan thinks?" Charley asked. Matty hardly respected her boss's opinion, let alone anyone else's. "Without the message from Casey, you would have looked for me eventually, right?"

As if this were a stupid question, Matty rolled her eyes. "Of course I would have. We had that cake for you, remember? I'd have found you for that."

According to Vivi at the front desk, they hadn't brought out the cake until ten thirty. A full two hours *after* Charley had left the club.

"Then we're good," she said, understanding her place.

Charley had always been content to accept people for who they were. So Matty was self-centered. She was also drama-free, moderately tidy, and didn't chew with her mouth open. All bigger deal-breakers than a lack of social backup.

"I knew you'd understand." She finally stopped pacing. "He's such a jerk. How did you spend a whole evening with him?"

Though Charley had tagged him with a matching insult less than an hour ago, she didn't like Matty doing the same. "You two have clearly gotten off on the wrong foot. If you get to know him, you'll see that Dylan isn't a jerk at all. He's actually a really nice guy."

"Jesus, Charley. Tell me you aren't falling for his aw-shucks routine."

Checking the computer, she found a minute to go before the weather. "I'm not falling for anything, Matty. You hating all men doesn't mean I have to."

The accountant threw her hands in the air. "He lied to you."

"He didn't lie," Charley confessed, acknowledging a truth she hadn't admitted until that moment. "I never asked him what he did for a living. Not in those exact words. So he didn't volunteer the information. Fine. I'll deal with that. But he never lied."

Blonde hair swayed as she shook her head. "You're so naive. He's using you. You work in radio, and his little dream depends on getting airplay. What better way in than to butter up to the DJ?"

The truth became glaringly obvious.

"We both know that I have no pull when it comes to what gets played on this radio station, and I doubt Dylan is delusional enough not to know that. The truth is, you don't think a guy like Dylan would ever be interested in me without some ulterior motive. Someone who isn't petite and blonde with curves in all the right places. That's what you're really saying, isn't it?"

"Men are scum," Matty replied. "That's what I'm saying. If you want to learn that the hard way, go for it."

Charley didn't offer a response as the final seconds of the last commercial counted down. Instead, she grabbed the forecast and reached for her headphones, remaining silent as her roommate left the booth.

Chapter 10

"Mitch?" Dylan called, after ringing the doorbell and knocking several times had been met with silence. He'd stepped into the house, surprised to find the door unlocked. "Mitch, it's Dylan. You here?"

An odd noise from his left drew his attention to the living room. Once he reached the sofa, the situation became clear. The coffee table and floor were littered with empty liquor bottles while what looked like the last quart of vodka rested on Mitch's chest.

"Wake up," Dylan said, shaking his manager. "You've been sober for a year. What the hell happened?" As he spoke, he rounded the couch and collected the bottles scattered across the expensive area rug.

Mitch wedged up on his elbows, sending the vodka bottle rolling under the table. "I took a long walk off a short wagon," he answered, dropping back and rubbing his eyes.

Voice like sandpaper, he smelled like a tub of gin, and his clothes—a Hawaiian shirt and khaki shorts—were wrinkled and stained. Lord only knew how long he'd been in them.

"Where did you get all of this?" Dylan asked.

"I've been stocking up for six months." Bare feet swung to the floor. "Tucking them here and there, like a diabetic hiding candy bars."

"Why would you do that?"

"How the hell should I know?" Mitch shifted to a sitting position and reached for the vodka. After a long swig, he balanced it on his knee. "Did you blow them away at the radio station?"

Dylan felt good about his performance, but like anything, he remained dubious. "The interview went well. I played the right chords and hit the right notes."

"That's what I like about you, Monroe. You're determined without being delusional."

Speaking of delusional.

"We have a show at the Marathon on Friday," Dylan said. "I need you there, and I need you sober. Can you do that?"

The Marathon Music Works was Dylan's favorite place to play in the city, and they'd been lucky to land a Friday night opening.

"Boy," Mitch growled, "don't talk to me like I'm a damn idiot. I'll be sober, shaved, and spit-shined by the time they open those doors. You worry about putting on a show. I'll handle the rest."

Until a week ago, Mitch had handled everything that Shooting Star Records hadn't, and some things that they should have. He'd convinced the *Tennessean* newspaper to run an article on the Louisiana boy about to make good, scored Dylan tickets to the Country Music Hall of Fame dinner Saturday night—offering the perfect opportunity to schmooze some big names and maybe land an opening gig on an upcoming tour—and booked the Friday night show at the Marathon.

Though Mitch's reputation on Music Row wasn't the best, Dylan believed in second chances, and Mitch Levine had proven time and again that signing him on as manager had been the right decision. Until the last week, they'd been cruising along, knocking down one door after another.

So why now? Why dive into a bottle when they were so close to their goal?

"Is this week some anniversary or something? The date of a painful memory that you had to drink your way through?"

Mitch rubbed his scruff-covered chin. "A drunk doesn't need a special occasion to fill his glass."

"It doesn't look like you bothered with a glass."

"I started with one. I'm not sure what happened to it."

"Why did you drag me down here?" Dylan asked.

The answer had to wait until Mitch had finished off the last of the vodka and tossed the bottle down with the others. With a belch, he leaned back and stretched pale, hairy legs to rest on the glass tabletop.

"I have an idea for branding," he declared, words noticeably slurred. "We need to play up that pretty face of yours and make you the most eligible bachelor in country music."

Dylan rejected the idea immediately. "I doubt an unknown is going to knock Chesney off that pedestal. I say we let the music lead and forget about the face."

"Which is why you pay me the big bucks. Or will," he clarified. "The country music demographic swings female. The girls want a guy with a nice ass, a pretty face, and music they can dance to. When you've got all three, you use 'em for all they're worth."

The man had a point. Though Dylan wasn't sure how he felt about his manager pointing out his nice ass.

"What exactly do you have in mind?"

"I've got a contact at *Country Today* magazine, and they're working on a list of the most eligible bachelors in the genre. The article won't come out until the end of the year, but they're doing the interviews and photo shoots this month."

Sounded like a good opportunity, but this didn't explain why Dylan had to drive twenty minutes out of town.

"Give me a date and time and I'll be there. But you could have told me this over the phone. Why am I here, Mitch?"

The older man met his client's gaze for the first time since he'd walked in. "You're here because I owe you an apology, and that needed to happen in person. For obvious reasons, I couldn't come to you."

Dylan nodded. "Fair enough."

"You're the only client I've got, Monroe. The drinking chased the rest off, but you stuck with me, and I owe you better than this. I'm sorry I went AWOL on you. It won't happen again."

"I appreciate that," he said, sliding his hands into his pockets.

Mitch had offered representation after Dylan's first deal had fallen through, when no one else would even take his calls. With dogged determination and unwavering support, he'd spent three years promising another deal, and now they had one. Mitch had more than earned Dylan's loyalty.

"Then we're good?" Mitch asked.

"Yes, sir. You need help cleaning this up?"

Mitch dropped his feet to the floor and teetered on the edge of the sofa. "I've got it. You want something to drink? I think there might be water in the kitchen."

Dylan shook his head. "I've got rehearsal at two. Do I need to do a quick search for more of the hard stuff and toss it out?"

"Nope. This is every last bottle I had." The manager stood up, wavering until he caught his balance. "Damn, that first step's a doozy."

"Are you going to be okay?" he asked, truly concerned.

"I'll feel like shit for a few days, but I'll make it. When I lock in a date on the magazine stuff, I'll let you know. Otherwise, I'll see you Friday night."

Waiting a beat to make sure the man remained upright, Dylan pulled his keys from his pocket.

"Call me if you need me," he offered, heading for the exit.

"Yeah, yeah," echoed behind him. "I'll be fine."

"The radio visit was a success," Clay said, sitting at the head of a conference table surrounded by his gifted, if small, staff. "How can we build on this?"

Ralph Sampson, Shooting Stars's radio liaison, chimed in first. "Willoughby has already agreed to add the single to the Eagle rotation, and we've locked in two stations in Shreveport anxious to play a hometown boy. I've drafted an email sharing news of the adds, as well as our streaming numbers as of noon today. The message will hit the inbox of every major market programmer on our list first thing tomorrow morning, and I may update it with more streaming numbers before hitting Send. I'll target midsize and smaller markets on Friday, hopefully with an edit to include other confirmed adds."

"I'm working social media from all angles," said Daphne Bukowski. "The pics we got from the station meet and greet are garnering lots of attention. If we can up the shares on Twitter, we could crawl onto the Emerging Artists chart on Billboard, but that's a slow build right now." The tiny blonde tipped up her glasses as she flipped a page in her notepad. "Newsletter subscriptions are up over the last twenty-four hours, as well as our Facebook and Instagram followers. I need Dylan to be more active on his accounts. He's the draw for the younger female audience. He needs to give them something to follow."

"Higher numbers is what I like to hear, and I'll talk to Dylan about his online activity." Clay turned to Lenny Cooper. "How are we looking on the distribution side?"

The balding father of two lowered his Tennessee Titans mug to the table. "We're good. The single went live with no problems on all major outlets, and preorders for the album doubled overnight. Though we're talking unknown artist numbers, not the kind you'd see for a Luke Bryan or a Miranda Lambert release."

That was the downside to stacking veterans of the business. They knew the realities of the industry and when their talents were being underutilized.

"We need to start looking at new artists," added Naomi. "Now that Dylan is up and running, we're ready for another project. Running a label with only one act won't get us very far, especially if that one act doesn't take off."

Clay knew Naomi well enough to know her comment didn't mean a lack of faith in Dylan's abilities or appeal. She was simply speaking the truth. Something the others had been hinting at for the last couple of months.

"I'm glad you brought that up," he replied. "I've got my eye on someone right now."

"Who?" asked Daphne.

"Chance Colburn," he announced, well aware that the name wasn't likely to garner positive responses. What Clay hadn't expected was total silence. "I've never known any of you to keep your thoughts to yourself. Spit 'em out now or forever hold your peace."

"He's a risk," Lenny muttered. "Foxfire dropped him for a reason."

Daphne leaned back in her chair. "He's a known womanizer. I can't imagine we could clean up his image enough to make him viable."

The person in charge of polishing images uncharacteristically held her tongue.

"Do you agree, Naomi?" Clay asked. "That's your territory, after all."

As the team awaited her response, the most senior member of the staff (not counting Clay) drove the tip of her pen so deep into her day planner, the cover developed a permanent divot. "Your call," she replied, failing to make eye contact with anyone in the room.

Interesting.

"Colburn hasn't caused a scandal in nearly two years. Foxfire only dropped him because his last album never hit the charts." Clay swiveled in his chair but kept a side eye on his publicist. "By some miracle, his hard living hasn't damaged his voice, and I think, with the right songs, he could make a comeback."

"Is he clean?" Ralph queried.

Clay shared the only answer he could. "For now. But who knows what will happen once he leaves rehab. Which is why he's still only a maybe." Rising from his chair, he added, "Until then, let's focus on the artist we have and make sure he generates enough revenue to keep us all employed." As the crew rose from their seats, he added, "Ralph, keep me posted on the adds, and compare them to the stations on the tour we start next week. I want to know what we're dealing with prior to hitting the road."

"You've got it boss."

Before she could make her escape, Clay said, "Naomi, I'll let you know what I decide on Colburn. If we take the risk, I'll need all your expertise to make it work."

Through gritted teeth, she said, "Whatever you say, sir," and left the room.

He couldn't help but wonder if her dislike of Chance stemmed from his reputation alone or personal experience. Either way, she'd have to get on board, because Clay had already made his decision, and Chance Colburn would be a Shooting Stars artist whether his staff liked it or not.

Turned out, getting ready for a date when she had no idea of their destination proved quite difficult. Jeans might be too casual, but Charley doubted he'd take her someplace fancy without a hint of warning.

In the end, she settled for a dark-wash denim skirt that showed off her legs and a simple white top that buttoned down the front. Hoop earrings and a touch of gloss finished off the look. Not bad for a farm girl with no fashion sense.

Trotting down the stairs, Charley sent up a prayer of gratitude that Matty was still at work. They'd been a bit cold with each other since their disagreement over Dylan two days before, and the last thing she wanted was the glare of death looming disapprovingly when he arrived. Which he did, right on time, while she was slipping on her cowboy boots.

"Just a minute," she yelled toward the door, nearly falling over in the effort.

She'd waited until Tuesday afternoon to text Dylan her address. Truth be told, Charley had spent the twenty-four hours prior debating whether or not to venture down this path. Nothing had changed in her estimation of Dylan Monroe. If anything, he'd grown even more dangerous now that she knew a little more about him.

Other than the one transgression of not telling her exactly what he did for a living, he scored high on every test. He'd admitted he was wrong, he'd shown a passion and talent for something she held dear, and in an interesting twist, he'd called Matty out for not protecting her friend. Even if Charley hadn't been in need of protecting, a little display of concern would have been nice.

On the downside, Dylan made Charley laugh, turned her on, and adopted the role of protector without question or prompting. The epitome of everything she'd vowed to avoid.

"This 'wildest dream' stuff better be good," she muttered, opening the door to find a casually dressed Dylan. "You're wearing a ball cap."

Straightening the Saints hat, Dylan said, "What's wrong with it?"

Not a damn thing, she nearly said aloud. "Nothing. I expected the black cowboy hat, that's all."

"I don't wear it everywhere," he replied. "Especially not when it's pushing a hundred out here." Assessing her from head to toe, he said, "You look gorgeous."

Charley clung to her purse strap. "I feel overdressed. Let me put jeans on."

Full lips curved in a devilish grin. "No way in hell." Before she could retreat upstairs, Dylan took her hand and dragged her out the door before reaching back to close it. "There should be a law against covering up those legs."

"Calm your jets, Monroe. No need to come in guns blazing." She allowed him to lead her to his truck, ignoring the heat sizzling up her arm. "I only agreed to this to find out what you think is my wildest dream. If it sucks, I'm catching a cab home."

"Do you always say exactly what you're thinking?"

Since she was thinking how much she wanted to drag him up to her room and rip his clothes off, that would be a firm negative. "Only sometimes," Charley replied. "So where are we going?"

"You'll see when we get there," he replied, opening her truck door.

"Is it far?" she asked, attempting to climb into the passenger seat. Not an easy feat in a denim miniskirt.

"Need some help there?" Dylan asked in his typical white-knight fashion.

Charley turned on the running board and hopped until her bottom landed on the seat. "Got it," she quipped.

"Nice job," he commended. "Not too far."

Dylan closed the door and crossed around the front of the GMC. Charley was buckled before he joined her inside, and they were on their way seconds later, traveling in silence, which was fine with Charley.

The silence ended when they reached the exit for the interstate.

"Did you know Gallatin Pike runs almost directly from my place to yours?" he asked.

"I did not." Charley turned her attention to the passing scenery. "Do you always make geographical small talk?"

"I'm sorry," Dylan replied, passing a slow-moving Nissan. "Am I boring you, princess?"

Possibly deserved, but still an annoying quip. "And to think," she said drolly, "I went to the trouble of telling Matty you weren't a jerk. Guess I spoke too soon."

Deep laughter filled the cab. "Matty thinks I'm a jerk, huh? That doesn't surprise me."

"She didn't like you calling her out about Saturday night."

He shrugged. "I only pointed out the truth." Cutting his eyes to her, Dylan added, "You need better friends, Charley. People who actually care about you."

Curious, she asked, "Do I seem like a damsel in distress to you?"

"Not in the least," he replied.

"Then why are you always coming to my rescue?"

A deadly smile split his lips. "Lucky, I guess."

Charley laughed. "Who's lucky? Me or you?"

"Maybe we both are."

A semi merged from an on-ramp, and Dylan eased over to give him space. As they cruised along, his fingertips brushed her thigh. If she had any sense at all, Charley would have pulled away with a firm warning to keep his hands to himself. Instead, she leaned into the armrest and settled her hand on his forearm, pretending the contact meant nothing.

Chapter 11

Though Dylan liked the spunky, take-no-shit version of Charley, he liked the quiet, lean into him version, too. He'd half expected her to smack him for the knee touch, but as she often did, the feisty DJ with the killer legs surprised him with an affectionate touch of her own. The unpredictability was nearly as enticing as the glossy lips and honeysuckle scent.

"Here we are," he said, pulling into the lot behind the old stone building.

Leaning forward, she glanced up at the looming gray structure. "You brought me to a church?"

"Not exactly."

Exiting the truck, Dylan hustled around to open her door. "You got it?" he asked as she refused his hand to climb out on her own.

"I should have put on jeans," Charley muttered, skirt riding dangerously high by the time she scooted to the ground.

Dylan didn't mind the free show, but the woman was too damn stubborn for her own good. "I'm about to introduce you to some friends of mine. Think you can pretend that you aren't here against your will?"

A huff accompanied the violent tug on the skirt hem. "I told you I don't like surprises. They make me cranky."

"You know what? We don't have to do this."

Charley locked eyes with his. "Are you freaking kidding me? I'm here now. You can't leave me hanging."

He stood his ground. "Are you going to behave?"

Brown eyes narrowed, and he could almost see the steam exiting her ears. "Yes, Mr. Monroe. I'll be a good little girl and play nice with your friends."

If he hadn't been one hundred percent certain that she might faint with excitement once inside, Dylan would have called the cab for her.

"Come on, then."

Leading her to the glass doors, he let Charley enter first, urging her down the three steps inside to reach the studio lounge.

"What is this place?" she whispered. "It looks like 1994 threw up in here."

She had a point. The artwork and furnishings were dated, along with the giant rear-projection television, but the kitchen in the back left corner had been updated since he'd last been there, and the giant pool table had been replaced only last year.

"Around here, money is spent in other areas." Like state-of-the-art consoles and the latest in recording technology. Dylan had been fortunate to record his album here.

Before Charley could comment on the worn green carpet beneath their feet, a familiar face entered from the other side of the room.

"Hey there, buddy. What's shaking?" Aiden D'Angelo grasped Dylan's hand and offered a quick hug. "I heard you on the Eagle the other day, man. 'Bout time those radio shits took notice."

Dylan cringed. "Aiden, I want you to meet Charley Layton, midday personality on Eagle 101.5."

The engineer engulfed Charley's hand in his smooth black ones and held it to his chest. "Present company excluded from my prior statement, of course."

Seemingly cured of her crankiness, she met Aiden's beaming smile with one of her own. "Of course. You aren't a shit until you have your own office. Sadly, I'm still only a lowly radio turd."

Dimples deepening, he said, "I like you already."

Aiden possessed a legendary way with women, and based on the enamored look on Charley's face, she was not immune to his charms.

"Well then," he cut in, sliding an arm across her shoulders. "Are we ready for the surprise?"

"Yes, sir. Come right this way." Aiden released Charley's hand with a wink before leading them into the long hall toward the main recording space. The narrow passage forced them to progress single file.

At the second door on the right, Aiden turned the knob and stepped through, but Charley halted as soon as the music hit her ears. Spinning, she stared wide-eyed at Dylan.

"Is that . . . ," she mouthed.

He nodded. "It sure is."

Charley smacked him in the chest. "Get out."

"No," he corrected. "Get *in*. We need to close this door."

She hustled inside to stare in shock through the window before the large console to see Jack Austin singing into a microphone. Her expression matched that of a four-year-old meeting Mickey Mouse for the first time.

Aiden motioned toward two high stools off to the side. Dylan had to help Charley find her seat, since she never took her eyes off the glass. The vocal continued for another minute before the music faded out.

"Sound good, boys?" asked Austin into his microphone.

Paul Story, a producer Dylan would give his left nut to work with, gave a thumbs-up. "I think we got it, Jack. Come in and listen."

The award-winning artist locked his headphones over the music stand and headed out of the tracking booth.

"Oh my God," Charley hissed, digging her nails into Dylan's arm. "He's coming over here. What should we do?"

"We shouldn't do anything," he replied.

"But what if he asks what we're doing here? Are we allowed to be here? This feels wrong. We shouldn't be intruding like this."

"Relax," he said, taking her hand. "Aiden cleared the visit. Just smile and get ready to say hello."

"I can't talk to Jack Austin," she growled, her voice increasing from a harsh whisper to a loud outburst.

"Sure you can, darling," said the man himself. "I don't bite."

For half a second, Dylan feared she might actually pass out as the color drained from her face. And if he ever questioned the sturdiness of his own ego, this encounter allayed his fears, because seeing the raw joy in her eyes made his night.

"I . . . Um . . . Hello," she mumbled without blinking. "I'm Charley."

"Layton, right?" Austin asked. "I've been listening to you on the radio. You're good."

Pale cheeks turned hot pink. "Really? You listen to me?"

Jack shared a crooked grin. "You're on the biggest station in town for five hours a day. Would be hard to miss you."

Charley's nervous laugh devolved into a snort. "Sure. Right. Of course."

"Hey, Monroe," he said, offering a hand. "How are you, kid?"

They'd never met, so the instant recognition took Dylan by surprise. "Good, sir. Real good."

"I like what you're doing so far." The shake was firm and friendly. "Keep it up. We need some young talent in this town willing to shoot for more than the drunken college crowds."

Feeling as if he'd been blessed by the pope, he nodded. "Yes, sir."

Pointing to the partition window, Austin asked Charley, "Did you like what you heard?"

After a quick fish impersonation, she found her voice. "I . . . I loved it. I mean, I only heard the last bit, but that part was great."

"Paul, let's hear the whole thing."

Pulling over another stool, he settled on the other side of Charley, who was doing her best to act natural. Dylan doubted she even realized her hand still rested in his, her thumbnail driving into his flesh.

"Relax," he said again, loosening her grip to reveal a deep divot. "Remember to breathe, baby. You're turning a little blue."

As the music began, she took a deep breath, shoulders lifting and falling before she leaned his way.

"Thank you," she whispered. "You were right. This is a dream come true."

Talk about an out-of-body experience. The only thing that would make this crazy moment even better was if Grandpa were here with her. This would be the highlight of the year for him.

Charley had feared she was only dreaming, but after pinching herself twice already, Jack Austin remained on the stool beside her. As the song faded out, he turned her way.

"Still like it?"

"Yes," she replied. "That opening verse sucks you right in."

Tapping his chin, Jack narrowed his eyes. "The intro needs something."

The older man Jack had called Paul said, "I don't agree. The riff is great the way it is."

"No," the singer argued, shaking his head. "There's an element missing. Play it from the top."

The other guy sighed but did as asked, stopping the playback at the first line of the lyrics.

"Banjo," Charley blurted, stunned she'd spoken aloud.

"What?" the two men asked in stereo.

She cut her eyes to Dylan, desperate for a save.

"I agree," he said. "Banjo would make the song stand out and add an unexpected edge to your sound."

Jack left his stool to pace the small room. "She might be onto something."

Paul didn't appear as receptive to her input. "It's been done."

"Everything's been done," the singer countered.

Great. She'd started a fight. Why the heck had she opened her mouth?

"I like the banjo idea," Aiden chimed. "Tater Beaumont is working over at Starstruck today. I bet he'd come by and cut something. Couldn't hurt to ask."

Thanks to her early days of running the Bluegrass hour back in Kentucky every Sunday, Charley recognized the name as a virtual icon in mountain music. A banjo legend.

"Call him," Jack ordered over Paul's protests. To Charley he said, "If this turns out as good as I think it will, you just might get a production credit."

"What the fuck, Austin?" snarled the man Charley now assumed to be the producer.

The artist ignored his outburst. "Would you be willing to listen to the rest of the tracks before we lock them down? I could use a fresh take from someone sitting in the trenches all day."

Full-on angry now, the man at the console stood fast enough to tip his chair backward. "This is bullshit. I'm the producer here."

"You've been producing for twenty-five years," Jack announced. "Your ideas are outdated, and your standards are subpar. In case you haven't noticed, the average age of artists on the charts right now is twenty-eight fucking years old. I'll be forty-two this year. This ancient shit isn't going to compete anymore, Paul. Get on board or get out of the way."

Silence loomed like a fart in church. Charley held her breath as Dylan tensed beside her, and a quick glance to Aiden revealed a satisfied smile on the man's full lips. Apparently, this little blowup had been coming for a while, and Charley's slip of the tongue had lit the fuse.

Without another word, Paul stormed out of the room, slamming the door behind him.

"About fucking time," Aiden drawled, high-fiving Jack.

"I'm so sorry," Charley said. "I didn't mean to cause any trouble."

Jack waved her words away. "I should have done that months ago. Once we lay down the banjo part, I'll have Aiden burn you a CD."

"You're serious about that?"

"Hell yes. I don't doubt we have the right songs, but like I told Paul, the sound isn't there. Any input would be appreciated."

Now she really was dreaming. "I'll do my best," Charley promised.

"Appreciate it. Now, how's your pool game, Monroe?"

"Rusty," Dylan answered.

"Let's dust it off, then, while Aiden gets Tater over here."

Leaping off his stool, her escort rubbed his hands together excitedly. "Yes, sir."

Never in a million years could Dylan have predicted how this night would turn out. At least now his left nut was safe, since he'd never be working with Paul Story. Best-case scenario had been Charley getting an autograph, a picture with her favorite artist, and a story she could someday tell her kids. Never had he imagined she'd get all that and a production credit on a future Hall-of-Famer's new album.

"Surreal," she repeated for the fourth time. "That's the only way to describe what just happened. Sur. Real."

Dylan scooped a chunk of fudge out of his banana ice cream. "I'll never again hear the word *banjo* and not think of you."

"I don't even know where that came from," Charley squealed before shoving a spoonful of cherry ice cream into her mouth.

"Years of listening has given you more musical insight than you knew. It's a genius idea." One he wished he'd thought of. "Down Here Down Home" would be killer with a banjo behind it. "And that song is going to be better for it."

"If I'd known that was Paul Story," she said, "I never would have opened my mouth. He's worked with everyone from Willie to Reba. Who am I to be voicing an opinion in his presence?"

"Someone with a fresher ear," Dylan replied, repeating Jack Austin's words. "How's your ice cream?"

"Awesome," Charley mumbled around a piece of cherry. "How long did it take you to make your album?"

"Six months," he answered. "We spent the first couple months finding the right songs and the next four recording the album."

Brown eyes narrowed over her waffle cone. "I bet my best boots that you have enough songs to make several albums, Dylan. Why spend a month looking for others?"

"Having the songs doesn't mean they're good enough to go on an album."

"But they're your voice. That's what listeners want."

Dylan wiped his mouth with a napkin. "Like I said in the interview on Monday, the songs on the album are all tunes I can relate to. They're my life and my history."

"Not the same," she countered. "I know that lots of artists have successful careers without writing their own songs, but you have the talent to do both. Why not use it?"

"Charley, you've heard one song. And not even a completed song. For all you know, every other thing I've written could be total crap."

With a knowing smile, she said, "But they aren't, are they?"

He didn't think so, but he'd been wrong before.

"The album is done, so it's a moot point anyway." Biting a corner off his cone, he turned his attention to the pedestrians passing by outside.

Taking the hint, Charley changed the subject. Somewhat. "Have you always wanted to be famous?"

This was a common misconception that drove Dylan a little nuts. "I've *never* wanted to be famous. I want to sing for a living. I love performing and feeding off a crowd. The fame is only part of the package, not the draw."

Charley nodded. "I see we've hit a nerve," she muttered, loading her spoon. "For me, it would be a deal-breaker."

"You don't want your fifteen minutes?" he asked.

She shook her head. "Not at all."

Dylan pointed out what seemed obvious to him. "As a disc jockey on one of the most listened-to country stations in a country music town, you're asking for a bit of fame, aren't you?"

After a quick bite, she licked a drop of ice cream from the corner of her mouth, and the blood flowing to his brain immediately changed direction. "People might know my name, but that isn't the same thing."

Pressing the cold cone to his forehead, he said, "That's what fame is, darling. People knowing your name."

"But they won't know my face," she insisted. "In your line of work, once a person makes it big, he can't go anywhere without getting mobbed by fans. I'm a little radio DJ. A faceless voice coming out of their speakers, killing time between the music people like you make."

"You're seriously underestimating yourself. Fans are going to know who you are. Jack did."

"That's because you told them I was coming."

"Nope," he corrected. "I told Aiden I wanted to bring a friend by. I never gave them your name."

Blinking, she said, "Then how did he know it was me?"

Dylan pointed out the obvious. "He's a fan, just like he said." Her modesty was cute, if naive.

The comment earned him a scoffing wave. "You aren't listening. I don't have fans. *You* have fans." Eyes cutting to his left, she added, "In fact, I'm guessing there's one a few tables down."

"What are you talking about?" he asked, spinning to scan the crowd behind him.

"Don't turn around," she snapped. "The lady in the Johnny Cash T-shirt has been watching our table since she sat down with her ice cream. I'm guessing you've played around town a lot?"

"I've done my share of working the bars, but we haven't played a show in Nashville since January, and that was after being on the road for the better part of 2016."

"Oh," Charley drawled. "Then I bet she's a tourist excited to see the hot singer who stole her heart and melted her panties."

Dylan had never been accused of that one. "You're giving me more credit than I deserve."

The white plastic spoon twirled in the air. "Granted, I've never seen you live, but I'd lay odds I'm right. Admit it. The women *love* you. Which is why being your girlfriend would suck."

He'd officially lost control of this conversation. "You don't think that when you intro some band at a big show that every guy in the audience isn't wondering how he can get your number?"

"Not remotely." Ducking her head, Charley whispered, "Don't look now, but she's coming this way."

"She's probably headed to the bathroom."

"We're in a corner, goober. She's coming to talk to you."

Before Dylan could argue further, a woman appeared beside their table, only she wasn't looking at Dylan.

"Excuse me," she said. "I hate to bother you, but aren't you Charley Layton?"

His non-famous friend was too busy gaping in shock to respond.

"She is," Dylan replied for her. "How do you know her?"

"Oh, I listen to her every day. You're so much better than that awful man who was there before you. That Hugh person? He never played my requests and was even rude on the phone when I'd call. But you're so nice. I'm Sharlene," the woman offered, holding out her hand. "We talk at least once a week, so I feel like we're old friends. Would it be weird if I asked for a picture?"

Dylan used every ounce of control not to burst out laughing. Charley still couldn't speak, but she nodded and rose from her chair as Sharlene handed him her cell phone.

"Oh." Sharlene paused, staring at his face. "You're pretty. Charley, honey, you're a lucky woman."

"That's what I keep trying to tell her," he quipped, standing to take the picture.

Once he'd captured the image, Dylan passed the phone back to its owner, who turned once again to her favorite radio personality.

"Thank you so much. My friend Brenda is never going to believe that I met you, so I had to have a picture as proof."

Charley finally found her voice. "Tell her I said hi."

"Oh my gosh, she'll love that." Sharlene hugged the phone to her chest. "I'll let y'all get back to your night. Thanks again for being so sweet."

As her biggest fan walked away, Charley slowly lowered into her chair, looking as if she'd been sideswiped.

"A faceless voice coming out of their speakers," Dylan mocked.

"Did that really just happen?" she asked, reaching for her ice cream.

He failed to keep the grin from his face. "Yes, ma'am, it did. What were you saying about being famous?"

Bewildered brown eyes met his. "Did you put her up to that?"

"Yes," he said dryly. "I found a total stranger, told her we would be here, and recruited her to cut in at the exact moment you said you would never be famous. You're onto me."

For a second, he thought she might throw her napkin at him. "I doubt that'll happen again."

"I don't know," he said, scooping up another bite. "I'm going to have to think twice about being your boyfriend after learning I'll have to share you with your fans."

A crooked smile lit her face. "Shut up, Monroe."

Dylan would not let it go.

"The look on your face was priceless," he proclaimed. "Flipping priceless."

"Ha ha," she countered. "So one person happened to recognize me."

Dylan tapped on the steering wheel. "Don't forget Brenda. She'd recognize you, too."

The man turned out to be right about *one* thing and acted as if he'd rescued baby kittens while solving the meaning of life.

"A couple nice ladies who listen to the radio is not the same as having a crowd of screaming girls pressed against a barrier hoping you'll make their dreams come true by sweating in their general direction."

"That's gross," he said, shooting Charley an appalled look as he pulled the truck into a parking lot. "I don't want to sweat on anyone."

Once again being a pain in the ass, Dylan refused to share their destination upon leaving the ice cream parlor. She was surprised to see a familiar landmark looming in front of her.

"The Parthenon?" Charley asked as a flood of memories filled her mind.

"Saturday night you said you hadn't gotten to explore the area. So we're exploring."

This was one attraction she could have skipped. "I wish you'd have told me we were coming here," she said as Dylan exited the truck to cross around the front. When he opened her door, Charley was still buckled in.

"What's the matter?" he asked. "You don't want to see it?"

Charley sighed. "I've seen it before." Her heart hitched into her throat as her chest tightened.

He stepped back as if to close her door. "I guess I should have asked. We can go someplace else."

"No," she said with a hand on his arm. "We can stay."

Since moving to town, she'd avoided this place, assuming the grief would be too much. But Charley found herself longing to walk the paths again. To tread the ground where she and Mama had shared a cherished afternoon. As they approached the imposing edifice, she was grateful for his silent strength beside her. They walked in silence as her mind drifted back in time. Back to the days before she lost the most important person in her life.

As they climbed the stairs to reach the giant columns, she brushed her hand over the stone surface, still warm from the summer sun. "Strange how some things change while others stay the same." Charley caught the scent of wildflowers on the wind and couldn't help but look around for a familiar face.

Dylan glanced around, too. "What are you looking for?"

With a faint shake of her head, she replied, "Nothing."

They strolled down the narrow corridor between the columns and the main structure, and she could practically hear her mother's laughter. Picture the smile, so much like her own, that she'd give anything to see again.

"You want to tell me where you are?" he asked, snapping her back to the present.

Despite her vow not to get personal, she shared the story. "Mama and I came here when I was thirteen. It was our last vacation together before she got sick. The doctor had given her the cancer diagnosis the week before, but we'd had the trip planned for months, and she refused to cancel. The day we spent at this park was one of the happiest days of my life." With a sad shrug, she added, "At the end, when repeated chemo treatments had done their damage, she said she was going to get better and we'd come back."

Charley didn't notice the tear rolling down her cheek until Dylan brushed it away.

"I'm sorry," he said, voice somber. "I shouldn't have brought you here."

"I'm glad you did." She wrapped her arms around herself. "I haven't felt Mama around me this much in a long time. I should have known that this is where I would find her."

Dylan leaned against a column and pulled her close. "I lost my grandmother to cancer. She always loved to hear me sing. I'd give anything if she could see me now."

Rubbing her thumb along his jaw, Charley smiled through her sadness. "She *can* see you, Dylan. And I'm sure she's as proud as can be."

"I hope so." He tucked her head against his chest, and his heart beat out a steady rhythm against Charley's cheek.

They stood there, consoling each other, until the last sliver of sunlight had faded behind the trees.

"Enough," she said, stepping from his embrace. "The only thing Mama ever asked was that I smile every time I think of her. She'd give me a good scolding if she found me here crying over a happy memory."

"Grand would smack me in the back of the head and tell me to toughen up," Dylan said with a laugh. "She used to say that death was part of life, and if a person couldn't handle the first, they sure as heck couldn't handle the second."

A practicality and strength that Charley admired. "I'd have liked her."

"And she'd have liked you," he offered. Dusty-blue eyes held hers as his lips lowered for a kiss.

"We should see the lake," she said, stepping away. The moment had grown too intimate, and Charley recognized the dangerous precipice she could so easily, and willingly, step off.

This was supposed to be her last date with Dylan Monroe. At least, that's what she'd been telling herself for two days. But this didn't feel anything like an ending. This had *beginning* written all over it.

"Are you turning skittish on me, Miss Layton?" he teased.

She preferred the joking Dylan over the vulnerable, heart-aching one any day.

"You promised no funny business, remember?"

The devilish grin returned. "I said I'd get you home by midnight and in bed alone. I didn't promise not to enjoy the time we had before then."

The promise in his words turned her knees to butter. Charley cleared her throat. "We're exploring landmarks, not each other."

"No reason we can't do both."

This man would be the death of her.

"Are you going to take me for a stroll around that lake or not?"

Dylan raised his hands in surrender. "By all means, let's go see the lake." Taking her hand, he led them halfway down the narrow corridor before adding, "It's darker over there anyway."

Heaven help her.

Chapter 12

The glow from the Parthenon sent trails of white light skimming across the water. The occasional duck could be heard in the distance as they walked side by side along the water's edge. She'd dropped his hand before they'd reached the water, withdrawing more and more as they walked.

"I get the feeling there's something you're not telling me," he said, sliding his hands into the pockets of his jeans.

Chestnut hair floated on the warm breeze. "I don't know what you mean," she replied, eyes focused somewhere in the distance.

Dylan kicked a small pebble with his boot. "Have I done something wrong?"

She cut her eyes his way. "You've done everything right. That's the problem."

"How is that a problem?" he asked, not following. "I thought we were having a nice time."

Charley veered off the path to sit on a short stone wall. Dylan followed, taking the spot beside her.

After a heavy sigh, she said, "Tonight has to be our last date."

He leaned forward to see her face. "Why?"

"Because you're the exact kind of guy I've vowed to avoid."

"Not all musicians are assholes, Charley."

"Being a musician isn't the problem."

"Then what?" Dylan asked, rising off the wall. "What kind of a guy am I?"

Toying with the hem of her skirt, she kept her face downcast. "You're kind and smart and protective without making me feel weak. You're the kind of guy a girl could give her heart to and never look back."

None of which sounded like a bad thing. "Not sure I've earned all of that praise, but if I have, I'm not seeing the problem here."

"No, I'm sure you aren't."

"Come on, Charley." Dylan returned to his seat and took her hand. "Help me out here. You're talking in circles."

She entwined her fingers with his. "Since I was nine years old, I've wanted to be part of this country music world. By twelve, I was creating pretend radio shows in my bedroom, spinning Grandpa's old albums on an ancient turntable and talking into a hairbrush. Now that I'm here, I don't want to give it up."

Dylan tried piecing that one together and wound up more confused than before. "I love that you're making your dreams come true. Who's asking you to give them up?"

"You wouldn't have to ask. I'd just do it."

He'd gone from being a prize among men to a crusher of dreams in a matter of seconds.

"Charley, would you ever ask me to give up playing music?"

"Of course not," she replied, turning wide eyes his way. "If I ever made you give up music, you'd hate me within a year. Probably sooner."

Exactly the answer he expected. "Then what makes you think I'd ever do that to you? You're great at what you do, and you should do it for as long as you want to."

"But what if we had kids?"

Leaping off the wall, he ran a hand through his hair. "Whoa. Hold on now. Who said anything about kids?"

This was supposed to be a simple date. Maybe a little making out in the truck and a plan to see each other again. But she goes and drops munchkins into the mix? Dylan had a career to launch. He didn't have time to be changing diapers. And babies spit up a lot, too, didn't they? He definitely wasn't ready for that.

Charley crossed her ankles, appearing way more relaxed about this subject than Dylan was. "Don't you want kids?"

"Sure," he hedged. "Someday. But not anytime soon."

"I don't, either," she snapped. "I'm talking years down the line."

Dylan exhaled. "What are you doing scaring a guy like that?"

Her laughter joined the rustling of the trees. "You act like I suggested we snip off your right nut. Get a grip there, buddy. I'm saying that you're a give-up guy. A guy a woman would willingly give up anything for, and I don't want to give anything up."

"I don't want you to give anything up."

"And I don't want to be in the spotlight, either."

"What spotlight? I've released one single. I'm lucky if ten people know my name right now."

"Come on." Charley waved a hand up and down in front of him. "You've got the big time written all over you. Movie-star good looks. A voice half the singers in this town would kill for. And your album is amazing."

Straightening, he said, "You've listened to my album?"

She crossed her arms. "I bummed a copy off John. I can't stop listening to it."

"You really think it's good?" Dylan asked, returning to the wall.

"I said it was, didn't I?"

"Yeah." He smiled. "You did." Dropping his guard, he admitted his fears. "I really need this thing to take off. I've already blown one shot, and there's no way I'll get a third chance at this."

Charley bumped him with her shoulder. "The songs are great, Dylan. Even though I still think you should be using your own, there's no denying you feel every lyric that you sing. The listeners pick up on stuff like that."

"Clay says the same thing." Including about using his own songs, though Dylan didn't voice that detail. "Now I have to charm my way through a ten-day radio tour, and hope I land an opening gig for the fall."

"I'm sure you will. And that's another reason we don't need to do this anymore." She rose to her feet. "You'll be leaving town soon."

Dylan shook his head. "Not for eleven days, and I won't even be gone two weeks."

She crossed her arms. "But it's only a matter of time before you are. You'll be out on the road, fending off female advances, and I'll be here sharing the latest big news about you with my listeners. As it should be."

"Wouldn't you like to get that news firsthand before everyone else?" he asked, rising and pulling her against his body. "We're good together, Charley. Why not enjoy the moment and let the future sort itself out?"

"I'm a planner," she explained, pulling away. "I like to know what's coming my way."

Dropping a kiss on her forehead, he lowered his voice. "You can plan on more nights like this one. All you have to do is say yes."

Squeezing his arms, she rested her forehead on his chest. "Yes to what? You haven't asked me anything."

"Charley Layton, will you do me the honor of going out with me again?"

She sighed as she lifted her head. "I suppose after tonight, you've earned that much. I'll be the mouthy Kentucky girl you dated until a supermodel came calling."

Brushing his lips across hers, Dylan whispered, "I'll take you over a model any day of the week."

At exactly eleven forty-five, Dylan parked his truck in front of her apartment.

"Before midnight, as promised," he said, pointing to the clock on the dash.

"Only because I turned down going back to your place twice," Charley reminded him. The offer had been tempting, but the man's persistence already knew no bounds. Revealing how difficult saying no had been would only give him more ammunition.

Unhooking his seat belt, he shrugged. "Can't blame a guy for trying." With a wink, he dropped to the ground and crossed around the front of the truck.

Charley considered opening the door herself, but she didn't want to ruin his chivalrous streak. Once he pulled it open, she took the hand he offered and climbed out.

"You don't have to walk me to the door," she said as he fell into step beside her. "It's less than twenty feet, and you can see me the whole way. If anyone tries to mug me, I'm sure you could step in."

"Walking you to the door has nothing to do with preventing a mugging," Dylan assured her. "I'm holding out for a proper goodbye. Or were you hoping I'd nod off and you'd sneak away again?"

She shoved him away. "You're such a jerk."

"And you're beautiful," he muttered, as they stepped up to the door. "Thank you for coming tonight."

"You're welcome. Thanks for one of the most amazing and unexpected encounters of my life." She laughed, tugging on his T-shirt. "And for the visit to Centennial Park. I wouldn't have gone on my own."

"Stirring up painful memories was not my intention." Dylan took her in his arms and tipped up her chin with strong fingers. "Are we good now?"

Charley wasn't good at all. She was confused and anxious and in way too deep for her own comfort. If he could crash so far through her walls in only two dates, she was bound to be utterly besotted after a month. Which meant if she were smart, she'd make this goodbye a permanent one.

But then she looked up into his eyes and goodbye was the last thing on her mind. "Yeah, we're good."

Dylan twirled one of her loose curls around his finger. "I'll have your name on the list at the door for Friday night. We go on at nine, but if you come early, I'll bring you backstage to meet the guys."

During their walk in the park, Dylan had described his bandmates as family. Which made meeting them akin to going home to meet his mother.

"I have a remote from five to seven, so I'm not sure what time I'll get there." A valid excuse since the remote was in Mount Juliet, outside the city.

"No problem. Text me when you get there, and I'll come find you." He tucked the curl behind her ear and ran his hand down her arm. "Guess this is goodnight."

Nodding, she watched his eyes drop to her mouth. "Yep. This is it."

"One kiss before I go?" Dylan asked, his lips hovering above hers.

"Just one," Charley breathed, rising on tiptoe.

The moment his mouth closed over hers, a sigh rolled through her body, followed by a trail of budding heat. She threw her arms around his neck and put every ounce of longing into the contact, proving how little control she had where this man was concerned. His hands squeezed her bottom, and she mewed in response, sucking on his tongue while the stubble along his jaw turned her cheeks cherry pink.

When he pulled away, she followed, moving on instinct as her lungs filled with air. "I'm not sure I can let you go," Dylan mumbled.

"Then don't," she replied, flattening her palms against his chest, feeling his body heat through the thin cotton.

"Is that an invitation to come in?" He nibbled her bottom lip, pulling her close enough for her to feel his erection against her core.

"Oh yes," Charley uttered, but the porch light flickered on and off. "Or maybe not."

Dylan exhaled into her neck. "Looks like your roommate is home."

"We agreed this wouldn't happen, right? So she's saving us from ourselves."

His head rolled from side to side. "I don't want to be saved."

Charley chuckled as she planted her hands on his cheeks and lifted his face. "I'll see you in a couple days."

"That's a long time."

"You'll survive." She pushed against his chest. "Go on. Before she opens the door and huffs."

After a hard kiss on her mouth, he stepped back. "Is she your roommate or your mom?" Cringing, he sighed. "Forget I said that."

"It's okay." Sobering and definitely a mood killer, but okay. "Be careful driving home."

Dylan backed his way to the truck. "Keep saying stuff like that and I might think you like me."

"Nah," she said. "I like the truck and don't want to see anything happen to it."

He pressed a hand to his heart, "You're a mean one, Charley Layton."

"Yeah, yeah," she replied, lingering at the door long enough to watch his taillights fade in the distance.

The flashing porch light had been a sign. Matty was pissed and ready for a fight. They'd had one minor argument since Charley moved in, not counting the disagreement at the station on Monday. On a groggy Sunday morning, she'd used the last of Matty's skim milk in her coffee and nearly lost her head when Mount Matilda went off. Since then, Charley had taken great care to use only the groceries she purchased for herself.

This situation was different. Charley had done nothing wrong by going out with Dylan, nor did she need Matty's permission to do so. With her hand on the doorknob, she braced herself, prepared to remind Matty of these important facts. But when she stepped inside, her roommate was nowhere to be seen. Slightly deflated, she dragged off her boots and set them on the bottom step before heading to the kitchen for a bottle of water.

When she flipped on the switch, Charley nearly leaped out of her skin at the unexpected figure standing in front of the sink.

"What did you do?" Matty asked. "Send him upstairs without you?"

Struggling to calm her racing heart, Charley crossed to the fridge and jerked it open. "That wasn't cool, Matty. You scared me half to death."

Voice snide, she said, "Just trying to be a considerate roommate."

Charley took a drink of water before responding. "Dylan is on his way home, and I'm going to bed. Goodnight."

"Are you going to see him again?" the blonde asked, following her from the room.

She'd agreed to spend more time with Dylan until he went on tour, which was sure to happen soon with the single taking off on radio. But Charley hadn't decided how far to let herself fall, and she wasn't ready to discuss the situation with a person who'd already made her opinion abundantly clear.

"That's none of your business," she replied as diplomatically as possible.

"Jesus, I'm your roommate, Charley."

"That's right. My roommate, not my guardian," she clarified, spinning at the base of the stairs. "I get it. You don't like Dylan, and you don't have to like him. But I do, at least enough to spend a little more time with him. And I don't need your permission or approval about who I go out with."

Tugging her robe tight across her chest, Matty tapped a foot on the beige carpet. "I'm trying to look out for you. I'm trying to be your friend."

"Then be my friend," Charley exclaimed. "Not my big sister."

Slamming her hands through her hair, Matty dropped onto the arm of the couch behind her. "This has disaster written all over it."

Anger gone, Charley set her water on the end table and took Matty's hands. "Not every guy is like Tristan. Once you stop seeing *him* in every man you meet, you might fall in love again."

A month after Charley had moved in, she'd learned the story of how a wide-eyed girl from Cookeville had met a guy online and pulled up stakes to be with him in Nashville, only to end up paying the bills while he played the bar scene, sleeping his way through half the town.

Matty shook her head. "They're all the same in the end. Every last one of them."

Bitter and cynical were a sad combination.

"You know that isn't true."

Ice-blue eyes met Charley's. "Every guy I've dated, Charley. Every one of them cheated. That means either they *all* cheat, or they only cheat *on me*. Either way, I lose."

Charley suggested an alternative. "Is it possible that you've been picking the wrong guys?"

"What are the odds I'd pick the wrong guy nine times?"

That *was* a troubling statistic.

"Nine, huh?" Charley mumbled, doing some quick math. "When you consider there are a hundred thousand or so options, that's really not a bad percentage."

She caught the throw pillow before it smacked her in the nose.

"I'm going to bed," Matty said. "If you're going to keep seeing him, at least have your dates on weekends like normal people. I can't keep staying up this late on a weeknight."

"You didn't have to wait up," she reminded the mother hen.

"Someone has to look out for you, Charley. I dropped the ball on your birthday, and now look where we are. Your one night with a hot piece of ass has turned into you breaking your own rules." She lingered at the foot of the stairs. "You're the one who said he was dangerous."

Her feelings hadn't changed on that front, but Dylan had allayed her fears enough to make dating him feel less like tap dancing through a minefield. There'd been no talk of rings or till-death-do-you-part, after all. So why not enjoy his company for a little while?

"I'm not breaking my rule so much as making an exception."

Matty tilted her head. "Does that mean you're toying with the possibility that you could have the man, the dream, *and* live happily ever after?"

Could Charley have it all? Love. Happiness. Professional fulfillment. Or were those all just promises made on the cover of a magazine? She really hoped not.

"I don't have a definite answer on that, but maybe."

Tapping the tip of her nose, Matty said, "And that right there is why you need saving. Keep your feet on the ground, woman. Or else you'll land on your ass eventually."

"That's almost poetic," Charley quipped.

"Just because I work with numbers all day doesn't mean I can't put pretty words together." The mother hen kissed Charley's forehead. "Night, girlie."

Her roommate trudged up the stairs, and Charley meandered to the kitchen for a late-night snack. Sitting at the table with her bowl of cereal, she considered Matty's advice. Practicality ruled every decision Charley ever made, until she'd walked away from the only home she'd ever known to chase a dream in Nashville. Even then, she'd resisted the urge to move before finding a job and a place to live. Hence, practicality still played a part.

There was nothing practical about dating Dylan Monroe. Or dating any musician at all, but especially not one on the verge of making it big. Charley didn't like to make sweeping assumptions, but pickers and singers weren't exactly known for fidelity.

However, based on her limited time with the man in question, plus the word of his female roommate, Dylan was not the sleep-around kind of guy. Which to most women would be a plus, but not to Charley. He was long-term. The real deal. The kind of man a girl could hitch her wagon to. But hitching would bring her right back to the initial issue of following in her mother's footsteps.

In the end, that was the deal-breaker—giving up her own dreams to jump on board someone else's. So as long as they both agreed that this was the line they'd never cross, Charley's reasons for avoiding Dylan went away. Mostly. There was still the matter of trusting that he meant what he said.

Putting the now empty bowl in the dishwasher, Charley headed off to bed feeling cautiously optimistic about her newfound romance. Whether she'd feel the same come morning was anyone's guess, but if the smile on her face was any indication, the chances looked good.

Chapter 13

Clay Benedict traversed the concrete floor of Marathon Music Works to reach the bar on the far-left side. "Jack on the rocks," he informed the female bartender. The room wasn't as packed as he would have liked, but the show didn't start for another forty-five minutes. He spotted Mitch Levine at the other end of the bar, staring into a glass.

Mitch's battle with the bottle was the stuff of Nashville lore, and Clay knew full well he'd recently fallen off the proverbial wagon. Once upon a time, the older man had managed some of the best-known acts in the business, and he'd made a fortune for both them and himself along the way. Most of the money had gone down his throat in the form of alcohol, but he'd managed to pull things together often enough to keep himself financially afloat.

Unfortunately for him, the Nashville music scene operated like a nosy small town, where everyone knew everyone else's business, and transgressions could scar a member for life. Somewhere in the last decade, Mitch had become a pariah of sorts, with few labels willing to work with him or any of his artists.

Essentially, signing with Mitch Levine Management had become a death sentence for any artist, and more than one had missed out on promising opportunities because of their connection with the unrepentant drinker.

When Clay had found Dylan singing in a bar in Printer's Alley, he'd known the boy had star potential. He also knew that he'd signed a previous record deal, but as was typical of the business, it hadn't worked out. Likely, shortsightedness on the part of some exec who wouldn't know a Dobro from a mandolin.

After sitting through the entire show, Clay had worked his way through an impressive crowd of adoring females to reach his potential new artist. As soon as he'd expressed interest, Dylan had shared the name of his manager, which gave Clay second thoughts. But Mitch had been clean and sober at the time, and he'd deployed well-honed negotiating skills that landed Dylan a deal any artist would be happy to have.

The new wave in label contracts involved signing over what some had termed 360 rights, meaning the label took a cut of all elements of the artist's career, including touring, merchandising, and even endorsements. In Dylan's case, and because he was the first artist signing to a brand-new and unproven label, Shooting Stars took a piece of his record sales and nothing else. If his career went as Clay hoped, they would renegotiate for another album with new terms that balanced out the pie in both directions.

"We missed you on Monday," Clay said as he set his glass next to Mitch's drink. "Dylan said you had another meeting. Is there a new development I should know about?"

"We both know that was bullshit, but I appreciate you playing along. As of now, the hidey-holes are once again empty, and I'm back to sucking down water." Mitch tipped the lemon from the side of the glass into the liquid. "I do have something to share, though. *Country Today* has agreed to include Dylan in an article about eligible bachelors in country music. The issue will hit stands in December and hopefully boost album sales during the holiday."

"Nice job," he commended. "Do we need to supply an image, or are they shooting their own?"

"Photo shoot lined up for next week."

"Good timing, since the radio tour starts the week after that. Daphne is pushing through social media, and Ralph has locked in ads at nearly fifty major market stations, including Dallas, Houston, and Denver. According to Lenny, the streaming numbers are looking really good. If we keep the pressure on, the single should hit by the end of the month."

Mitch turned his back to the bar. "Maybe then the boy will calm down."

"He seems calm to me." Clay had been pleasantly surprised by Dylan's quiet demeanor—considering the level to which his life was about to change.

The older man shook his head before sipping his drink. "Damn, I hate this stuff." He set the glass on the bar. "Dylan hides it well, but he's nervous. That first deal falling through messed with his head. I've spent three years rebuilding his confidence, and I thought for sure signing with you would settle his fears."

Everything he'd seen from Dylan assured Clay that the boy could handle whatever came his way, but fear of failure ran through the heart of every artist in this town, whether they admitted to it or not.

"The numbers will reassure him. By the end of the year, every other label in town will be kicking themselves for passing him by."

Eyes on the stage, Mitch said, "Damn straight. Shortsighted bastards."

"And with his success comes redemption for you," Clay pointed out. "I'm assuming that's a nice bonus."

Mitch nodded his agreement. "It sure doesn't suck."

Charley entered Marathon Music Works at eight fifteen, but only because Sharita refused to let her hide in the car. Not that she didn't want to see him. Truth be told, she couldn't wait to lay eyes on him. Meeting his bandmates was the problem. What if they didn't like her? What if they didn't approve? This was a lot of pressure, considering she'd known the man for less than a week.

If she were lucky, Dylan would be too busy getting ready for the show to come out and get her. But since she'd promised, Charley sent a short text alerting him to her arrival.

"I love this place," Sharita said, scanning the crowd with a smile on her face. "My buddy Malcolm shoots concerts here, and he's trying to get me on the list of approved photographers. God, that would be awesome."

The cocoa-skinned intern rarely went anywhere without her camera, but due to venue rules, she'd been forced to lock her baby in the trunk of Charley's car. A second-year student in the photography program at the Art Institute, Sharita's duties at the station included creating amazing images from any event in which the Eagle participated. To her credit, several artists had requested her shots for their promotional efforts.

In addition to being a talented photographer, Sharita was a fun, upbeat person, and Charley enjoyed having her along on remotes.

"Did you let him know we're here?" she asked, having dragged from Charley the reason they were attending this particular show. "I can't believe you scored a date with Dylan Monroe."

There were times in the last couple of days that Charley hadn't believed her luck, either. Dylan had sent a text Wednesday night, seconds before she'd turned off the light for bed. The naughty conversation had carried on for at least two hours, which had made sounding perky and alert on the air Thursday morning much more difficult. She'd ended up napping the previous night away, which worked out well since somewhere around eleven o'clock, they'd picked up where they left off.

Before the conversation had ended at two in the morning, Charley had crossed into new territory, enjoying the previously unknown pleasures of sexting.

"I sent a message," she said, "but I don't know if he'll see it before the show starts."

"Oh, he got it," the intern said. "And if that look on his face is any indication, he's really happy to see you."

Before Charley could respond, Dylan swept her off her feet as his mouth landed on hers, stealing her breath and burrowing through another layer of her heart.

"Hi," he said when he finally let her breathe.

"Hi," she replied, too dumbstruck to say anything else.

The black hat teetered high on his head while a goofy grin split his face. "I missed you."

Ignoring the heat climbing up her cheeks, Charley said, "You talked to me last night."

Dylan shook his head. "But I didn't get to do that."

As Charley's toes dangled in the air, the woman beside her coughed. "I'm Sharita," she said. "Remember me?"

"Sure I do," he said, lowering his cargo to the floor. "You took the pictures. How did they come out?"

"Great," she replied, beaming with pride. "With a jaw like that, you're a photographer's wet dream."

Taking the odd compliment in stride, Dylan smiled. "Thank you, ma'am. You girls ready to come backstage?"

Sharita smacked him on the arm. "Are you serious? I get to go, too?"

Hugging Charley close against his side, he said, "Hell yeah you do."

"Up top," the younger woman ordered, and the pair high-fived. "I'm so glad I did that remote today." She hadn't been scheduled to accompany Charley for the dealership broadcast, but she'd shown up anyway, claiming nothing better to do. Being out of school for the summer wasn't easy on a person with so much energy to spare.

Leading them around the edge of the crowd, Dylan tugged Charley along, glancing back several times to make sure Sharita was still with them.

"You've made a fan for life, you know that?" Charley yelled over the crowd noise.

As they reached a set of doors to the left of the stage, he said, "I like her enthusiasm. And no one's ever called me a wet dream before."

Charley found the last statement shocking. He'd certainly turned up the heat in her dreams for the past week.

Once through the doors, they made an immediate left into a cozy-looking room with an exposed-brick wall, plush gray sofas, and a foosball table. She recognized Casey sitting on the arm of a sofa, sticks in hand, tapping out a rhythm on what looked like a small wooden crate. Two other guys, dressed in jeans and graphic tees, lounged on the opposite couch. The moment the threesome entered the room, Dylan broke all contact with Charley.

"Hey, guys," Dylan said, "I've got a couple ladies I want you to meet."

The two strangers rose to their feet while Casey barely spared them a glance. "Hey," he mumbled, the drumsticks never missing a beat.

"He gets intense before a show," Dylan clarified. "Ignore him." Gesturing toward the others, he made the introductions. "This is Lance Roberts and Easton Atwood. Lance plays bass, and Easton is the best guitar player you've never heard of."

Handshakes were exchanged.

"Guys, this is Charley Layton from the Eagle and photographer extraordinaire, Sharita . . . I'm sorry, honey, I forgot your last name."

Instead of answering, the doe-eyed intern stared at Easton as if he'd descended in a flash of white light with flapping angel wings. To be fair, if Dylan weren't standing beside him, the guitarist *would* be the best-looking guy in the room. Spiked black hair. Deep blue eyes. Stubble-covered chin. She didn't blame Sharita for falling under his spell.

"Lewis," Charley supplied. "Sharita Lewis. It's nice to meet you, guys."

"So you're the voice in my radio," Lance said. "It's nice to put a face with the name."

"Thanks for coming to the show," Easton said, seemingly unperturbed by Sharita's silent adoration. "And thanks for playing the single."

If either man knew of her personal connection to Dylan, they didn't betray the knowledge.

Shrugging off the gratitude, she said, "Wish I could take credit, but I only play what they tell me to. Nearly every time it comes around, the phones light up. I'd say you've got a hit on your hands, gentlemen."

Dylan rubbed his hands together. "From your lips to the music god's ears. You want something to drink? There are plenty of options."

A mini liquor buffet covered a table along the far wall, but Charley had to decline for the both of them. "I'm driving, and Sharita is underage. Do you have any sodas, by chance?"

"We've got a couple of those," Easton replied, navigating Sharita to the display with a hand on her back. "Pick whatever you want."

The musician had no idea he'd made a young girl's year. Without a word, her friend chose a can of Coke before turning to Charley, dreamy-eyed and smiling like a postlobotomy patient.

Charley snagged a can for herself, turning to find Dylan had remained with his bass player.

"We should probably go find a spot to watch the show," she said, annoyed that they were back to playing games.

"I'm not in a hurry," Sharita said, taking a side step closer to Easton and whipping her phone out of her pocket. "We need to get a picture."

Playing the good sports, all three men posed for selfies with Sharita before huddling in for a group shot. Casey remained on his perch, and Charley lingered near the door, waiting impatiently for her chance to escape. By the time they'd all admired the images and made sure that

Sharita tagged them properly on Instagram, Charley's patience had worn thin.

"Sharita, I'm heading back out front. Come find me when you're done here."

"I'll walk you out," Dylan said, dragging himself away from an impromptu Snapchat tutorial.

Charley charged through the door. "Don't bother. I can find my own way."

"Hey," he said, grasping her hand once they were in the hall. "What's wrong?"

She jerked away. "One minute you're kissing me in front of a roomful of people, and the next you're pretending we barely know each other in front of your buddies. What that's about, Dylan?"

Closing the door to the room they'd just left, he pulled her to the side. "I'm not playing a game. This is an important time for us, and I don't want the guys to think I'm distracted, that's all."

A distraction? She'd give him a distraction. "If you remember correctly, I'm the one who said we shouldn't do this. I tried to walk away. If spending time with me is such a *distraction*, there's a simple way to remedy the situation."

"Dammit, Charley. I didn't say you're a distraction." Snagging her hand, he dragged her farther into the dark hallway. "These guys have been through hell and back with me. They've given up family time, lost girlfriends, and lived hand-to-mouth all so we could get to where we are now. *My* name is on that contract, and it's my responsibility to make sure this thing works. I want you in my life, but *this* has to come first right now. They need to trust that I'm all in. That this deal is my top priority. Do you understand?"

She understood perfectly. "I know that you're committed to this, Dylan, and something tells me the guys in that room know it, too. This was obviously a bad idea. Good luck on your road to stardom, and rest assured I won't be getting in your way."

Stepping around him, she walked off without looking back. In her head, she knew it was better to get out now than later, but her heart didn't feel quite so lucky.

"What are you doing out here, man?" asked Casey when he found Dylan leaning against a wall behind an empty road case. "We go on in twenty minutes."

"I'll be ready," he said, but his mind was somewhere else. "You know that I've been seeing Charley, don't you?" Dylan had been vague about his plans for Wednesday night, but Casey wasn't stupid.

The drummer shrugged. "That's your business."

"You don't think the other guys will have a problem with it?"

Leaning on the large black case, Casey crossed his arms. "They know what this shot means to you. So long as you don't start skipping practice or ditching commitments, it's all good."

Dylan leaned his hat back to scratch his forehead. They'd put their faith in him once before, and he'd taken them all to the bottom. That they'd stuck with him anyway felt like an incredible gift he had no idea how to repay. "Did you see the email from Ralph?"

"Fifty-four stations," he said. "We're taking off, buddy. The train has left the station."

"Yeah, but is there room on that train for Charley?"

Casey narrowed his eyes. "If Pam and I were still together, would you expect me to drop her for this?"

"You were together for two years. Charley and I have had two dates."

Two amazing nights that topped any he'd experienced to date. And not because of the sex or the sexting. They just . . . fit. When Charley was around, Dylan felt as if he could accomplish anything he put his mind to.

"But you like her, right? I've known you for six years, and I've never seen you fall this fast. That's gotta mean something."

Pulling off the wall, Dylan crossed his arms. "The timing sucks, though. We leave town in a little over a week and won't be back for ten days."

"Dude, if you can't leave the girl for ten days, how are you going to handle going on tour?"

Good question. He knew what being a working musician required, and he understood that any personal life would have to come second to the music. Dylan had seen couples make it work and others who didn't survive the first month. Until Charley had come along, he'd never met a girl worth taking the risk himself. Which made him a royal idiot for what he'd pulled a few minutes ago.

"What do you think about adding 'Better Than Before' to the set list tonight?"

His best friend flashed a grin. "I'm up for it, but you need to make sure Easton knows his solo."

That was one thing about surrounding himself with master musicians. Dylan never had to worry about the guys behind him.

"He'll know it. Now let's hope she stuck around to hear it."

As they headed back to the lounge, a familiar figure stepped through the doors to the front of house. Pam froze in place, blue eyes locked on Casey.

"Hey," the drummer said.

"Hi," replied his ex.

As if they'd run out of words, the pair stared in tense silence, prompting Dylan to step in.

"We're glad you could make it, Pam."

"Yeah," Casey agreed. "Glad you made it."

She nodded. "I kind of feel like I've been in this with you guys since the beginning. Only seemed right to come watch the first big show."

"That's why I put you on the list," Dylan said.

Pam's smile didn't reach her eyes. "Anyway, I found this on the kitchen table." She extended a green ball cap to Casey. "I know it's your lucky hat, so I wanted to make sure you had it before showtime."

The hat had been a present from Pam to Casey, given a month into their relationship. He'd worn it for every gig since.

"Based on recent developments," Casey said, "I figured the luck had run out on that one."

Hurt filled Pam's eyes as she tossed the hat onto a black case. "Right. That makes sense." With a quick wave, she added, "You guys have a good show."

As she marched toward the exit, Dylan elbowed Casey, who brushed him off. "Forget it, man."

Dylan had reached his limit.

"Pam, wait. Those pictures you found were never intended for Casey."

"Dude," Casey growled.

"He doesn't even know who she is," Dylan continued. Casey had insisted he keep his mouth shut before now, but Pam deserved to know the truth whether his friend liked it or not.

She stopped walking and turned around. "Then why were they on *his* phone?"

"Easton thought it would be funny to give Casey's number to a woman who wouldn't take no for an answer. He thought she'd call, Casey would tell her wrong number, and the woman would go away."

Jaw tight, she said, "But she did more than call."

Dylan nodded as Casey slapped his hat against his thigh.

"Why didn't *you* tell me that?" Pam asked, closing the distance and shoving Casey hard in the chest. "Why did you let me believe the worst?"

"I didn't let you believe anything," Casey argued. "You didn't ask me about the pictures. You threw them in my face and said, 'Fuck you, we're through.' Like I hadn't earned a little trust after two years."

Fists clenched, her jaw twitched. "You should have told me the truth."

Slamming the hat back on his head, he said, "You weren't interested in the truth."

Anger and betrayal were a dangerous mix, and Dylan should have known better than to start this now. Before he could soothe the situation, Easton walked into the hall.

"What's going on out here?"

Talk about bad timing.

Pam threw herself at the guitarist, sending him flying against the wall. "This is all your fault. Where the hell do you get off giving out Casey's number?"

"Whoa," Easton said, hands up in surrender. "I didn't know she'd send him pictures. I offered to explain, but Casey wouldn't let me."

Shaking her head, the furious woman raged at the men around her. "You're all a bunch of assholes."

With that parting shot, she stormed into the club, leaving three stunned males staring after her.

"Nice, dickhead," Casey murmured to Dylan as he stomped into the lounge.

As he passed, Easton said, "Man, I—"

"Forget it," the drummer snapped. "We've got a show to do."

Dylan grabbed the discarded ball cap off the case. "She's right," he said to Easton. "We're all a bunch of assholes."

Chapter 14

If Charley were on her own, she'd be in her car carrying her distracting ass home. But, alas, she was Sharita's ride, and the young intern had yet to find her in the crowd, which had more than doubled in size since their little foray backstage. So far, Charley had recognized four people from the radio station, spotted Clay Benedict in the VIP section at the back of the floor, and rolled her eyes at the flustered females tugging Dylan Monroe shirts over their heads as they pushed their way to the front.

In their whirlwind romance, if one could call it that, Charley hadn't had time to think about where she'd landed. In fact, she'd been too tied up in lust (she refused to entertain the other L-word) to consider the practicalities of what she was getting into.

Her declaration that she didn't want to be in the spotlight held true. Which was another reason this fiasco should end tonight. As Sharita had pointed out, Dylan belonged on film. Magazines were sure to come calling. Television appearances would be next. Award shows and the dreaded red carpet would follow, spinning the guy she'd met one

Saturday night at a club into a bona fide star, sought after and untouchable by mere mortals.

Charley wouldn't last long in that scenario. Not when Dylan could have any woman he wanted.

Checking her phone for the time, she knew the lights would drop any minute, so she scanned the room once more for Sharita. Though the band's newest fan wasn't likely to leave before the show drew to a close, Charley could at least see if someone else from the station might offer the intern a ride. Stretching on her toes, she spotted Sharita tunneling in from the side of the crowd and hopped into action to catch her. Except the minute she breached the mass of bodies, the lights went down and the audience surged forward, carrying Charley as if she'd been caught in a dangerous riptide.

Beams of light crisscrossed the stage as the band members reached their positions. Seconds later, they kicked off "Working at Home," and Charley's chest tightened as Dylan stormed onstage, guitar strapped to his chest and hat down low.

Though the crowd had no way of knowing the song, since the album hadn't been released yet, they clapped along, bouncing to the beat and feeding off the energy of the music. As much as she wanted to run, Charley found herself as mesmerized as the strangers around her. Dylan possessed a natural stage presence, appearing as comfortable beneath the lights as he had sitting next to the water in Centennial Park. His smile could power a city block, and passion filled every strum of the guitar.

The same guitar he'd settled in her lap six days before.

As the first song faded to a close, the crowd went wild. Regardless of what happened between them, Charley couldn't help but smile. The fans loved him. The applause died down as he stepped to the microphone and thanked everyone for coming out to celebrate the release of his new single. Seizing the opportunity, Charley turned her back to the stage and let the crowd funnel around her as she worked her way to the edge.

When she finally reached open air, Dylan said the last thing she expected to hear.

"I'm not sure if Charley Layton is still out there, but I hope she is." He shielded his eyes from the lights and scanned the audience in front of him. "I owe Miss Layton an apology. You see, I was a bit of a jerk earlier tonight, and I'd like to make it up to her. So if you're listening Charley, this one's for you. It's called 'Better Than Before.'"

Easton drew a mournful cry from his guitar as Dylan swung his acoustic around to his back. The slow song subdued the crowd, who listened with rapt attention, swaying from side to side. When his soulful voice filled the room, Charley's heart soaked in every gorgeous note.

> They say I'm a lucky man,
> And boy I know they're right,
> Because the day she smiled my way
> Is the day I saw the light.
>
> I thought I had it all,
> Wasn't missing anything,
> Thought love would keep me down,
> Said I'd never buy a ring.
>
> But a girl like that doesn't come along every day,
> You've got to hold on to her tight, before she walks away.
> Don't take her love for granted, and she'll show you so much more,
> 'Cause life with her beside me is better than before.

Dylan stepped back as Easton took the spotlight, mesmerizing the crowd with a solo that echoed the sentiment of the lyrics. The chords hung in the air, lingering like a prayer suspended in the artificial fog hovering around his feet. Solo fading to a close, the guitarist retreated into the darkness, leaving Dylan center stage once more.

At some point during the song, Charley had made her way back to the front, unaware that she'd taken a single step. Resting her arms on the thin metal barrier, she waited for Dylan to look up, ready with a smile when he did. The moment their eyes met, she kissed her heart goodbye. Dropping to her level, he sang the rest of the song for her.

> There are times I get it wrong,
> Forget the things I've learned.
> I lose my way, but she's right there
> To give me love I haven't earned.
>
> And if I ever lose her,
> It'll tear my world apart.
> She's the breath that keeps me going,
> She's the beat inside my heart.
>
> And a girl like that doesn't come along every day,
> You've got to hold on to her tight, don't let her
> walk away.
> Don't take her love for granted, and I promise
> you for sure,
> Life with her beside you will be better than before.

Somewhere in the back of her mind, a dying cynic pointed out the cheesiness of the moment, but the smile stayed on her face as Dylan leaned in to seal the deal with a kiss. The crowd fell away when his lips touched hers, and Charley wrapped her arms around his neck, cursing the barrier between them. By the time the kiss ended, they were breathless and both a little stunned.

Not until the crowd roared with applause did Charley remember where they were.

After his kiss with Charley, Dylan experienced the best hour onstage of his life. The crowd pulsed with energy, and at the end, several fans in the front were singing along with the new single. Less than a month and they already knew the words. The entire night had been a rush, with the only downside being Charley's early departure.

Dylan had wanted her to stick around and celebrate with him and the guys, but thanks to an early-morning remote, she insisted on heading home. Though not without a long goodbye kiss and a commitment to attend the Hall of Fame dinner with him the next night.

"What the hell was that about?" asked Mitch when he found Dylan packing up his guitar.

With the success of the show, he expected his manager to be in a better mood.

"What was what?" he asked, snapping the case shut. "The show was great. The crowd loved us."

The older man didn't seem to share Dylan's assessment.

"I'm talking about that damn kiss. Where do you get off pulling a stunt like that?"

Kissing Charley hadn't been a *stunt*, and Dylan took offense to Mitch's tone. "I didn't plan that, but I damn sure don't regret it." Lifting the guitar, he said, "The crowd didn't seem to mind, so what's it to you?"

Mitch followed him to the back exit. "What part of 'eligible bachelor' do you not get?"

"I kissed her, Mitch. I didn't propose."

"Listen, boy. Pictures of that kiss are already peppered all over the Internet, and they're tagging you in every one of them. A simple search is all it'll take for the magazine to find them, and then we're screwed."

Dylan dragged the keys from his pocket and unlocked his truck. "That eligible-bachelor bull was your idea," he reminded Mitch. "If it doesn't happen, it doesn't happen. We've got the radio tour next week, and by the time that article is scheduled to come out, I'll have hopefully spent weeks on a major tour, gaining more exposure than *Country Today* could ever get us."

The manager poked him in the back. "Do you think I do this shit for my health? I had to bow and scrape to get you in that article. You don't toss off opportunities like this over a piece of ass."

"Hey," Dylan snapped, spinning on his heel. "Charley isn't 'a piece of ass.' She's the woman in my life, and I won't have you or anyone else disrespecting her. You manage my career. I'll manage my personal life. Is that clear?"

Jaw working from side to side, Mitch stood his ground. "When your personal life threatens to fuck up your career, that's my business. Do you have any idea how many people are riding on your success? You've got a whole damn label to yourself. You're it, buddy. You go down, so does Shooting Stars Records."

"And so do you, right, Mitch?" he growled. Dylan knew what was on the line and exactly how much weight rested on his shoulders. The last thing he needed was someone reminding him how many people would be hurt if he didn't get this ship off the ground. "I've worked my ass off for this chance, and if you think for one second that I would do anything to screw it up, then you don't know me at all. This is about the music, not my relationship status. As long as there's no ring on my finger, I'm a bachelor. That should be enough for your magazine article. And if it isn't, too damn bad."

Dylan yanked his door open and slid his guitar behind his seat. To his credit, Mitch backed off and let him close the door. Running on pure adrenaline, he cranked the engine and slammed the GMC into drive. By the time he made a left from the parking lot onto Clinton Street, he'd cursed Mitch six ways from Sunday.

Tonight had been the best show of his life. That's what should have been the focus. Mitch should have been dancing a freaking jig after seeing that crowd's reaction. Hell, the entire week had been a success, according to his label. When he'd talked to Clay after the show, the exec had been all smiles, patting him on the back and congratulating him on blowing the roof off the place. Not once did he mention what happened with Charley.

The first time he'd taken this ride, Dylan hadn't even gotten this far. Four months of his life sat on some computer hard drive, deemed unworthy of even getting a shot. This time was different. Shooting Stars believed in him, and he would not let them down.

Maybe this wasn't the time to start a relationship. Maybe diverting even a fraction of his energy to something other than the work would bring it all crashing down. Or maybe, he reasoned, Mitch was overreacting. Dylan couldn't blame the man for being nervous. Once upon a time, he'd climbed to the top only to watch it all fall apart. Then again, Mitch couldn't blame any artist for his legendary descent. The mistakes he'd made were his alone.

Determined to do right by all involved, he vowed to appease the magazine, if necessary, and reassure Mitch that his priorities were still in order. No matter what, this opportunity would not slip through his fingers. Too many people were counting on Dylan to be successful. And he would be. Because, at this point, failure was not an option.

Chapter 15

"We're live from Esmeralda's Pancake House, raising money for the good folks at Central City Food Bank." Charley dodged a fast-moving intern balancing a tray on her shoulder. "The staff and personalities of Eagle 101.5 are here to serve up some scrumptious food and collect money for a great cause. We'll be here for another hour and a half, so if you've longed for Ruby Barnett or Beau Treble to serve you up a waffle, your dream can come true today, folks. We're at 515 Flanders Avenue. Hurry over and have breakfast with us. Charley Layton, sending it back to Freddy in the studio."

As Charley set the microphone on the table, a familiar face came rushing into the restaurant. "There she is, Brenda. That's Charley right there."

"I know what she looks like, Sharlene. You were right. She is prettier in person."

Sharlene of the awkward ice cream shop encounter all but bounced Charley's way. "Remember me?" she asked. "From the other night?"

When a person had a fan club of one, she tended to remember. "Of course I do," she replied. Turning to the curvy woman with cherry-blonde hair, she added, "And you must be Brenda."

"I am!" she exclaimed. "How did you know?"

"Good guess," Charley replied with a smile. "Are you ladies here for breakfast?"

"We sure are. Which tables are you serving?" Sharlene asked.

Sorry to disappoint them, she pointed to the microphone. "I'm currently handling the live spots, but Ruby is taking care of the first several tables by the window."

"Did I hear my name taken in vain?" the morning hostess interrupted. "How you ladies doing?"

Neither of Charley's fans appeared as excited to see Ruby as they'd been to see her. "We're great," Brenda said. "But we were hoping Charley would be our waitress this morning."

"Well, why can't she be?" Ruby asked.

"I'm doing the live spots," she explained. Since Charley hadn't been at the station long, the assumption had been that listeners wouldn't want a lesser-known personality as their server. That left Charley on broadcast duty.

Ruby waved her words away. "Don't be silly. I can do this. These ladies came all the way down here to have you slap some pancakes in front of them, and by golly, that's what they'll get." Sharlene and Brenda danced with excitement as an apron got tossed over Charley's head. "Now y'all have a seat right at that first table, and Miss Layton here will deliver your menus in one second."

"Yes, ma'am." Brenda led the way as the ladies hurried to take their seats.

"Are you trying to get me in trouble?" Charley asked. "John made it clear that I'm not supposed to serve."

While tying the narrow strings behind Charley's back, Ruby drawled, "Rule number twenty-three, honey child. Never hide your best assets when there's money to be made. If in the eyes of those ladies you're our best asset, then tote your scrawny little ass over there and make some money."

"But—"

"I'll take care of Willoughby." Ruby spun her around and shoved two menus at her chest. "Have you ever waited tables before?"

"I used to carry around trays of cookies at church gatherings."

"Close enough." Tucking a pen over Charley's left ear, she said, "Everything is right there on the menu. Take the order. Talk 'em up. Collect the cash. Think you can do that?"

Slightly offended, she grabbed a notepad off the counter behind her. "I'm not an idiot, Ruby. The next break is in ten minutes. Someone needs to call Freddy and let him know he won't be cutting to me."

"Where are you going?" asked the program manager as Charley turned toward her customers.

"Personal request," Ruby answered for her. "We're here to give the people what they want, and those two ladies over there want our newest addition."

John appeared skeptical. "I didn't realize you were so popular."

"I didn't, either," Charley mumbled. "Better not keep them waiting." Circling her boss, she crossed the short distance to Brenda and Sharlene and set a menu in front of each of them. "What can I get you ladies to drink?"

"Water for me," Brenda replied.

Sharlene said, "I'll have some orange juice. You must be walking on air after last night."

"Last night?" she asked, making note of their drinks.

"That kiss!" Brenda all but shouted. The woman seemed to have two volumes—loud and louder. "It's all over the Internet. I've watched the video three times this morning already."

Freezing with her pen above her paper, Charley cut her gaze from one smiling fan to the other. "There's video?"

Sharlene giggled as she picked up her phone. "Girl, let me show you. Though you lived it, so I guess you know better than anyone what happened."

Seconds later, Charley stared at Sharlene's phone screen as Dylan Monroe planted a passionate kiss on her lips, and she all but threw herself at him. When they finally broke apart, the crowd went wild, and the video cut off.

Stunned into silence, she didn't know whether to curse or cry. Being in the spotlight sent chills of panic down her spine, but until that moment, Charley had never contemplated the concept of going viral.

"Did you say all over the Internet?"

"I've seen it on Instagram, Facebook, and Twitter," Brenda said. "And my daughter saw it on Snapchat."

Scrunching up her nose, Sharlene said, "For the life of me, I cannot figure that snap thing out."

"Kenzie has tried to teach me," Brenda lamented, "but I don't get it, either."

Charley had an account on all the usual sites, but she rarely checked them unless she was on the air and needed something to talk about.

"By the way," Sharlene whispered conspiratorially, "you weren't tagged in a few of the posts I saw, so I went ahead and did it for you."

A nervous laugh escaped Charley's lips. "I appreciate that. I'm going to grab your drinks, and I'll be right back, okay?"

"Sure," they said in stereo.

Returning to the table where she'd left Ruby, Charley said, "Have you been online today?"

The redhead flashed a wicked grin. "That was one hell of a kiss, girlfriend."

"Why didn't you tell me?"

Ruby picked up the microphone. "Tell you what? That you got kissed off your feet by the hottest thing to come out of Louisiana since Tim McGraw? I assumed you knew."

"Not that part," Charley hissed. "I didn't know it was on video."

"Nothing happens in this world anymore that isn't caught on camera from at least three different angles." The older woman turned down the radio to her right. "I thought that might be the Dylan you met last weekend. Looks like you hit the jackpot, chickie."

"Wait. You knew?"

Instead of answering, Ruby went live. "Good morning, guys and dolls. This is your friend Ruby Barnett coming to you live from Esmeralda's Pancake House here in East Nashville, where the Eagle 101.5 staff is working their little tootsies off to rake in all the cash we can for the Central City Food Bank. If you come in now, you can plant your tookus at one of Charley Layton's tables, and maybe she'll tell you what it's like to kiss the hunky Dylan Monroe. I think we all want to know what that's like, am I right, ladies?"

Tossing up her hands, Charley marched off toward the kitchen, where she bumped into Payton Cheswick, one of Ruby's sidekicks on the morning show.

"Layton, you sly dog," he said. "I know that cutie Monroe doesn't swing my way, but damn, I'm still jealous. You work fast, girlfriend. High five."

Annoyed, Charley left him hanging. "I don't want to talk about Dylan."

"Why?" Payton asked, following her to the drink station. "That kiss is all anyone is talking about. Hell, I bet his record sales have doubled overnight."

Charley filled two cups with ice. "We didn't kiss to sell records."

"That's not what I meant. Come on," he pressed. "Why are you mad?"

Water sloshed onto the counter as she slammed down the clear pitcher. "I'm all over the Internet lip-locking some guy in front of an audience. How is anyone going to take me seriously after that? I'm a professional, dammit. Now I look like a . . . a groupie. Willoughby already treats me like a puppy he has to house-sit until my owners return. What if he uses this to get rid of me?"

Without warning, Payton dragged Charley to the far side of the kitchen and looked around as if making sure they were alone.

"If you tell Ruby I said any of the things about to come out of my mouth, I'll deny it to my dying day. The truth is, Charley, you're better on the air than folks who've been doing this gig almost as long as you've been alive. Ruby couldn't hold a candle to you if she hadn't been doing this since Jesus was knee-high to a camel, and Willoughby is only the program manager because he sucks on the air." Glancing around one more time, Payton lowered his voice. "You're a natural, darling, and nothing makes radio people more jealous than someone who can slap on those headphones and do what you do."

Blinking, Charley struggled to process this information. "You really think they're jealous?"

Perfectly manicured brows shot up a wrinkle-free forehead. "Sugar, I know they're jealous. You're in no danger of going anywhere. I'll admit, fraternizing with the artist types is usually frowned upon, but the higher-ups love you. And this Dylan Monroe stuff? That's already landing your name in the news, which in turn brings the station free publicity. That's a win all the way around."

So in some weird way, both she and Dylan had benefited professionally thanks to one spontaneous kiss. If she examined that fact too closely, the whole thing would feel tawdry and shallow, so she focused on Payton's compliments about her talent. Deep down, Charley knew she was good, but in Kentucky she'd been a big fish in a tiny pond. In Nashville, she often felt like a minnow swimming with the sharks.

Turned out, she wasn't a measly minnow after all.

"Well then," Charley said, making her way back to the drinks. "I guess going viral isn't the end of the world."

"And I bet kissing Dylan Monroe isn't, either," he hinted.

Flashing a smile, she cleaned up her mess. "It is not, Payton. It definitely is not."

By the time Dylan arrived at Charley's place, he'd had one of the strangest days on record.

First thing in the morning, he'd been summoned for a meeting with Mitch, Clay, and the label publicist, Naomi Mallard. At first, he'd feared the worst. That stations had started playing the song and received so many complaints that they'd taken it off the air. To his relief, Dylan's imagination had been way off.

The entire conversation had revolved around social media. Dylan had the accounts and posted from time to time, but he didn't live by the latest trend in his newsfeed or feel lost if he hadn't checked Instagram in a couple of days. According to Naomi Mallard, that had to change. Or at least his amount of personal postings did.

According to the publicist, a heartfelt moment intended to win Charley's forgiveness had turned into an Internet sensation. Several fans had caught the kiss on video, and by morning, Dylan was trending, the video had been shared thousands of times, and his number of followers was shooting up on every platform. In some cases, triple what he'd had the day before.

Clay and Naomi were ecstatic about the new development, while Mitch feigned approval. Dylan couldn't help but wonder what Charley thought of the whole thing.

Her spotlight comment kept coming back to him. Charley didn't like attention. Considering her response when Ruby had dragged her onstage in front of two thousand people, there was no telling how she'd react to being seen by twenty thousand overnight. His afternoon text to check on her hadn't alleviated his concerns, either. Charley's only response had been a question about what to wear that evening. Dylan had to ask Naomi, since he had no idea what to tell a woman to wear to anything.

The answer came back cocktail dress, and he'd passed it along, receiving an ambiguous "Okay" in response. Whether it had been an

I-can-do-that okay or a fucking-great okay, Dylan didn't know, so his heart lurched into his throat as he knocked on her door.

A full thirty seconds later, the thing finally opened, and Matty the Dragon offered a cold yet noncombative greeting. "Come on in. Charley is almost ready."

"Thanks," he replied, stepping inside and hovering near the door. "You look . . . comfortable."

Not the greatest compliment, but he was trying.

"Unlike Charley, I have a date with Netflix." She settled on the couch and grabbed a bowl of popcorn off the coffee table. No invitation to sit was offered, so Dylan continued to stand. Rocking on his heels, he straightened his tie before leaning against the wall to wait. A couple of minutes later, he was rewarded for his patience as Charley descended the staircase wearing a solid blue dress that hugged her curves, stopped midthigh, and revealed enough cleavage to be tasteful yet still make his mouth water.

Simple black heels finished off the look, turning her legs into objects of perfection. By the time she met him at the bottom, Dylan's brain had turned to mush, and his dress pants had grown uncomfortably tight.

"Sorry I'm late. I couldn't find one of my earrings." She pointed to a tiny gold hoop, and Dylan resisted the urge to drop a kiss below it. "Are we ready?" Charley asked when he made no move to leave.

Speech failed him, so he nodded and reached for the door.

"Try not to make the evening news," Matty quipped around a bite of popcorn.

Charley ignored the snarky comment, leading Dylan out of the apartment. They reached the truck without exchanging another word, but before opening her door, there was one thing he had to do. Locking his hands on her satin-covered hips, he took her mouth with his, relaying every emotion churning through his system—from lust and longing to admiration and pride.

When he pulled away, her hand lay against his cheek, and her eyes smiled into his. "So the dress was the right choice, then?"

Dylan nodded. "The dress is perfect, but only because you're wearing it."

"That's the second-nicest thing anyone has said to me today."

He glared in challenge. "Who's been flirting with my girl?"

Straightening his lapel, she shook her head. "Payton would rather flirt with you than with me, but he said something nice about my skills as a DJ, and I value an observation about my brain a little more than one about my body. Not that I don't appreciate the compliment. Or the sexy man who gave it."

He wiggled his brows. "You think I'm sexy?"

"I do." She grinned.

"I'm getting a sense that you aren't mad about our make-out session going viral."

"Not sure *mad* is the right word. I was more embarrassed than anything, but then I remembered what led to the kiss, and I figured there were worse ways to become famous on the Internet."

"Much worse ways." Dylan laughed, opening the passenger door. "Watching you climb up here might be the best part of my night."

Charley smacked him playfully on the chest. "Don't be ogling my legs."

"You can't show 'em off that pretty and expect a man not to ogle."

Her husky chuckle aroused him almost as much as the heels. "Play your cards right, and I might let you do more than ogle before the night is over."

For a brief moment, Dylan considered skipping the dinner altogether. But if he did that, he'd be proving Mitch right, and he wasn't about to give his manager the satisfaction. Even for a few extra hours of Charley naked beneath him.

After dropping a hard kiss on her lips, he lifted her into the truck, eliciting a surprised yelp from his gorgeous date and scoring a delicious peek under her skirt.

"I'm holding you to that promise, Layton," he said, enjoying her carefree laughter as he closed the door.

Chapter 16

"So now I have to step up my game on social media," Dylan said as they crossed the Cumberland on Korean Veterans Boulevard. "Before leaving the house, I shared a picture of Bumblebee getting hair on my pants with some complaint about trying to look nice and he isn't helping."

"Remember back when we were kids and didn't stare at a screen all day?" Charley pined. "Good times."

"But think of all those selfie opportunities we missed." He grinned her way. "And the food that never got its day to shine. Chocolate gravy on a Sunday morning, or deer meat on the grill." Dylan shook his head. "How was life ever worth living without fifteen likes on a pic of your peanut-butter-and-jelly sandwich?"

"Grandpa *loves* chocolate gravy. Makes me feel bad that I never got Granny to teach me how to make it."

They stopped at a red light at Second Avenue. "That's easy. Sugar, cocoa, and flour. Add a little milk, whisk, and put it on the stove."

Now this was a revelation. "You cook?" Charley asked. She had not been blessed with the magical powers required to throw seven ingredients in a pan and turn out something edible.

Dylan nodded proudly. "I can put together a meal now and then. Granny had bad knees, but she refused to give up working in the kitchen. When she couldn't stand at the counter anymore, I became her understudy, so to speak." The light turned green, but he had to wait for the straggling tourists to scurry across before driving on. "Five foot nothing and as sweet as the day is long, but if you didn't follow her orders exactly as she rattled them off, Granny would tear you up one side and down the other."

"I think we might have had the same grandmother." Charley chuckled. "Except Gram knew I had no business being in the kitchen, so I got the scolding if I dared get too close. Mama was a wonderful cook. Together they could put out a spread that would feed an army. And all in a matter of hours." Sighing, she watched a young girl skip along the sidewalk. "Unfortunately, that tradition died with them."

"Doesn't have to," Dylan said. "You could cook if you wanted to."

Charley shook her head. "You've clearly never seen me in a kitchen. I can barely boil water."

"You mean like you have no musical abilities? We proved that wrong, didn't we?"

"We both know I didn't play a thing on that guitar."

"Sure you did." He smiled. "And we'll get you cooking, too. Like anything else, it takes a little practice."

Though his faith in her was naively misplaced, Charley appreciated the belief all the same. Dylan made a right to cross over to Demonbreun Street, only to find a line of black cars in front of them, mostly limousines.

"I thought this was a dinner." She watched a highly recognizable artist climb out of one of the limousines and make her way up the stairs. "Is that a red carpet?"

"They're celebrating a biopic documentary of Merle Haggard," he replied, edging forward as the black SUV in front of them did the same. "I didn't get the red-carpet memo, either."

As if saving them from some great embarrassment, a valet sprinted around the front of the truck and waited for Dylan to lower his window. "Are you here for the event?" he asked.

"Yeah, but it looks like we might be in the wrong line."

"No problem. I'll take it from here, and you two can make your way in."

Dylan glanced over to Charley with a shrug and said, "Sounds good, man. Thanks." To Charley he said, "I guess we're walking the red carpet. You good with that?"

"No," she answered, watching another chart-topper climb the stairs. "But I'll give it my best shot."

Taking her hand, he dropped a kiss on her knuckles. "Thank you."

Before she knew it, Dylan had rounded the truck, helped her down, and was escorting her along the sidewalk to the entrance.

"Thank heaven I asked what to wear," she whispered in his ear, careful not to smack her temple on the brim of his cowboy hat. "But I still think I might be underdressed."

A major label executive she'd only seen pictures of to that point exited the SUV they'd been following with a woman closely resembling a disco ball on his arm. Charley's little ten-carat gold earrings didn't seem all that fancy anymore.

"You look gorgeous," Dylan assured her, stopping to turn her way mere feet from the main stairs. "In jeans and a T-shirt you'd be the envy of any woman here, and I'm damn proud to have you on my arm." After tucking her against his side, he lowered the midnight-black hat. "Naomi says the trick to this stuff is to smile but look bored at the same time."

Choking out a laugh, she said, "How do we do that?"

"I have no idea, but let's give it a try."

Charley's anxiety ebbed as her adrenaline levels rose. Though she knew they were legitimate attendees, she couldn't help but feel as if they were crashing a party and at any minute would be exposed as frauds.

But then she remembered that on her arm was a talented rising star in the ranks of country music, and her fears subsided.

The carpet led to the center set of doors at the entrance, but not before meandering past a mixture of press and paparazzi roped into an area on the left. To Charley's surprise, someone called both their names as they reached the end of the press line. With studied precision, Dylan turned to face the flashes, holding tight to her hand as she did the same by his side. She could only assume that "smile but look bored" translated to "look happy to be there but not enamored with the attention." Something she could definitely pull off.

What should have taken seconds took upward of five minutes as the line moved slowly, the press calling out for this or that star to offer a pose. Two more photographers hollered for Dylan, and by the time they reached the end of the press area, Charley's vision had become nothing but flashing dots. Which meant she failed to see the man with the microphone waiting for them around the bend.

"Next in line we have the newest star on the scene, Mr. Dylan Monroe. How are you, buddy?" asked Owen Overstreet, as if he and Dylan were longtime friends.

Once Charley's vision cleared, she recognized the reporter from a local Nashville news station. Matty's parting words came back to her, and she nearly burst out laughing.

"I'm good, man. It's nice to be here," Dylan replied as if being interviewed on a red carpet were an everyday experience. If he hadn't been squeezing her hand so tightly, Charley never would have guessed he was nervous.

"So the new single is getting a lot of buzz. How has this week been for you?"

Rubbing the back of his neck, he said, "It's been crazy, but a good kind of crazy. Played an amazing show last night at the Marathon here in town, and we hope to spend a lot more time in front of the people going forward."

Giving Dylan a friendly nudge, the reporter said, "I think we've all seen how well that show went for you last night." Nodding toward Charley, he added, "And I see the other half of the most famous kiss this week is here with you. Miss Charley Layton, looking beautiful. Are you having a good time tonight?"

Startled to find herself on the opposite side of an interview, she said, "We haven't been here long, but it's fun so far."

Oddly enough, as the attention shifted her way, Dylan's grip loosened.

"What's it like to be Dylan Monroe's girl?"

Scrutinizing her date, she offered a subdued smile. "Pretty good, actually." Turning the tables, she passed the question on to Dylan, mostly because she knew the reporter wouldn't. "How about you? What's it like to be Charley Layton's guy?"

Owen shifted the microphone in Dylan's direction. "Are you kidding?" he replied. "Look at her. I'm a lucky man, my friend."

"And hearts are breaking all over Nashville right now." Waving them on, Owen said, "You kids have a good time tonight, and thanks for stopping to talk to us. We move on now to our next guest coming down the red carpet . . ."

Charley didn't hear the rest of the reporter's statement as Dylan led her toward the entrance with a hand on the small of her back. An usher opened the doors as they approached, and as soon as they stepped inside, he placed a kiss on her cheek. "You're amazing, you know that?"

She did not know that, but she felt damn proud of herself in that moment. No cold sweats. No racing heart. And no panic attack. Who knew having Dylan by her side would cure her phobia?

"I'm used to microphones and being put on the spot. How about you, though? You handled that like a pro." She brushed a speck of lint off his shoulder. "I'm impressed.

"Then I faked it better than I thought. For a second there, I almost forgot how to talk."

Even knowing him for only a week, she understood the confession couldn't have been an easy one. "You'll get used to this. According to Owen back there, you're the newest star on the scene, remember? That's going to become a regular occurrence."

Taking her hand once more, he said, "Maybe you should handle all my press, and I'll sing the songs."

She didn't like him *that* much. "Not a chance, cowboy." Charley glanced into the glittering room ahead of them. "What happens now?"

"We mingle," he supplied, moving them forward. "But first, we get drinks."

Once he'd downed half a Jack and Coke, Dylan started to relax. He also noticed more than one man in the room admiring his date. Even a few women cut discerning looks Charley's way. As expected, the beauty in the blue dress didn't notice the attention. Clay flagged them down from a table near the front, and as they made their way through the room, Mitch came into view, his scowl deepening with every step that Dylan and Charley took.

The next few minutes could go south in a hurry, so he maneuvered Charley to Clay's side of the table, keeping her a safe distance from his unhappy manager.

"Nice to see you again, Charley," Clay greeted with a warm handshake. "You look beautiful."

"Thank you," she replied, a pretty blush dappling her cheeks. "The press outside threw me for a loop. I thought I was attending a nice dinner, not a movie premiere." Squeezing Dylan's arm, she added, "Your star here did great. The photogs even knew his name."

"That's partially thanks to you and that little public display of affection last night."

"We didn't kiss to get publicity," Dylan cut in. "Though we're happy to have it," he added as Mitch sent him a warning glare. Aware he could no longer put off the inevitable, he motioned to the man across the table. "Charley, I don't think you've met my manager yet. Mitch Levine, this is Charley Layton."

"Hi," Mitch said, not rising or extending a hand.

"Um . . . hello," Charley replied, casting a questioning look Dylan's way.

Pulling out the chair next to Clay's, he said, "Have a seat, honey."

"We need to talk," interrupted Mitch as Charley lowered herself into the chair. The older man rose slowly to his feet. "Come on."

Dylan didn't appreciate being summoned like an errant child, but he followed anyway, reluctant to cause a scene. When they reached the far wall, Mitch picked up where he'd left off the night before. "I thought you were bringing Casey to this shindig. First that damn video, and now this? What are you thinking?"

"I'm thinking I had two tickets to a nice dinner, and I'd rather have a beautiful woman by my side than a lanky redhead in a ball cap."

"This isn't a joke, Monroe. I got a call from *Country Today* this afternoon. They wanted to confirm that you're still an eligible bachelor and will remain one until their article comes out."

Why was he so hung up on this one article? "I'm not putting my life on hold for a magazine article. In case you weren't paying attention in our meeting this morning, sales doubled after that video went viral. The song is in radio rotation from coast to coast and getting more adds every day. The label is happy, I'm happy, and you should be, too."

Mitch shook his head. "You've got one song doing okay. One song, Dylan. Ever heard of a one-hit wonder? You want a career, you need to work the angles. You have to make the fans want you before they'll want the next single. I'm doing what you hired me to do, son. But you've got to be on board, or we're all wasting our time."

Seeing the light, Dylan leaned an arm on the wall. "I like her, Mitch. There's got to be another way."

"So like her," he said. "But do it in private. In public, play things down for a few months. You barely know this chick, anyway. You two could be over in a matter of weeks, and you'll have blown a prime opportunity for nothing."

Dylan wanted more than a few weeks with Charley, but he wanted his career just as much.

"Fine," he agreed. "If the magazine calls again, let them know I consider myself free and available. I'll explain things to Charley. She's not big on all the attention anyway, so the reprieve will probably be a relief."

"You'll thank me for this someday."

Annoyance trumped gratitude in that moment. "Did you say the article comes out in December?"

"That's right," Mitch answered, mood noticeably brighter. "If she's really the one, four months of keeping things quiet won't hurt anything, right?"

Four months of pretending didn't sound all that attractive to Dylan, but he agreed to the plan. "I guess not."

"When did you and Dylan meet?" Clay asked Charley, relatively certain he knew the answer.

The concerned young woman continued to watch her date across the room. "Last weekend. I was out with friends celebrating my birthday at the Wildhorse when Dylan asked me to dance."

"Things are moving pretty fast then," he noted. "I suppose a girl has to grab an opportunity when it comes her way."

Now he had her attention. "Excuse me?"

"Not that I blame you." Clay nodded toward Dylan. "A guy with a face like that, about to be launched into stardom. Happy birthday to you, right?"

Charley slapped a tiny blue clutch onto the table. "I'm not with Dylan for an *opportunity*, Mr. Benedict. In fact, I had no idea when I left that club with him that he could even carry a tune. I didn't learn that he was the launching artist for Shooting Stars Records until John Willoughby walked into my radio booth Monday morning and told me so."

Exactly what Clay wanted to hear. But then he put two and two together. "So Dylan didn't tell you anything about being a singer or that he had a single already available, but you didn't call him out on the air?"

Jaw tight, the brunette reached for the glass of white wine she'd carried to the table. "I don't know what woman did you wrong, but let me assure you, not all females are hateful she-cats. Now if you're through insulting me, I'd be happy to spend the rest of our time together in silence."

No wonder Dylan liked her so much. A woman with this much fire could keep any man coming back for more.

"For the record, my last statement was meant as a compliment, but I admit that my delivery could have been better. You see, Miss Layton, I've put a great deal of money into Dylan Monroe, and I tend to keep a close eye on my investments." Reaching for his own drink, Clay tapped his glass to hers. "I apologize for having to test you, but if it's any consolation, you came through with flying colors."

She fought not to smile, but lost the battle, and for half a second, Clay wished he were ten years younger.

"So this means we're on the same side?" Charley asked.

"I believe we are."

"Then I have a question for you."

"Fire away, my dear."

Charley leaned back with her glass. "Why doesn't Dylan's album include songs he's written himself?"

A question Clay had asked Dylan on several occasions. "I've been harassing him to write his own songs since we started this process, but his answer is always the same. He doesn't write songs."

"That's bull," she snapped. "He played one for me the night we met, and it was great."

Now it was Clay's turn to lean forward. "Dylan played you a song? Are you sure he wrote it?"

"He said he did, and I don't have any reason not to believe him."

Why would an artist keep his songwriting a secret? Especially in this town, where one hit song could set a man for life.

"Do me a favor," Clay said. "Don't tell Dylan that we had this conversation."

Brown eyes turned suspicious. "Why not?"

"Because I'd like to get to the bottom of something first." Mitch led his client back to the table, so Clay quickly added, "And I'm guessing he'd be unhappy about you telling me. So let's keep it our little secret for now."

"I hadn't thought of that," Charley mumbled.

"Sorry that took so long," Dylan said, settling into the chair beside his date. "You two okay over here?"

"We're good," she replied a little too quickly.

"Everything good with you and Mitch?" Clay asked, opting for deflection.

"We're good, too," the young man said, avoiding eye contact.

Silence settled over the small party. If Clay was a betting man, he'd say he and Charley weren't the only ones keeping a secret tonight.

Chapter 17

"He is not preparing me for the cheating," Charley argued for the fourth time in the last week.

"You're deluding yourself, woman. Dylan flat-out told you that he's going to see other women." Matty tossed a handful of socks from the washer into the dryer. "How are you not seeing this?"

Lifting herself onto the counter, Charley continued to eat her chocolate ice cream. Which she'd been craving all day.

"I'm going to explain this one more time," she said, tapping her spoon on the rim of her bowl. "He isn't going to see other women. That's the whole point. He needs to make it look like he isn't seeing *anyone*, including me. Mitch has convinced him that playing up this ridiculous eligible bachelor thing is going to get him more attention and somehow translate into more sales and more . . . I don't know. More whatever it takes to make it big."

Truth be told, Charley didn't like anything about Mitch's idea, but she could understand the reasoning. A lot of male artists came into the business with a wife in tow, and even families, but these days everything was about image and tweets and likes. Gone were the days an artist could break through with nothing more than a nice smile and a great song. So she had to stay in the shadows for four months. Charley didn't need to be in the limelight anyway. Though that trip on the red carpet *had* been fun.

"Right," the cynical roommate replied. "You've given the man a free pass, Charley. No guy passes up a free pass."

There was simply no convincing Matty that all men weren't lying, cheating scum.

"When Dylan isn't doing interviews, rehearsing with the band, or shooting a video, he's with me. He doesn't have time to see other women."

Charley would have loved to have been at the video shoot earlier in the day, but since Mitch had lined up a special behind-the-scenes extra edition, she'd have had to hide from the cameras the entire time and miss all the action. Not a fun way to spend the afternoon. Plus, she'd worked a remote in Franklin during the morning.

Matty slammed the dryer shut. "What about when that reporter from the magazine spent the whole day with him? You weren't around then."

"Convincing a reporter that he belongs on a most eligible bachelor list would be a little difficult with his girlfriend tagging along."

"I always hated that term. After a certain age, it sounds stupid."

Rolling her eyes, Charley licked the bottom of her spoon. "Then what would you prefer I call myself?"

Two cranks of a knob, followed by the push of a button, and the ancient machine rolled into motion. "I have no idea. I haven't been a guy's *anything* in so long, I haven't had to think about it." Lifting a full basket onto her hip, Matty began loading the washer. "I can't believe this doesn't bother you. Sneaking around to see each other. Letting him tell the press that you two are just friends. All to con some teenage girls into dreaming they have a chance with him, hoping they'll buy all his records and tweet about how amazing he is, and I think I just threw up in my mouth even saying that."

"Did someone up your drama queen medication this morning?" Charley hopped off the counter and set her now empty bowl in the sink. "I'd better jump in the shower. Dylan is picking me up in an hour, and with him leaving for the radio tour in the morning, this is definitely a shave-my-legs night."

Though Clay Benedict had mentioned his large investment in Dylan, that money apparently didn't pay for five-star travel accommodations for a radio tour. Ten days in a van with Mitch, Casey, a driver, and a record label rep did not sound like a pleasant way to see the country. Hopefully, by the time the tour ended, his single would be climbing the charts, and all the hours on the road would have been worth it.

"You're wasting those amazing legs on a man who doesn't deserve them," Matty mumbled.

Stopping on her way out of the room, Charley said, "You think I have amazing legs?"

A pair of black yoga pants flew at her head. "Of course I do, you little hussy. They're almost as tall as I am, for crying out loud. I'd kill to have legs like that."

In the short time she'd known her, Matty had never expressed even a hint of self-doubt. Except for the bit about men cheating on her. But when it came to looks, either the woman's mirror was broken, or her eyes were.

"Matty, you're like a Mensa poster child wrapped in the body of a beauty queen."

"That explains why I was the president of the chess club *and* Miss Putnam County 2006," she said with a perfect curtsy. "But that doesn't change my short, stubby legs into those filly ones you've got going on."

Carrying the yoga pants back to the basket, Charley helped bundle the rest of the clothes into the washer. "Right when I think there's ice running through your veins, you go and say something nice like that."

With a flip of her hand, Matty splashed cold water at her room-mate's face. "I'm still a bitch," she said with a laugh. "A short, jealous one."

Charley dabbed her face on her sleeve as she backed away. "There's a heart of gold in there somewhere. You can't hide it from me."

"Don't you be telling people that," came a shrill voice from the kitchen as Charley hustled up the stairs. "I have a rep to protect."

Dylan had never realized the benefits of being normal. No cameras. No photo shoots. And no pretending he didn't have a beautiful girl waiting in the wings.

None of this was fair on Charley, and that's why he'd insisted on having the night off before heading out on tour tomorrow. Visiting radio stations meant their days would start at the butt-crack of dawn, and it required reaching the first destination a day early. A Sunday drive up to Louisville, where the tour started, wouldn't be too bad, but he was already dreading the longer trips.

The high from the video shoot still churned through his system. They'd worked long hours for two days straight and visited four different locations in and around the city before wrapping late in the afternoon. Thanks to shooting the outdoor party-in-the-sticks scene hours before, Dylan had been in dire need of a shower before racing off to Charley's. As soon as he parked outside her door, his cell phone dinged.

"One night, people. That's all I asked."

Checking the screen like a good little artist, he saw the text from Mitch and swiped to read it.

We've got an opening gig. Tour kicks off 17th in Jacksonville. Runs three months.

Staring at the screen, he read the words three more times.

"I'm going on tour. Dude, we're going on tour."

He fired off a text to the guys, repeating the exact words he'd said aloud, and then jumped from the truck and ran to Charley's door, ringing the bell three times before she finally opened it. Swooping her into his arms, Dylan spun circles on the stoop. "I'm going on tour, baby. We did it."

Understandably confused, Charley braced her hands on his shoulders. "I didn't know you were this excited about visiting radio stations."

"No," he said, dropping her to her feet. "A real tour. I'm going to be an opening act."

"For who?" she asked, reminding him of a detail he'd missed.

"Shit. I don't know." Jogging back to the truck, he checked the phone and found the next message.

Wes Tillman twenty-year anniversary tour, and Clay is paying for a bus.

Turning to rush back to her, Dylan nearly knocked Charley to the ground. "Jesus, darling, I didn't know you were behind me."

She waved away the apology. "Forget that. Tell me. Who's the tour with?"

"Wes Tillman." A man Dylan had grown up listening to who'd won every award available and would likely be in the Hall of Fame within the decade.

"I thought he retired."

"I guess he changed his mind." Spinning her off her feet once more, Dylan hooted with excitement. "Do you realize how much I can learn from this? From Tillman? And how many people are going to see us?" He put her down and paced away. "Charley, this is what I've been working for, and it's happening. It's really happening."

"I know! I'm so excited for you. When does it start?"

Checking the phone again, he said, "The seventeenth and lasts for three months. That's three days after I get back from the radio visits."

"Oh," Charley said with less excitement. "I guess we won't get to see each other much between now and Christmas, then, huh?"

Dylan didn't like that part, either, but he was determined to make things work. "You can come see me on the road."

"When? I work five days a week and run remotes on the weekends."

"You can request one weekend off, can't you?"

"I guess, but they earn me a hundred dollars a pop, so it would cost me money."

Grasping her shoulders, Dylan locked eyes with hers. "This tour could take me to the next level, honey. Soon, you won't need to worry about an extra hundred dollars a week."

Charley backed out of his grip. "I make my own money, Dylan, and I have no plans to stop doing so anytime soon. You said you'd never ask me to give up my job."

"No." He shook his head, following her retreat. "That's not what I meant. You're a fantastic DJ, and I want you to do that for the next thirty years if that's what you want. But that doesn't mean I can't take care of you, right?"

"We've been seeing each other less than a month . . ."

"Feels a lot longer for me," Dylan said, tucking a stray lock behind her ear. "Look, Charley, we don't have to come up with all the answers right now. Tonight I want good Mexican food with my girl and to show you exactly how much I'm going to miss those pretty legs of yours. Is that all right with you?"

To his relief, a hesitant smile brightened her face. "So you're only going to miss my legs?"

Tipping up her chin, he said, "I'll miss all of you, darling. From head to toe." Lowering his mouth to hers, he took her lips in a slow, wet kiss that promised all the ways he planned to love her by morning. Charley kissed him right back, pressing against him with her arms draped around his neck. When they wound their way back to reality, the woman in his arms stared up at him with unease in her gaze.

"You won't forget me when you're out there with all those screaming girls, will you?"

Dylan squeezed her tight. "Nothing in the world could make me forget you, Charley Layton. Not ever."

Charley's appetite had not come along for the ride tonight. Not that the food at Mas Tacos por Favor wasn't excellent, but the butterflies in her stomach left little room for anything else.

Dylan wanted to take care of her. That smacked strongly of long-term commitment and feelings that shot way beyond a casual dating scenario. But it wasn't *his* feelings that scared her. It was her own. Because Charley could not deny a zing of elation when Dylan had tucked that hair behind her ear.

Feels a lot longer for me.

She felt the exact same way. Charley couldn't believe that she'd met him only three weeks before. When she glanced his way, it felt as if he'd always been there. Holding her hand. Making her smile. Riding to her rescue.

The problem was reconciling her independent nature with Dylan's white-knight tendencies. She *did* need him, but not to pay her bills or fix her car. Well, maybe to cook her a meal now and then. The one night they'd spent together during the week, he'd made some amazing fried chicken that she wouldn't mind having on a regular basis.

In fact, the chicken had been so good, she'd nearly bragged about it to Grandpa on the phone the next day. She'd stopped herself in the nick of time. Confessing she had a new man in her life would result in both Grandpa and Elvis arriving at her door within days, demanding an introduction.

Tonight, to prove to herself that she hadn't crossed some imaginary line long ago drawn in her head, Charley had insisted on paying for dinner. Until now, she'd let Dylan pick up the tab every time they went out. Which shifted the balance a little too far for her comfort. No matter the difference in their bank accounts, and by all indications, the difference was substantially in his favor, she needed to edge the needle closer to the middle.

And to prove that he understood her almost better than she understood herself, Dylan never flinched when she offered to pay. How could he know her so well so fast? Was it all an act? Was Matty right, that guys had some sixth sense, allowing them to say all the right things until they got what they wanted and moved on?

Cutting her gaze to the man in the driver's seat, she searched for some sign of the truth. Some unforeseen fault that would prove he wasn't as perfect as he seemed.

As if sensing her eyes on him, Dylan looked over. "You're awfully quiet over there. What are you thinking?"

"That you're too good to be true," Charley admitted. "That I'm going to wake up one day and wonder how I missed the signs. How you tricked me so thoroughly into falling for you."

Shifting his attention between her and the road, he said, "I like the falling for me part, but not the other. Where's this coming from?"

Charley shrugged. "Survival instinct, maybe?"

"Are you sure that isn't Matty's voice in your head?"

"Could be some of that, too," she admitted. "But doesn't this scare you even a little bit? Or am I the only one freaked by the speed of this ride?"

Staring ahead, Dylan replied, "Men aren't supposed to admit when they're afraid."

Leaning against the window, Charley crossed her arms. "I won't tell if you don't."

The passing streetlights illuminated his jaw, revealing a muscle tick below his ear. "Okay, then. Yeah. I'm scared shitless. About all of it. The deal. The tour. You. But that's a good thing, right?"

In Charley's mind, being scared was a sign to turn back. "How so?"

"The way I see it, if you aren't scared, you aren't living." He turned the truck into the parking lot behind his townhouse. "So I'll take scared over easy any day."

When he put it that way, Charley felt like a coward.

"That's deep, Monroe."

He smiled as he cut the engine. "That's what I thought when I read it in a fortune cookie." Stretching an arm across the seat back, Dylan toyed with her hair. "We've got the place to ourselves tonight. What do you think we should do?"

Feeling generous, and a bit aroused already, she let the fortune cookie crack go.

"You said something about showing me how much you're going to miss me."

"I did, didn't I?"

"Yes, you did."

"I do have something in mind, but it could take all night. And you might want to stretch first."

Charley laughed as he leaned toward her. "Are you taking me to a Zumba class?"

With a nibble of her lower lip, he said, "Something better."

Shoving her hands into his hair, she nearly dragged him over the console, offering a kiss that said she was up for anything he could dish out.

When the kiss ended, they were both a little breathless.

"We need to go inside," Dylan muttered, pressing his forehead to hers.

"Yeah." She nodded. "Let's go."

Chapter 18

It was a miracle they made it into the house. Neither was willing to stop kissing long enough to watch where they were going, which made getting the key in the lock damn near impossible.

Once inside, the keys hit the floor along with Dylan's hat, Charley's purse, and whatever mail had been left too close to the edge of the table.

"What the—"

"Ignore it," he hushed. "I'll get it later."

Unable to wait any longer, he tugged the cherry-red top over her head and dropped his lips to her cleavage.

"Wait," she fussed. "Are you sure we're alone?"

Lifting her off the floor, he pushed her back against the wall and felt her legs hug his hips. "I'm sure. And if anyone dares to come through that door right now, I'll kill him with my bare hands."

"You know how to make a girl feel special," Charley mumbled, digging her nails into his shoulders as he licked along the edge of her bra. "Mmm . . . ," she moaned, arching forward. "I like that."

Dylan caressed her bottom as he ground against her. "I like it, too."

Delicate hands shot into his hair as his tongue dipped behind the slip of satin. When he found the sensitive pink tip, she gasped, holding him to her.

"A bed," he murmured. "We need a bed."

"Yes," she agreed, locking her ankles against his ass as they moved away from the wall. "What are you doing?"

"I'm taking you upstairs," Dylan said as they passed through the living room.

"You're going to drop me."

At the base of the steps, he looked up into wide brown eyes. "You trust me?" he asked.

Relaxing her grip, she nodded. "I do."

"Then let's go."

As Dylan took the stairs at a steady pace, Charley let her hand trail up the railing. "This is kind of fun."

"The fun hasn't even started," he assured her, reaching the top and crossing the hall to his bedroom. With a kick behind him, the door swung shut, and he finally had her where he wanted her.

The weekend before, they'd discussed Mitch's eligible bachelor scheme on the way home from the dinner, which had led to Charley suggesting they end the night going their separate ways. He'd understood. She'd needed time to process his proposal that they play things low-key to keep everyone happy. And then he'd spent a sleepless night worried about her response.

If she'd have backed out then and there, Dylan wouldn't have blamed her. But she hadn't. And tonight, he'd show her how much her understanding meant to him.

Lowering her to the bed, he remained standing and reached down to remove his boots. Charley leaned back on her elbows, pushing her breasts forward to strain against the black satin holding them in. Satin that wouldn't be there for long if Dylan had his way. Once both boots were off, he leaned to join her on the bed, but she shook her head.

"I like to watch you undress," she said with a lopsided grin.

"I remember." Dylan remained on his feet and tugged the black T-shirt over his head. "That reminds me. You owe me a shirt, little lady."

Lashes lowered, Charley scooted higher on the bed. "I sleep in it."

Undoing his buckle and sliding off the belt, he drawled, "I'd like to see that sometime."

"Come back to me in ten days and I'll show you."

"I'll come back to you, baby." Tucking his thumbs inside his jeans, he added, "Always."

As if unable to resist, Charley lifted onto her knees and kissed the center of his chest. "Good. 'Cause I'll be waiting."

Taking over, Charley held Dylan's smoky gaze as she drew the starched denim down his powerful legs. He obliged by lifting one foot, and then the other, so she could toss the jeans aside.

"I believe I have a debt to pay," she purred, tracing the shape of his erection behind the boxer briefs. "This looks like a good time to pay up."

"You don't owe me anything, honey, but I'm happy to take any payment you want to make."

Tasting the warm flesh below his naval, Charley slid her hands around to test the firmness of his ass. "Magnanimous yet accommodating." She chuckled. "I like that in my men." When she kissed him through the cotton, his body went rigid and his teeth clenched. "You okay up there?"

"I'm good," Dylan replied in clipped tones.

"You're about to be." Charley let her nails scrape down his rib cage before tucking them behind the waistband and casually pulling. Inch by inch, she kissed her way down until the material crested over her target and Dylan sprang free, pulsing and ready. "There we go," she murmured, licking the tip.

Dylan moaned as his hips swayed forward, and Charley took the invitation to trail her tongue down his length. "You're killing me, baby."

Taking him in, she gripped his thighs, the muscles rippling as his knees locked and a growl echoed off the walls. Salt and heat danced on her tongue as she took him deeper, sucking hard down and back as his hands fisted in her hair. Aroused and wet, Charley picked up her pace, hands locked on his ass while Dylan rocked for her, giving more until her lips reached the base of his shaft. Drawing back far enough to tease the tip, she sucked one more time, eliciting a roar from his lungs as she swallowed his essence and felt him quiver with release.

Licking her lips, Charley looked up to see Dylan's head thrown back and his rippling abs pulled tight. Seconds passed before his chest constricted, his lungs filling with much-needed air. Fingers still buried in her hair, his head tilted her way, gray eyes darkened by desire.

"You're amazing," he breathed, leaning to drop a kiss on her mouth. "Fucking amazing."

Dylan's praise aroused her nearly as much as the look in his eyes. "I'm glad you liked it."

"Liked it?" he asked, lifting her to her feet and turning her back to him. His scruff tickled her neck as he whispered in her ear. "I loved it, honey."

A callused hand slid under Charley's bra to cup her breast, while the other slid down the front of her shorts, where his fingers teased her clit. Wrapping her hands around his wrists, she rubbed her bottom against his erection as a purr escaped her lips.

"That's it, baby. That's it."

Body on fire, she leaned her head against his shoulder, lost in the sensations spiraling through her limbs. Abandoning her clit long enough to unbutton her shorts, Dylan worked the denim down her legs, leaving only her black thong in place.

"You're so hot, Charley. I can't get enough."

"Me neither," she panted as he slid the flimsy strip of satin to the side to work her folds. "Don't stop," she mumbled, writhing against his hand. "Please, don't stop."

"Never," he growled, driving a finger inside.

When she arched forward, he pinched her nipple, sending shards of pleasure and pain to her core. Charley teetered on the edge, ready to break apart at any second.

"Dylan, I can't hold on."

"I've got you." Another finger slid inside. "So wet. Come on, now. Come for me, honey."

Panting for air, she nodded as his thumb pressed hard against her clit and stars exploded behind her eyelids. The orgasm slammed her body, but Dylan held her tight, riding the crest with her until she went limp in his arms. Chest heaving, she dug her nails into the arm braced across her chest.

"I think you outdid me," she whispered. "That was incredible."

"And that was only the opener," he murmured, biting her earlobe, his hand still locked on her breast. "The fun is just beginning."

"Let me grab something, darling," Dylan sighed into her ear. "Don't move."

Charley did as asked, remaining at the foot of the bed in her matching black bra and thong. Looking at her was enough to set him on fire. Touching her threatened every ounce of his control. But he was determined to make this a night she wouldn't forget, and he'd made sure they were prepared.

Retrieving a condom from his nightstand, Dylan returned to her, trailing his index finger down her back to reach the narrow strap tucked between her gorgeous curves. Charley shivered, and he raised her hair to kiss the back of her neck.

"Perfection," he breathed against her skin, tearing open the small blue packet and rolling the condom down his shaft.

Unclasping the bra, he slid the straps slowly down her arms and tossed the delicate number off to the side. Every dip and crevice begged for his touch, but Charley didn't move. Only stood her ground, letting him touch and taste. The contour of her shoulder. The crook of her neck. The small of her back. And all the while, he grew harder until he couldn't hold back any longer.

Drawing out the moment, Dylan slid the panties down her thighs to land silently around her feet, and with a gentle push, Charley landed on her hands and knees, knowing instinctively what he wanted her to do. Without prompting, she arched and drove back against him, letting him know she wanted the same.

Hands locked on her hips, he drew her to him, finding her wet and open, and slid inside only to have her clench around him.

Chestnut hair swung forward as her head dropped with a sigh. Dylan slid in the rest of the way, teeth clenched for control. He wanted to go slow. To make this last. But his body had other plans. Withdrawing, he drove in deep again, thrusting hard enough to draw a gasp from Charley.

Kissing her back, he said, "I'm trying, baby. I'm trying to go slow."

Charley shook her head. "No. More. Give me more, Dylan."

Her plea snapped his control, and he leaned up, bracing his feet wide to take her over and over, faster and harder. She matched his intensity, meeting him drive for drive, plunging them both into mindless pleasure as the world went white-hot, searing his brain and scorching his lungs.

Dylan buried himself one more time, the release burning through his chest as Charley screamed his name, her body trembling against him. When any sense of reality returned, he found himself tucked behind her on the mattress, arms wrapped around her shoulders as they both gulped for air.

Charley had heard women say that a man had made them see God, but she'd never really believed it happened. Lo and behold, she was wrong.

"Maybe you leaving town all the time isn't going to be such a bad thing," she said, flattening her back against Dylan's abs. "Rounds like that might make the separation worthwhile."

Dylan chuckled, shaking them both. "Not sure I can guarantee that kind of performance every time. I even impressed myself."

Rolling to face him, she threw a leg over his hip. "You can't set a bar that high and expect a girl to go back to anything less."

Caressing her thigh, he licked her bottom lip. "I'll promise to deliver my best whenever you give me the chance."

"I see a lot of chances in your future," Charley assured him, running her thumb across his lips. With a heavy sigh, she said, "I'm going to miss you."

"I'm going to miss you, too."

"Ten days is a long time."

"Not as long as three months. Are you sure you can't get away to come see me?"

She'd been scrimping since her first day on the job, saving all her pennies to eventually get a place of her own. Missing out on a couple of weekend remotes wasn't going to threaten Charley's plans.

"I could probably work something out once I see the dates."

"Wait." Dylan scrambled to the end of the bed and returned with his phone. "I bet the schedule is online." A few swipes and "Wes Tillman tour" typed into a search engine turned up the information they needed. "We start in Jacksonville, go up the East Coast, across the north, and then out west."

"Well, that sucks. Is there nothing within driving distance?" she asked.

"Looks like the tour wraps up here at the Bridgestone in December, but there's a show in Knoxville on Halloween."

Charley brushed her hair out from under her ear. "That's six weeks into the tour."

Dylan continued to stare at the phone as if the dates might change. "Cincinnati isn't that far. We'll be there the third week in."

"But that's a weekday," she pointed out. "It's easier for me to get away on a weekend."

"Okay, then, what about Little Rock? Four weeks in on a Saturday night."

Remembering a trip they'd taken when she was a kid, Charley said, "That's at least a seven-hour drive from here. It would suck, but I could do it."

Setting the phone on the bed behind him, Dylan rolled to his side. "Why don't you let me buy you a plane ticket? Then you can come see me anywhere."

Letting him buy meals was one thing. Letting him buy plane tickets was another.

"I'd rather not cost you that much."

Planting a quick kiss on her lips, he said, "They don't cost that much. I want to see you."

She traced the line of his jaw. "I want to see you, too. But what happens if we get caught on camera somewhere? What are you going to say? That your *friend* Charley just happened to be in the neighborhood. In Indianapolis."

"This damn article better be the greatest thing to ever happen to my career, or I'm kicking Mitch's ass."

Charley felt the same way, but she'd agreed to these terms and would abide by them.

Cuddling in closer, she said, "Maybe we should stop worrying about what happens weeks from now and focus on the moment. You did promise me a long night, remember?"

"I like the way you think, Miss Layton." Dylan shifted her up onto his chest. "And I really like when you're up there."

Leaning up enough to brace her hands against his chest, she straddled his hips. "Are you offering me a ride, Mr. Monroe?"

"That I am," he replied, skimming his hands along her thighs. "Ride away, darling."

Chapter 19

Clay almost felt bad watching the crew load into the van. Almost.

"I expect nothing but good results," he said, clapping his hands like a coach rallying his team. "Pictures and videos need to be shared on all platforms. Ralph, you've got the label accounts for the next ten days. Make him look good."

"Will do, boss."

"Dylan, you've got the easy part. Flash a smile, sing 'em a song, and leave them wanting more."

"Right," the groggy artist replied. "No pressure there at all."

Having watched Dylan and Charley say their goodbyes, which they did more than fifty feet from the departing van, Clay knew exactly why his young hopeful could barely keep his eyes open.

Turning to his PR expert, Clay said, "Naomi, any words of wisdom before we send them off to make a mess?"

She shook her head, sending the black-as-night ponytail swinging. "Dylan is a publicist's dream. He'll be great." As if unable to help herself, she added, "But don't party so hard I have to explain why you were dancing on a table with your shirt over your head."

"What a killjoy," Casey murmured with a lopsided grin.

"Do what she says, Flanagan." Clay and Naomi stepped back from the van. "Drive safe, Clifford. And no buying cigarettes on the company credit card."

"Yeah, yeah," grumbled the bus driver, put out by his demotion down to a minivan. The only reason he'd agreed to take the quick ten-day job was the promise of being Dylan's official bus driver once the Tillman tour hit the road.

With a wave, Casey closed the side door, and the Odyssey rolled into motion.

"They're going to be miserable by the time they hit Milwaukee," Naomi predicted.

Aspiring artists often lived on the notion that life in the lights would be one big luxury ride. If they were lucky, they learned the truth.

"I doubt it'll take that long. Wednesday they've got a drive from Columbus to Philly." Clay swatted away a persistent fly. "If they don't kill each other by the end of that one, the rest of the tour will be a breeze."

Naomi turned to her left and spotted the woman sitting in the older-model Ford Bronco. "Is that . . ."

"We're supposed to pretend we don't see her," he whispered.

"Why is she lurking over there?"

"Because Mitch got Dylan into some eligible bachelor article that comes out later in the year, and he's convinced the lovebirds to keep their romance private so as not to make our young star appear ineligible in the meantime."

Cutting disbelieving eyes his way, she said, "That's the dumbest thing I've ever heard."

Clay agreed, but he also understood that fans wanted to see their idols as accessible, and what was more accessible than a single man?

"Once the article comes out in December, they're free to go public. Though I get the feeling Mitch would prefer they not make it that far."

Leading his publicist to her car, he asked, "Have you thought any more about my Chance Colburn idea?"

As expected, Naomi visibly tensed. "No, I haven't."

A lie, and they both knew it.

"I don't know what your history is with the man, but I suggest you find a way to deal with it. I've sent the contract to his manager. Chance is expected to sign next week."

Lips pursed, she locked eyes with his. "Why would you risk a fledgling label on Chance Colburn? Broadway is crawling with artists, any one of whom would be a safer bet."

Clay didn't need to defend his decision to anyone, but in this instance, he made an exception.

"We've spent the better part of a year launching a brand-new artist. A total unknown. Add up the man-hours and the advertising alone, and we've spent roughly a quarter of a million. Signing Colburn means cutting that price tag in half, at least. He has awards on his shelf, two platinum albums on his wall, and a built-in fan base that we can build on." He opened her car door. "This is a sound business decision, Naomi. He's clean, and he's ready to work. With you by his side to keep the press positive, we all win."

Hazel eyes flashing, she tossed her ever-present planner onto the passenger seat. "That doesn't sound like a winning plan for me, but as I said before, it's your call."

As she slammed the key in the ignition, Clay asked, "Am I going to lose you over this?"

Naomi Mallard wasn't the only publicist in town, but she *was* the best. Losing her would put a major dent in the team, and in all honesty, he wasn't sure anyone else could handle Colburn.

Debating her answer, she tapped the steering wheel for several seconds before finally looking his way. "I'm not giving up anything for Chance Colburn. Not this time." With that cryptic reply, she shut the door and drove off.

So there *was* history between them. Clay wasn't sure if this development would play in his favor or not, but the decision had been made, and he wouldn't rescind the offer now. Naomi was a professional. She would do her job. With luck, Colburn would cooperate. Because if he didn't, the fragile walls of Shooting Stars Records could come tumbling down, and Clay would be damned if he'd let that happen.

Charley had to stop checking Dylan's Instagram account every five minutes. She'd done well for the first couple of days. They'd exchanged texts, with Dylan telling stories of Clifford the driver stopping every hour to smoke, and Ralph Sampson's previously unknown tendency toward car sickness. Getting the smell of vomit out of the van had required two scrubbings, three passes with a vacuum, and seven pine-scented air fresheners hanging throughout the vehicle.

But by Friday, every new picture he shared featured another pretty girl with her hands on Charley's man. She reminded herself that they were fans. Listeners excited to hug the hunky new singer passing through their town. The silent pep talks worked for a while, until she made the mistake of following Casey's Instagram account. That's where the evening shots were shared. The guys gathered around a table covered in beer bottles and fruity little umbrella drinks for all the pretty girls who'd joined them.

In no picture were there less than two skinny, boobilicious females hanging on Dylan's arms. Or his neck. The neck she wanted to strangle. In dire need of reassurance, she'd asked him about Casey's account and all the partying they were doing. Not only had he taken six hours to respond, but his answer had been less than reassuring.

We're having fun, babe.

That was it. That was his entire response. No *they mean nothing to me* or *I'd rather be there with you*. Just that they were having fun. Well, she could see that they were having fun. That was the damn point.

"You're going to drive yourself crazy," Matty warned as Charley punched a couch cushion.

At nearly midnight, Casey had shared a picture of Dylan surrounded by six women, one of whom sported an I'M THE BRIDE sash. They'd clearly stumbled into a bachelorette party, and Charley knew exactly what drunk women did the night before their weddings.

"I'm fine," she snapped, lying through her teeth.

"You knew this was coming."

Charley knew that Dylan was going out on the road to *work*. This did not look like work.

"I know that Dylan isn't doing anything wrong," Charley said, determined to be sensible.

Matty poured herself another glass of wine. Since Charley hadn't felt well for two days, she stuck with hot tea.

"This is going to be ten times worse when he goes on a real tour," her roommate pointed out, qualifying as the least helpful statement of the night.

"I've thought about that, and so far, I've come up with two solutions."

With a cynical expression, Matty said, "Do enlighten me."

"I can trust him and realize that none of this means anything. Or I cancel all of my social media accounts and go off the grid."

"Two entirely sensible options. Or maybe you accept that life with Dylan will involve watching women throw themselves at your man, and be confident in the knowledge that he'll always choose you over them."

Who was this woman, and what had she done with Matty?

"You don't even like him. You're the one who says all men cheat and break your heart and aren't worth the bullet it would take to put him out of your misery."

Pressing Charley's hair off her forehead, she mumbled, "Don't be silly. I'd never shoot anyone."

"But you don't—"

"Like him. Yes, I know." Matty shrugged. "Which makes this next statement even harder to say."

Charley waited with arched brows.

"The truth is, I think he's for real. I think he really likes you, and if he makes you happy, then you should have him."

Lifting her chin off the floor, Charley said, "Did you spike my tea? Because I'm not understanding the words that are coming out of your mouth right now."

Matty rolled her eyes. "Come on. He looks at you like you're the most beautiful girl he's ever seen. And when you talk, his face . . . changes. Like he's listening to poetry or the best song ever written. That boy is in love with you, Charley, and you love him, too. That's worth ignoring a little drinking on the road."

"I don't . . . I . . . ," Charley stuttered, unable to process this new declaration. "I don't *love* Dylan."

"The hell you don't."

"I think I would know if I loved somebody," she scoffed, hopping to her feet. "I mean, I've only known him for, what? A few weeks!"

As if she'd suddenly become an expert on the subject, Matty said, "Love doesn't have a set time frame. It can happen in three years. Or it can happen in three weeks. So you got the fast track."

That was impossible. Charley paced the length of the couch, forcing Matty to pull her legs up or be stepped on.

"You're clearly seeing things that aren't there. Besides, you don't even believe in love."

"I don't believe in love *for me*," the jaded woman corrected.

"Nope. You said for everyone."

"Fine." She threw her hands in the air. "I'm a bitter woman. We say stupid shit. I don't really *not* believe in love. I'm annoyed with it. I don't necessarily like it or appreciate what it's done to me, but I haven't written it off entirely."

Charley dropped onto the sofa. "You really think he's in love with me?"

"Please. That boy is so far gone, he doesn't know which way is up."

"And I love him, too?"

Matty leaned forward. "Don't you?"

Before she could answer, Charley's phone dinged and she dove at it like a pigeon on a crust of bread.

I miss you, baby. A few more days. Can't wait.

Staring at the screen, she whispered, "Yes. Yes, I do."

Overwhelmed by the rate of change in her life, on Saturday morning Charley sought out the sanest person she knew. She'd gotten up early to place the call, knowing she'd miss him otherwise.

"Hello?" he answered after the third ring.

"Hi, Grandpa," Charley said, never so happy to hear his voice. "How are you doing?"

"I'm shuffling along, as always," Maynard Layton replied. "Haven't heard from you in a while. How's my baby girl?"

A pinch of guilt mixed with a heavy dose of homesickness. "She's good. Missing home, though."

"Now, darling, you know you're welcome to come back anytime. Is the big city not treating you right?"

Charley plopped down on her bed and pulled her knees up. "The city is great, Grandpa. I've just been really busy. A lot of changes to get used to, you know?" With one change that seemed bigger than the rest. "Tell me what's going on up there. I want to hear all the gossip."

Though Gramps claimed not to be the gossipy type, he always knew the latest dirt and never hesitated to pass the news her way.

"Let's see," he mumbled, as if considering where to start. "Old man Bailey quit the radio station."

"He what?" Charley sprang up on the bed. "He's been there for nearly forty years. What happened?"

"Wilma at the co-op said they took away his job of picking the new music to play and gave it to Terry Parsons. Bailey got so mad, he quit right on the air. No warning or nothing. Then he packed his stuff and went to the house."

The change didn't surprise Charley, since Dean Bailey had little interest in the music he was supposed to be programming. The man didn't even have a radio in his truck and likely had never read a magazine in his life. She herself had attempted to show him how to find the latest industry news on the Internet, but Dean had only growled and walked away.

"I can't believe he'd just quit like that." Charley would have bet money that he'd take his last breath in the halls of that station.

"Heard it myself. Only later found out that it was a shock to the rest of the staff, including Fanny."

Fanny Carmichael had inherited the station from her father, and she'd been like an extra grandmother to Charley. She ran a tight ship, but had a heart of gold, and was a beloved member of Liberty society.

"Have you talked to her about it?"

Voice a little lower than before, he said, "She mentioned it over dinner the other night."

Charley flipped to her knees. "You had dinner with Fanny Carmichael? Are you two dating?" Gram had been gone for four years, and in that time, Grandpa hadn't so much as looked at another woman.

"Dating is for younger folk," he explained. "People in their sixties visit and hope neither one of them keels over in their soup."

He wasn't fooling anyone. "You are dating!"

"Don't be getting any ideas, now. Fanny and me are spending a little time together. That's all."

Knowing Grandpa wasn't sitting home alone every night put a smile on Charley's face. For a farmer, he was a social creature, and she was glad he'd picked Fanny to be with. Or maybe she'd picked him. Either way, the new development eased her worry about leaving him behind.

And since they were on the topic, Charley delved into the real reason she'd called. "I've been spending time with someone, too."

"Oh yeah?" Grandpa asked. "Do you like him?"

"I do," she answered. "A lot."

Reading between the lines, he said, "I see. When are you going to bring him home so we can meet him?"

Charley knew exactly whom he meant in that *we*.

"Maybe soon, but the last thing I need is Elvis scaring him away."

Her oldest friend, who'd grown up on the farm next door, found his greatest entertainment in chasing off any boy who dared try to date her. A former marine, and roughly the size of a barn, Elvis Marigold would do anything for Charley. Except let her have a love life.

Though, to be fair, she'd done her share of alienating his potential dates. It wasn't her fault that none of them had been good enough for the big jerk.

"If the boy can't stand up to Elvis, he isn't good enough for my baby girl."

Dylan would stand up to him all right, but that didn't mean Elvis wouldn't do something stupid like coax him out on a four-wheeler and then leave him to find his way back. Between the two farms, there were nearly two hundred acres of uncleared land, populated by enough wildlife to make the terrain even more dangerous for someone who didn't know the area.

And then, of course, there was Dylan's touring schedule, which made taking him home to Grandpa even more difficult.

"Maybe over Christmas," Charley replied, hoping she'd survive the three months until then with her sanity and heart intact.

As if sensing her troubled thoughts, Grandpa grew serious. "There's something you aren't telling me. Do I need me to come down there, honey?"

She'd give anything for him to come down and hug all her problems away, but Charley wasn't a little girl anymore. Nor did she really have any big problems. Most women would be ecstatic to realize they'd fallen in love with a man like Dylan. And she was . . . mostly.

But the night before, a traitorous thought had entered her mind. If she quit her job, she could travel with Dylan, and they wouldn't ever have to be apart.

Falling onto her side, Charley hugged a pillow against her chest. "Don't be silly. It's harvest time, and you're needed up there."

"If I'm needed down there, then to hell with the hay."

Her family may not have been as big as some, but Charley was loved more by this one man than anyone could ever ask to be.

"I love you, Grandpa. But I'm fine. I promise. I just needed to hear your voice."

Charley heard the screen door slam on the other end and knew that he'd stepped onto the porch. "You sure?"

Forcing confidence into her voice, she nodded, despite knowing he couldn't see her. "I'm positive. And I'll find time to come soon, okay?"

"You better. I've got a mess of okra with your name on it."

"Sound good. Tell Fanny I said hi, and I'll call again soon."

"Love you, baby girl."

"Love you, too, Grandpa."

Charley ended the call feeling better than she had before. The talk with Grandpa had put everything in perspective. So she was in love. This was not the end of the world. In fact, nothing had really changed. She still had the job she always wanted, lived in her dream city, and was loved fiercely by the best grandfather a girl could have.

That she also had Dylan was a bonus, not a cause for alarm.

A rumbling in her stomach reminded Charley that she had yet to eat breakfast. The queasiness that had plagued her the night before no longer lingered, so she headed for the kitchen in search of food.

Chapter 20

Getting through her shift had been a nightmare. How was Charley supposed to concentrate when Dylan would be home in a matter of hours? John had attempted to coerce her into a last-minute remote, but there was no way she was working tonight.

Though the stomach bug had returned on Monday, Charley had felt fabulous the last couple of days and was happy to be cured just in time for Dylan's return. She slipped on the new sundress she'd bought over the weekend, grabbed a light sweater, and waited impatiently for him to arrive. At six o'clock on the dot, a knock sounded at the door and Charley leaped to answer it, bolting into Dylan's arms the moment she saw his face.

"Someone is happy to see me," he chimed, spinning her as he had not two weeks before. "God, you smell so good. One more day in that van and I'd have cut my damn nose off."

Charley laughed as he set her down. "Men are nasty, aren't they?"

"Disgusting," he agreed. "Are you ready to see my surprise?"

He'd been smart not to share news of a surprise until earlier in the day. Patience was definitely not one of Charley's virtues, proven by the last ten agonizing days.

"What is it?" she asked.

"You'll see." Tipping up her chin, eyes like a coming storm stared into hers. "First, I need a proper hello."

Warm lips descended to hers as Charley rose up to meet him. This. This was what she'd missed. His kiss. His hands. His scent. They lingered there in the doorway with twilight darkening the sky, lovers getting reacquainted after too long apart.

Ending the kiss, he said, "I missed you."

Light-headed, she allowed Dylan to hold her steady. "I missed you, too."

"Now it's surprise time. Let's go."

After another kiss at the truck, they were on their way, though Charley had no idea where. Dylan regaled her with road stories, editing out the less appetizing elements of four men alone in a minivan, living on fast food and little sleep. She was so distracted that she'd failed to follow their course until a familiar building came into view.

"We're going back to the Hall of Fame?" she asked.

"Not quite."

A block down from where they'd made their last public appearance, Dylan turned right into a narrow thoroughfare, and then into the entrance of a parking garage in the middle of a tall contemporary building. Charley had noticed the word "Encore" over the entrance on Demonbreun Street and assumed they would be eating at a restaurant inside.

"Am I dressed okay for this surprise?"

Appreciative eyes scanned her body. "You look gorgeous."

That wasn't what she'd asked, but Charley didn't push. Once they were parked, Dylan played the gentleman, as always, opening her door and helping her down. In silence, they crossed to an elevator that carried them up one floor to what could have been a swanky hotel lobby in New York City. As if he owned the place, Dylan crossed to a friendly-looking man sitting behind a reception desk.

"How you doing tonight, Marvin?"

"I'm doing fine, Mr. Monroe. It's good to see you again."

"Marvin, this is my friend Charley. She doesn't know yet why we're here."

Light glistening off his bald, espresso-colored head, the man behind the counter grinned her way. "Then I won't spoil it for you." As if to share a dark secret, Marvin leaned forward. "You're much too pretty for this boy, Miss Charley. What are you doing with an ugly old thing like this?"

Putting a hand beside her mouth, she whispered loud enough for Dylan to hear, "He pays me in food. Don't tell anyone."

Marvin threw his head back with a loud guffaw and waved them on. At the elevator, Dylan squeezed her hand, waited for the doors to open, and then gestured for her to go first. At the fourteenth floor, he led her to a door down the hall to their left and pulled a key from his pocket.

Still silent, he pushed the door open, again gesturing for her to go first. Following the dark hardwoods down a narrow hallway, Charley stepped into the most opulent room she'd ever seen. Contemporary furniture in brown and cream rested beneath a one-of-a-kind light fixture, with bare bulbs hanging from cords draped at varying lengths. A luxurious gray shag rug set off the living space, but the real draw was the view beyond the giant sliding glass doors that served as the back wall.

In the distance was the Nashville skyline, glistening in the setting sun. The L&C Tower. The AT&T skyscraper, often called the Batman Building. And in the foreground—the Hall of Fame and Music City Center with its guitar-shaped outline, glowing red and orange in the late-summer sun.

"Is this a hotel room?" she asked, though he'd used a real key to get in. Not a key card. "I don't understand, Dylan. What are we doing here?"

Arms spread, he said, "This is my new place."

Certain she'd misheard, Charley shook her head. "Your what? You bought this place?" They'd never talked money, but there was no way an artist with only one song on the radio could afford . . . this.

"I did not," he replied, confusing her further. "A buddy of mine owns it. He's moving to LA for a year to work in a studio out there, and I'm renting it from him."

Okay. Maybe he hadn't lost his mind. "What about your roommates?"

"Casey and Pamela can handle it. Besides, I think they'd rather live alone now that they've made up." Crossing to the balcony, Dylan opened the door and extended a hand her way. "You have to come see this."

She could see fine from where she was standing. "I'm good," Charley snapped.

Waving his hand, he tried again. "It's gorgeous, babe. Come have a look."

Two steps forward revealed a surprise she hadn't spotted before. "The bedroom doesn't have a door."

The wall that should have separated the two rooms was open on both sides, affording little privacy for either space.

"Cool, isn't it?"

"Um, no," she said. "There's an entire wall of windows. How do you get dressed in here?"

Dylan laughed and dragged her to the open door. "We're fourteen floors up. No one can see in this window."

"People over there can," Charley argued, refusing to step over the threshold.

"I doubt anyone in the L&C Tower is looking through binoculars to see inside this condo."

"But they could." Dylan pulled her onto the cement balcony, and Charley's stomach did a flip. "Oh God," she said, covering her mouth.

Voice heavy with concern, he grasped her shoulders. "What's wrong, honey? Are you sick?"

"Heights," she mumbled around her hand. "I don't like heights."

The contents of her stomach churned into her throat, and, in a panic, Charley ran inside in search of a bathroom, reaching the toilet just in time. To her utter mortification, once the retching stopped she realized Dylan was holding her hair. With as much dignity as she could muster, she reached for some toilet paper to wipe her mouth before dropping back on her knees.

"I'm so sorry," she mumbled. "I've never reacted like that before."

"No. Honey." Dylan squatted next to her, brushing stray locks out of her eyes. "I didn't know. I shouldn't have made you go out there."

Tears stinging the back of her eyes, Charley fell apart right there on the bathroom floor. "I feel like an idiot. I was so excited to see you, and now I've ruined the whole night."

Lifting her to her feet, he cradled her against his chest. "Nothing is ruined, honey. I might not kiss you for a while, but nothing is ruined."

Snorting through her waterworks, she wrapped her arms around his torso. "Maybe Marvin has some gum."

"I'll bet he does. Will you be okay if I run down and get it?"

Charley nodded. "So long as I stay away from that balcony."

"That's fine," he cooed, escorting her to a stool in the kitchen. "No more balcony for you."

"Are you sure you're okay?" Dylan asked, leaning back on the couch with Charley's head resting on his chest.

"I'm fine," she replied, sounding much more like herself. The tears had really thrown him off. Charley had never seemed like the emotional type. "I've had a little stomach bug lately, but I'm sure it's nothing."

Entwining his fingers with hers, he said, "I don't like the idea of you being sick."

"I don't like it, either, but I've been better this week." Charley leaned up, the color back in her cheeks. "So you're really going to live here?"

He traced the outline of her delicate jaw. "After the tour, yeah."

"Is it going to sit empty until then? Seems a shame for a place this nice not to be used."

"Well," Dylan hedged, "I thought maybe you could stay here. Live here," he corrected.

Charley jerked to a sitting position. "You thought I'd live here?"

Not the reaction he expected. "Sure. It's a secure building. It's right downtown, so you'd be closer to work. And I'll be back before Christmas." Pointing to the sliding glass doors, he said, "Since we won't be opening those anymore, we can put the tree right in front of them."

Shifting farther away, Charley scrambled off the couch. "Dylan, I live with Matty."

"Not forever."

"No, but until the lease I signed runs out."

"When will that be?"

"That doesn't matter." Her cheeks flamed from pink to red. "You thought I would just drop everything and move in with you? After less than a month? That's a little fast, don't you think?"

Baffled by the anger, Dylan tracked her around the room. "Charley, no one is asking you to drop anything. I just want to take care of you."

"What is this *need* you have to take care of me?"

"Because I love you," he blurted, stunned by the admission, but certain in its truth. "Because I love you, Charley Layton. I think I've loved you since the night I met you. Since you kissed me under that streetlight and smiled at me over a ham, bacon, and egg burger. You stole my heart the same night you stole my shirt. That's why I want to take care of you."

The tears returned again. "Do you really mean that?" she asked.

"Of course I mean it, baby. I'm not asking you to give up a damn thing for me. And if you want to stay where you are, that's okay, too. But know that if you change your mind, my door is always open." Cracking a grin, he added, "Well, the door will be locked, but Marvin can let you in."

Charley flew into his arms to plant kisses on his neck. "I love you, too, Dylan Monroe. And I think we're both totally insane for saying it, but I don't care. Because I love you."

"Thank God," he murmured into her hair. "Thank you, God."

After a whirlwind day and a half, Charley was still reeling from Dylan's declaration Wednesday night. She'd also added vertigo to her stomach bug symptoms, which had returned for a brief time on Friday. At Dylan's insistence, she'd made a doctor's appointment, but since she hadn't seen a physician since moving to town, the earliest Charley could get in was mid-October.

She wasn't likely to need the appointment by then, but she booked it anyway, knowing she could easily cancel. Of course, Charley had assured Dylan that she'd keep the appointment, and that she'd visit an urgent-care office before then if things got worse.

"I'll call every day," he said, holding her close as they said goodbye next to her Bronco.

This time, they hadn't bothered to keep a safe distance from the others. Not parading their relationship in front of the press didn't mean they had to slink around like criminals when the cameras weren't around.

"No, you won't," Charley refuted. "We agreed. A couple check-ins a week. I'll follow the tour online, and you'll be busy with shows and live appearances. When you get back, the eligible bachelor article will be on the stands, and we'll be able to get on with our lives like normal people."

"That's all I want." Dylan kissed her for the third time, stealing her breath until someone whistled from the bus.

"Monroe, come on! We're pulling out."

With his forehead pressed to hers, he whispered, "I hate this."

Charley pushed him away. "Don't say that. This is going to be the most amazing three months of your life." Determined not to cry, she dug her hands into her jeans pockets. "I have to go anyway. I'm on the air in an hour."

Cupping her face, he said, "I love you, Charley."

She cleared her throat. "I love you, too. Now go get on that bus."

"One more kiss." His lips touched hers for three seconds too short before he jogged off toward the tour bus.

With one final wave, he disappeared inside and the door closed, a puff of exhaust choking the air as the lumbering machine pulled away.

"Sucks every time," said a woman behind her.

Charley spun to find Pamela Shepherd a few feet away. Since the morning they'd awkwardly met at Dylan's apartment, the two women hadn't crossed paths much, and they'd never exchanged more than a friendly greeting. According to Dylan, Pam and Casey were two stubborn people who'd finally come around in the last week. What they were stubborn about, Charley didn't know.

"How many times have you watched them drive away?" she asked.

Pam pursed her lips. "More times than I can count. But this is what you deal with when you date a working musician."

Though it was none of her business, Charley asked anyway. "*Are* you dating a working musician?"

The low-key blonde offered a sheepish grin. "Let me guess," she said. "Dylan is taking credit for Casey and me getting back together."

202

An odd statement. "Why would Dylan take credit?"

Eyes dropping to the ground, she said, "No reason. You know you've got a good one there, right?"

"I do," Charley replied without hesitation. "Doesn't stop the worry, though."

"What worry?"

Something told Charley that Pamela would understand her feelings. "There's a lot of temptation, isn't there? Out on the road?"

The other woman sighed. "Sure. Alcohol. Women." She didn't have to go into detail. "But they can find those same things here."

"I hadn't thought of that."

"Look," Pam said. "I made the mistake one time of not trusting Casey, and I nearly lost him. They're good men, Charley. Have a little faith."

Sound advice from a knowing source. "Thanks for the reminder."

With a smile, she said, "Anytime."

Chapter 21

On the day of Charley's doctor's appointment, Dylan had been gone for four and a half weeks. And after three weeks of feeling normal, her mysterious stomach bug had returned with a vengeance. Out of sheer annoyance, she kept the appointment, determined to take whatever the doc would prescribe to shake the crud for good.

Thanks to social media, Charley often felt as if she were on the tour with Dylan. There were constant radio visits, which she could stream online, and lots of pictures popped up on various social media sites. Her favorites were the ones of Dylan onstage. The sheer joy on his face made their time apart worthwhile.

Two quick raps on the exam room door had Charley tucking her phone back into her pocket.

"Good morning," greeted a chipper doc with a pair of reading glasses hovering on the tip of her nose. "I'm Dr. Robenzie, and you must be Miss Layton?"

"I am."

The doctor flipped through the chart in her hand with pursed lips. "Stomach bug, huh? Vomiting?"

"A couple times," Charley confessed. Since the unpleasant experience always seemed to follow greasy meals, she added, "I think it was something I ate."

With bright-blue eyes and a caring smile, the gray-haired woman said, "That's one option." She settled onto the round rolling stool. "Have you had this problem in the past?"

"No."

"Do you have any food allergies that might have slipped through?"

"I don't have any allergies that I know of."

The doc removed her glasses. "How long have the symptoms been happening? Is there shooting pain?"

Charley crossed her ankles. "It's been more than a month, and I haven't experienced any shooting pains. There's been a little heartburn in the last week, but I'm sure the wrong food is to blame for that, too."

As if contemplating her patient's response, Dr. Robenzie tapped her top lip. "Miss Layton, could you be pregnant?"

"I . . . What?"

"According to your information, your last menstrual cycle was the end of July."

"I've never been regular with that," she explained. "I mean, I skip months all the time. It'll show up."

The doc tilted her head. "Maybe not for another eight months or so." Rising from the stool, she said, "I'm going to send Nurse Phyllis in to get a urine sample. A quick test and we'll know for sure."

"Doctor, we use condoms," Charley assured her. "Every time. I mean, *every single time*. I cannot be pregnant."

"Technically, there's a two percent chance you could be." Patting her patient's knee, she added, "If it makes you feel better, think of it as ruling the possibility out."

Ready to leap off the exam table and run from the room, Charley grabbed the doc's arm. "But there is *no* possibility."

Sliding her hands into the pockets of her lab coat, the doctor grew serious. "If you've had intercourse since your last cycle, I'm afraid there is a possibility, Miss Layton. You can skip the test and leave now, but that won't change the outcome if you are."

Right on cue, Charley's gut rolled and she dashed off the table to the large garbage can against the wall. Since she'd skipped breakfast, there was nothing to come out, resulting in painful dry heaves. Once the sickness passed, she took the paper towels the doctor offered and wiped her mouth. As the towels fell into the trash, she accepted a cup of water and returned to the table.

"Are you ready for the test now?" Dr. Robenzie asked with genuine kindness.

Charley nodded. "Yes, I'm ready."

Dylan checked his phone for the fifth time. Still no word from Charley. Her appointment had been that morning, and she'd promised to let him know the results. That had been over ten hours ago. Of course, the radio silence sent his imagination soaring. What if it was something serious? What if they'd rushed her into surgery and she hadn't had time to call him? Would Matty let him know? Something told him that was a big no.

His intention to stream her midday show online had been shot to hell by a last-minute radio visit Mitch only informed him about thirty minutes before they had to be on the air. The station brought in fans for a meet and greet, and suddenly Dylan's day had been shot.

"You're on in five, Monroe," Mitch reminded him. "Unless you're telling the fans to get out here for the show, put the phone away."

"I'm expecting news from Charley," he replied. "She went to the doctor today."

"I don't care if she went to the moon today. You've got a show to do."

Shutting down the screen, Dylan stuck the cell behind the speakers. "What is your problem with Charley?"

"Women always cause problems," he grumbled. "This isn't the time for you to be getting involved."

Lightning struck. "This was never about some magazine article, was it, Mitch? You don't want me with anyone."

Checking his watch, the manager leaned forward to check out the crowd. "Like I said, this isn't the time. The crowd's a good size. Better than last night."

Many concertgoers didn't bother showing up for the opening acts, often choosing to tailgate in the parking lot rather than watch a performer they didn't know do a twenty-minute set.

"I don't give a shit about the crowd," Dylan snapped.

"You damn well better, boy. This is what matters," Mitch growled, pointing to the stage. "Those people out there will make or break you, so you damn well better get your head in the game and put your focus where it belongs."

Tired of the same old argument, he took a step closer to the old man to make his point thoroughly clear. "I can do *this* and still have Charley. I've told you before, Mitch. You have no say in my personal life. We agreed to keep the relationship quiet to make you happy. To give off some illusion that you insisted on. But once that article is out, this bullshit ends."

The lights dropped, and Easton said, "We're up, buddy," tapping Dylan on the shoulder as he trotted onstage.

Shoving past his manager, Dylan followed his guitarist, reaching center stage as the crowd surged forward with a roar.

"Holy shit, Charley. What are you going to do?"

She'd been asking herself that same question all day. "I have no idea."

"Are you going to keep it?" Matty asked, which was the toughest question of all.

Now she knew how her mother had felt twenty-five years before. And if her mother had made a different choice, Charley wouldn't be alive today.

"I think so," she murmured, hugging the throw pillow tighter.

How she'd gotten through her shift, Charley would never know. Years of training had kicked into autopilot, and the five hours passed as if nothing traumatic had happened. As if her whole world hadn't been turned upside down.

Matty flounced onto the couch beside her. "But how are you going to take care of a baby? And what is Dylan going to say? If that manager of his doesn't like you dating, he sure as hell isn't going to like this."

Mitch Levine was the least of Charley's worries. "I don't know what Dylan's going to say. I don't even know how to tell him," she admitted. "I mean, the subject of kids came up one time, and he acted as if I'd suggested we sever his arm and sell it for scraps."

"But he loves you, right? I mean, that should help."

"Help?" Charley turned sore eyes to her roommate. "He's launching a career. Dylan isn't in any position to be a father, and I'm in no position to be a mother."

"So you aren't going to keep it?"

"Stop asking that." Bolting off the couch, Charley marched to the front window and stared into the pouring rain. Fitting weather for a night like this. "I don't know what I'm going to do."

Warm hands wrapped around her upper arms as Matty put her chin on Charley's shoulder. "I'm sorry," she murmured.

"We used a condom every time. I kept telling the doctor that, and she smiled this condescending grin, as if I were being naive."

"Nothing's foolproof, right?"

Charley sighed. "Except not having sex at all. Which was working really well for me until Dylan came along."

"Yeah, well. That's my current method, and I'm here to tell you, it sucks donkey balls."

Laughter wouldn't come. "What am I going to do?"

Matty squeezed her arms. "You need to tell Dylan. This isn't your burden to carry alone."

"I don't want to hurt his career. We made a pact," Charley said. "He'd never ask me to give up radio, and I'd never ask him to give up music."

"Maybe no one will have to give up anything."

Now who was being naive? Something had to be sacrificed. Either she gave up the baby or gave up her career. Even if Dylan came around to the idea of starting a family, he wouldn't be around. Charley would be on her own, if not financially, then physically. She would bear the brunt of the work. The responsibility.

But even knowing the reality, she couldn't imagine making a different choice than her mother had.

"You should call him," Matty said.

"This isn't the kind of news you give over the phone."

"Where is the tour right now?"

"DC," she replied. Charley had the schedule memorized. "They move on to New York City next, for two shows over the weekend."

Matty turned her around. "Flights to New York can't be that much. We'll buy you a ticket."

The *we* part didn't go unnoticed. "I doubt I can afford one on such short notice."

"Let me—"

"I can't, Matty. But thanks for the offer." Charley turned back to the window. "I'm not ready, anyway. I need to have answers before I tell him. Figure out how to make things work. For all of us."

"All right, then. But don't forget that you have friends here, okay? And not just me. People at the station love you. They'll want to help."

Unless someone could turn back time, Charley didn't see any way for them to help her now. With a nod, she crossed to the stairs and headed for her room.

At the end of the set, Dylan took his final bow, high-fived several fans in the front row, and trotted into the wings, eager to check his phone. Only his phone wasn't where he'd left it.

"Hey," he called to one of the roadies. "Did someone pick up my phone?"

"I don't know. You'll have to ask around."

Which he tried to do, but with the set change in progress, no one had time to discuss a missing anything. Bodies hustled on and off the stage as Dylan hunted, wishing he'd gone with something other than a black case. The speakers were rolled away one by one, leaving an open space on the stage and no phone.

"Did one of you pick up my phone?" he asked the band, but none of them had seen it. Spotting the tour manager, he dodged a tech carrying a bass drum on his way to reach her. "Hey, Fran. Did anyone turn in a lost phone?"

She continued to scrutinize her clipboard. "Not tonight, hon."

Dylan sighed. "Thanks. Will you let me know if they do? It's an iPhone 7 in a black case."

"Got it," she said, making a note at the top of the page.

Continuing to scan the area, he remembered that he'd been talking to Mitch the last time he'd had it. No doubt the manager had feared it would get lost or swiped and had taken the cell with him.

"Fran," he called. "Have you seen Mitch?"

"Eight minutes to the next act," she said into her headset. "We need to move." Orders given, she finally looked Dylan's way. "He's on your bus."

"Thanks!"

Navigating his way through the mayhem, Dylan hurried toward the back entrance only to be cut off by none other than the headliner himself.

"Another good show out there tonight," Wes Tillman praised. "Glad we got you on this tour, Monroe. I have a feeling a few months from now, you're going to be a hot commodity."

High praise indeed. "Thank you, Mr. Tillman."

"Mr. Tillman is my dad," the singer quipped. "Call me Wes."

"Yes, sir. I can do that." Until tonight, Tillman hadn't shown much interest in his opening act, and Dylan had assumed he'd never even watched a set. Maybe he'd been wrong. "I'm honored to be included. As a relative unknown, this tour is a great opportunity for me. I've enjoyed your music for years, so it's a privilege to watch you work."

"Let me guess," the older man said with a chuckle. "You've been listening to me your whole life."

Dylan smiled. "Not all of it, sir. But most."

"I get that a lot. Since we have two days coming up in New York, my wife, Harley, is going to meet me there. Maybe take in some sights." With a tap on Dylan's arm, he said, "Why don't you come out to eat with us one night? Meet the missus and talk music."

Dumbstruck, Dylan mumbled, "I . . . Uh . . . Sure. That would be great."

Wes nodded. "Then it's set. Keep up the good work, and you've got a nice, long career ahead of you."

"Right. I'll do my best."

As Tillman walked away, Dylan scratched his head, nearly knocking his hat to the ground.

"What happened to you?" Lance asked, coming up behind him.

"Tillman offered to take me to dinner in New York City. He wants to talk music."

Lance whistled. "No shit?"

"No shit," Dylan replied, still stunned. "I'm going to talk music with a legend."

The bass player gave a hoot. "That's awesome, man. Welcome to the big leagues."

As his bandmate walked away, Dylan struggled to remember what he'd been doing before Tillman cut him off. "My phone," he said, jogging toward the exit. "Charley. I need to tell Charley."

Chapter 22

Charley made it to the end of the week without losing her mind. But barely.

Late Tuesday night, she'd sent Dylan a text that said she was fine. Which technically she was, since pregnancy wasn't an actual illness. To her surprise, she never received a response. Nor had she heard from him since. No calls. No texts. Nothing.

At the end of her Friday shift, Charley turned over the microphone, packed up her headphones, and raced to her car. She still didn't intend to share the news—whether good or bad she hadn't decided yet—over the phone, but she needed to hear his voice.

The call went straight to voice mail.

"Dang it."

It was four o'clock in New York on a show night, so he was probably doing some kind of publicity and turned off the phone. Once he went back online, she felt certain he'd see the missed call and get in touch. Only he never did.

Lying in bed that night, she couldn't help herself. Charley checked Dylan's Instagram first but found nothing new posted since Monday night. So she clicked over to Casey's account—and wished she hadn't.

Sprawled out in a corner booth was Dylan, arm around a pretty brunette who would have been in his lap had she crawled any closer. They were both laughing, the table in front of them littered with bottles and empty glasses. No umbrellas this time. Charley supposed New York City was too sophisticated for such tacky drink accessories. A check of the time stamp revealed the picture had been posted in the last half hour.

"I guess when you're having that much fun, you can't be bothered to call your pregnant girlfriend back home."

To be fair, Dylan didn't know she was pregnant, but still. He should have called. Or sent a text. At this point, she'd take a smoke signal.

Since she knew he wasn't too tied up to take a call, Charley rang his number. And again got his voice mail. This time, she decided to leave a message, only Dylan's normal greeting had been replaced by a programmed computer voice letting her know that the person at this number wasn't available. And then the line went dead.

"What the hell?" she said to the screen, dialing the number again only to get the same result. Tossing her phone onto the bed, she crossed her arms. "Stupid technology."

Feeling a pout coming on, she snatched up the phone and checked Facebook. Scrolling her newsfeed, she saw that a cousin had bought a new car, a politician had done something underhanded (big shocker), and a Hollywood socialite had dumped her cheating boyfriend.

"You tell him, honey," Charley said aloud. "Men are assholes."

Concerned she was starting to sound like Matty, she scrolled a little more and bolted upright in bed. There, on her screen, was Dylan Monroe, sauntering into a New York City restaurant with the same brunette on his arm.

"You son of a . . ." Words faded as she read the headline.

Rising Star Dylan Monroe Takes Potential New Love to New York City Hot Spot

That rat-sucking, good-for-nothing piece of shit. Five weeks on tour and all his I-love-you crap goes out the window? Really? Charley was that easy to toss away? And he didn't even have the guts to tell her so. What did he think? That she wouldn't find out? Cameras caught everything. That's what Mitch had said. They couldn't be seen together in the wrong places because cameras caught everything.

"Dammit!" she screamed, slamming the phone onto the bed as she leaped out of it. "Such an asshole."

Matty sprinted into the room. "What is it? Is there a bug?" she asked, prancing near the door.

"I wouldn't call a bug an asshole, Matilda," Charley sniped. "It's Dylan. He has a 'potential new love,'" she explained, using air quotes. "The son of a bitch has a new sucker on the line, and he doesn't even have the balls to tell me I've been replaced."

"Are you sure?" Matty asked, reaching for her arm.

"I saw the picture online."

"Being on the Internet doesn't make it true. You know that."

Charley grabbed the phone and swiped to Casey's Instagram. "There. Right there," she said, smacking the screen. "That's Casey's account, not some headline-seeking reporter. That looks pretty damn true to me."

Cast in the uncomfortable role of devil's advocate, Matty said, "They could be friends. Someone said something funny and they're all laughing. This could be totally innocent."

Running her hands through her hair, Charley paced the floor. "She's in his lap, Matty. His arm is around her."

"His arm is across the back of the booth."

Vertigo setting in, she collapsed into the chair in the corner and rubbed her temples. "He won't take my calls or return my texts. I may be naive, but I'm not an idiot. Dylan is through with me." Saying the words brought reality crashing around her like a summer downpour. "He doesn't love me, Matty. He never did."

Tears blinded her vision as Charley rocked forward and back, arms curled against her stomach.

"Oh, honey. You don't know that." Matty hit her knees and brushed the hair from Charley's face. "Tours are crazy. That stupid manager probably has him running in a million different directions. Wait and see. I bet he calls you tomorrow, hungover and fuming about some website suggesting he has a new girlfriend."

Shaking her head, Charley refused to be a fool any longer. "You were right. They all cheat. Every last one of them." Her voice hitched on a hiccup. "I should have listened." Holding a hand to her stomach, she whined, "And now look what I've done."

Matty held her roommate as she cried. "You aren't in your right mind, honey. You've got hormones playing hell with your common sense. Give the man a chance to explain."

Charley wanted to believe. Fought to find a voice or reason somewhere in her swirling mind that would put all the fears and worst scenarios to rest. But a week of growing anxiety, mixed with crazy-making hormones and an overdose of every emotion under the sun, smothered any glimmer of hope.

Lungs singed and nose burning, she ran out of steam somewhere around two in the morning. But her last thought before drifting off brought another round of tears.

She would have to go home.

"Where do they get off printing this shit?" Dylan stormed around the tiny living space of the tour bus. "We walked into a restaurant together. Since when does that mean we're dating?"

"The spoils of fame," Casey said, stretched out on one of the narrow sofas. "It's part of the game."

"I'm not playing any games. What if Charley sees this?"

The redhead glanced up from under his ball cap. "Same as with Pam. If she trusts you, she'll know it's bullshit. If not . . ." He shrugged. "Good riddance. You've always got Denise there."

"I have a feeling Denise's girlfriend, Laura, would have a problem with that."

"Denise plays for her own team?" Casey shook his head. "That's a crying shame."

Dylan dropped onto the opposite sofa. "Where is Mitch with my phone? He swore he'd get one today."

Sadly, the iPhone never turned up, and the schedule had been packed tight for the last three days. First on the road actually getting to New York, and then with constant appearances. Every time Dylan found a free minute to try calling the station, Charley's shift had ended. Then Mitch had a full day of meetings on Friday, doing God only knew what, while Dylan had done the early dinner with Tillman and his wife. He hadn't known Denise, one of Wes's backup singers, would be tagging along until she'd offered to share a cab.

"Maybe he's in a meeting," the drummer suggested, sarcasm heavy in his tone.

Ignoring the barb, Dylan leaned forward. "Let me see your phone."

"Why? So you can lose it, too?"

"I need to see if there's anything else I'll have to explain to Charley."

Rolling onto his side, Casey dragged the cell from his pocket and tossed it across the bus. "Zero, four, two, seven," he said. "That'll get you in."

Not surprised, Dylan said, "That's Pam's birthday, isn't it?"

"Shut up and worry about your own love life."

Their roommate had visited three stops on the tour so far, and with each, she and Casey spent more time alone. Dylan had caught the lip-lock goodbye before his drummer climbed back on the bus after the DC show, relieved to see the two lovebirds back to their old ways.

Keying in the code, Dylan went to Instagram first and spotted Casey's last post. "Dude. This picture is worse than the paparazzi one. You know that Charley follows you."

Casey crossed his ankles. "What? We were having a good time, that's all."

"It looks like Denise is in my lap. Dammit, this is going to make things worse."

"Maybe by the time you get your phone back to call her, she'll have cooled off."

That was the thing about cell phones. Dylan didn't have Charley's number memorized because she was always there with one quick touch of her name. The new phone would have his contacts, and as soon as Mitch handed it over, he'd make the biggest groveling call of his life.

"Do you have Mitch's number in here?" he asked.

"Nope," Casey replied. "He isn't my manager."

Dylan threw the phone onto his friend's chest. "Fine. I'll wait. But he better be here soon."

Shooting Stars Records had their second official artist.

Clay Benedict strolled into the recesses of Madison Square Garden, relieved to have the business portion of his trip concluded. Chance's recovery required he spend the rest of the year in sober living in Colorado, but after the first of the year, he'd be ready for the studio. With luck, a notebook full of soul-searching songs would be tucked neatly in his pocket.

Surrounded by the typical chaos that preceded a live show, he evaded a forklift carrying equipment cases and then shuffled out of the way of three roadies rolling two cases each. Once the path cleared, he spotted Mitch Levine coming his way.

"Mitch," Clay called. "Over here."

The older man squinted, dodging an abandoned spotlight like a pro.

"I thought you wouldn't be here until tonight?" he said. Not the warmest greeting.

"I finished my business early. Where's Dylan?"

"On the bus, I assume." Mitch carried two phones in his hands, and one of them dinged. "Hold this," he ordered, foisting an iPhone into Clay's hand before checking the other. Squinting again, he played trombone with the cell before finding the proper distance to read it. "Looks like the article in *Country Today* got pushed up a month. Holiday and year-in-review stuff shoved it out of December, so now they put it in November."

"Good," Clay said. "Then Dylan and Charley can stop sneaking around."

The manager grumbled. "I've got to take a piss. Keep that for me, and I'll be right back."

The always-classy man limped off without awaiting a reply. Clay hadn't planned to stand around doing nothing, but he also had no intention of following the old codger into the bathroom. So he waited. For five solid minutes. Checking his watch, he sighed in frustration. Tillman's manager expected him in less than ten. Roger Stacks had managed the first act Clay and Tony had ever signed. Due to their schedules, the men rarely found time to catch up.

At the point when Clay considered abandoning his post, the phone in his hand rang. The name Matilda Jacobs flashed across the screen. After five rings, the call went to voice mail, but seconds later, the iPhone rang again with the same caller. Assuming the call was important, Clay answered.

"Hello?"

"I knew it, you coward. You blocked my number. Bet you didn't think I'd figure it out, did you?"

"I—"

"I'm not interested in your excuses. I only called to do the one thing you apparently don't have the balls to do. To end this. And not that you care, but I'm pregnant. Congratulations, jerk. I'll be in Nashville for another week. After that I'm gone, so if you have anything to say to me, I suggest you say it quick."

Stunned silent, Clay held the phone to his ear, wondering how in the hell Mitch Levine had managed to get a woman pregnant.

"That's what I thought," the woman on the other end snapped. "Goodbye, you piece of shit."

The call cut off, and Clay was left staring at the cell in his hand when Mitch returned.

"What's wrong with you?" the old bastard asked as he returned from the bathroom.

"Who is Matilda Jacobs?"

"How the hell should I know?"

"You apparently got her pregnant, Levine. I assume the name should ring a bell." Mitch grabbed the phone and tapped away on the screen. A quick glance over his shoulder revealed an open search engine. "You have to Google the woman you knocked up?"

"Shut up, Benedict." Mitch continued to type until he found whatever information he sought. Extending the phone forward and back again, he focused in and read silently. "Well, shit. She said she's pregnant?" he asked.

"Among other things," Clay replied. "She also called you a piece of shit."

"She wasn't talking to me."

"She what?"

The old man waved a hand in the air. "Never mind. Don't tell Dylan. I'll take care of it."

"Does Dylan know this Matilda person?"

"Probably," came the reply. "Like I said. I'll take care of it."

Without another word, Levine shuffled off in the direction Clay had entered from. Definitely the most bizarre conversation of the week. Maybe the year.

❧

"I can't believe you called him a piece of shit," Matty remarked, staring from across their kitchen table.

It had been her roommate's idea to try calling from a different phone, and the mere thought that Dylan would block Charley's number had brought on an angry fit long before she'd dialed his number. The jackass thought he could write her off? Oh no. Charley made sure she had the last word.

"He deserves worse," she said, sliding the phone across the table. "Now he can't claim I took off without telling him."

"But what did he say?"

"Nothing." Charley pretended it didn't hurt. That she didn't care if the man she loved turned out to be a too much of a coward to face his responsibilities. "He didn't say anything."

Still rooting for a misunderstanding, Matty flipped her cell. "I bet he'll call once the news sinks in. You didn't exactly give him a chance to speak."

"I did, too," she argued. "And he didn't make a peep." Rising from her chair, she grabbed another sleeve of crackers off the counter. The salty little squares had become her constant companions, keeping the morning sickness at bay. "It doesn't matter anyway. I talked to Willoughby this morning. He thinks I'm going home to take care of a sick relative and agreed to have a part-timer handle my shift until a full-time replacement is found. Elvis will be down with a truck next weekend to take me home."

Matty hugged her knees against her chest. "You're doing this all too fast, Charley. You just got the news a few days ago. Heck, you only told him a few minutes ago."

"There's no need to wait around. This way, no one has to know why I went home."

The excuse rang hollow in her ears. Charley was running away. The panic had taken over, and all she wanted was to go home.

"But you won't start showing for months. At least stick around until Dylan comes home."

"No."

"But, Charley—"

"I can't do it, okay? I can't wait around, hoping, only to have him come back and tell me to have a nice life."

"But Dylan wouldn't do that, and you know it."

"I thought he wouldn't forget me while out on tour, either, and I was wrong."

"He hasn't forgotten you."

Charley slammed into a chair. "Nearly a week of silence, Matty. He wouldn't return my texts or calls even before the bomb I just dropped in his lap. I couldn't endure another two months of nothing, waiting around for some final blow. I couldn't survive that."

With a sigh, her roommate conceded the argument. "You're right. But what if he doesn't walk away? What then?"

"If Dylan decides that he's ready to be a father, then we'll talk." Staring at the floor, she added, "Until then, I've made a decision, and I'm going home."

They sat in silence for several minutes, the only sound the crackers crunching between Charley's teeth.

"I didn't want to be right," Matty muttered, dropping a hand on top of her friend's. "Not this time."

Charley slipped a cracker between her teeth, acknowledging the words with a bitter nod.

Chapter 23

This could not be happening.

"Mitch, I backed up those contacts before we hit the road. They should be there."

The manager feigned innocence. "All I know is what the chick at the store told me. There was no data under your account. No pictures. No contacts. Nothing."

Dylan nearly punched a window out of the bus. He'd already been out of touch for five days, and he had no doubt that Charley had been calling and sending him messages. Messages he couldn't see because his new phone was freaking wiped clean.

"How am I going to get her number?" he said to himself, hands fisted at his sides.

Maybe there was a home number. He hadn't seen much of Charley's apartment and couldn't remember seeing a landline, but that didn't mean there wasn't one. Matty was there first, so the line would likely be in her name. Dylan went into search in his phone and typed in Matilda . . . "Shit. I don't know her last name."

"Whose last name?" asked Casey as he entered the bus.

"Charley's roommate."

"Jacobs," he supplied. "Matilda Jacobs." As Dylan stared in amazement, the drummer shrugged. "What? She gave it to me the night I met her."

"You're good for something, buddy," he replied, typing the full name into the search bar. A few pictures popped up from social media, along with the information that she worked as an accountant at Sunburst Communications in the office of Eagle 101.5.

"She's an accountant?"

"Yep. She told me that, too."

Dylan took a seat on the sofa. "I thought she worked in sales or something."

Casey made a tsking sound. "That's pretty sexist to assume a beautiful woman can't also be smart."

"And it's insulting to assume people in sales aren't smart."

"If you two are going to carry on," Mitch said, "I've got shit to do." Neither man commented as the manager exited the bus.

"Why do you need the roommate's last name, anyway? I figured you'd be halfway through some pleading explanation by now."

Holding up the phone, Dylan said, "No contacts. Mitch says there was no data saved on my account."

"Mitch is a lying sack of shit."

Leaning back, he eyed his friend. "You were never this open about not liking Mitch back when he was getting us gigs and landing us this deal."

Casey grabbed a beer from the minifridge. "He didn't get *us* a deal, he got *you* a deal. A fact he's chosen to remind me of on three separate occasions in the last three months."

"We're a band. He knows that."

"Nope," he said, popping the top. "That's not how your buddy Mitch sees it. 'Your ass can be replaced at any time, Flanagan.' Those were his exact words."

Dylan surged forward. "That's bullshit. No one is being replaced."

Sober green eyes locked with his. "It's your name on the contract, bro. Your name is on the album. And the marquis outside this venue. Lance, Easton, and I are nothing but hired hands, and as soon as Mitch gets the chance, he'll replace us all."

"I won't let that happen."

"Do you know what he told Easton?" Casey asked, ignoring Dylan's declaration. "'Try to be uglier.' He doesn't want anyone thinking the guitarist in the background is prettier than his meal ticket up front." The bottle top flew into the trash. "Hell, I'm probably safe because I'm the wooden nickel in this outfit."

How had none of them mentioned this before? "Mitch Levine doesn't have the power to hire or fire anyone. He works for me."

"Like the rest of us."

"Hey." Dylan jerked Casey by the arm. "Have I ever treated you like some hired monkey keeping time in the shadows?"

"No," his friend conceded. "But you give that asshole too much power. That's all I'm saying."

"Where is this coming from? He's my manager. He manages my business. That's what I pay him to do."

Casey drove a finger into Dylan's chest. "He manages your life. He says, 'Jump,' you say, 'How high?' That shit with Charley and pretending you're a free man? That's boy band crap. We do this to make music. To entertain people. Not to get teenage girls to hang your picture on their bedroom walls."

"What's the ruckus in here, boys?" asked Lance as he and Easton climbed aboard. "We could hear you three buses down."

Holding Casey's gaze, Dylan said, "Our drummer here is pointing out how much of a pussy I am when it comes to Mitch. Either of you want to back him up?"

Easton spoke up first. "Your manager is an asshole, man. And you're the only one who doesn't see it."

Unbelievable. "Y'all know the history. You were there. No one else would come near me after that first deal fell through."

"They might have," Lance suggested. "Mitch locked you in six months out of that mess."

"Yeah. After six months of nobody on my side."

"*We* were on your side," Casey chimed. "Long before Mitch was."

Dylan didn't have a reply. He could only stare as guys he considered family filed off the bus one by one.

Charley had made a plan. And now she was changing it.

"You told him you'd be here for a week," Matty argued. "That was yesterday."

"There's no sense putting off the inevitable." Charley dragged her second suitcase to the top of the stairs. "Elvis will be here any minute to load the bed and dressers in the rental truck."

Matty wrestled the suitcase from her grip. "Give me that. You're in no condition to be tumbling down the stairs because of a heavy suitcase." Attempting to lift the black nylon, she grunted. "What do you have in here? A dead body?"

"The only person I'd stuff dead into a suitcase is on a tour bus, likely curled up with his new love."

"Oh my God, woman. You do not know that." The black bag thudded on each step as Matty dragged it behind her. "I hope this Elvis friend of yours is a strong guy, because there's no way we're going to get this in your Bronco on our own."

Elvis was, in a word, huge, but Charley didn't have to say so, since the man in question was standing in their living room.

"Y'all shouldn't leave your door unlocked like that."

"What the hell?" Matty screamed. "Get the fuck out of my house!" In her panic, she lost her footing and went flying forward, suitcase lunging behind her, thumping down the last five stairs. Thanks to Elvis, she landed upright on her feet, with her nose pressed against his overall-clad chest. He stopped the suitcase with one hand inches before it crashed into her.

Charley took advantage of her roommate's stunned silence to make the introductions.

"Matilda Jacobs, meet Elvis Marigold."

"This is your friend?" she mumbled, straightening off his chest and blowing a loose lock of platinum hair out of her eyes. "How big do they build 'em in Kentucky?"

"We come pretty stout up there, ma'am. Not like the puny little boys you've got down here."

The insult to all Tennessee males was delivered with a friendly smile that revealed perfect pearly whites, courtesy of the Marine Corps.

"Elvis, stop scaring the panties off my roommate and grab this suitcase."

Without question, he did as asked, shifting Matty gently to the left in order to reach the bag. "I didn't mean to scare her," he mumbled, saluting the little blonde with a tip of his ball cap. "It's nice to meet you, Miss Matilda."

"Matty," she breathed. He lifted the suitcase as if it weighed little more than a baseball. "You can call me Matty." As Elvis headed outside, she turned on Charley and mouthed, "Holy moly, he's hot."

This was a common response when females first laid eyes on Charley's neighbor. But since she'd known him since they were five years old, racing through the mud on their brand-new four-wheelers, he was too much of a brother to be anything other than plain old Elvis to her.

"Unless you plan to move to Liberty, Kentucky, I suggest you not get any ideas. Elvis runs his family's farm, and I doubt he'll ever leave home again."

"Again?" Matty queried, peeking out the door.

"Six years in the marines," Charley replied.

Watching Elvis toss the suitcase into the Bronco, she whispered, "Ooh rah."

Charley rolled her eyes. "Here's my cell phone. I need you to return it to the store tomorrow."

Matty glanced down to the phone. "Why? It's your phone."

"I was leasing it, and I won't be able to afford the same plan up home. Besides," she added, "it's nearly impossible to get a signal on the farm."

Blue eyes went wide. "What kind of foreign land are you from?"

"One with more cows than people." Charley slapped the phone into her hand. "I've already turned off the number. It took a chunk of my savings to buy out the contract, but I don't want any connections to down here."

Now Matty rolled her eyes. "This is insane. One guy turns out to be a jerk, and you give up your job, your home, and now your cell phone?"

"I've put the number at Grandpa's on the fridge, along with the address. I don't get much mail, so forwarding shouldn't be a problem."

"What do I do if Dylan shows up at this door?" Matty asked. A possibility Charley hadn't considered.

After half a beat, she said, "He won't."

Hands on her hips, Matty stared her down. "But what if he does?"

"Ask him what he wants," Charley instructed. "If he wants information about the baby, you can give him the house number. If he wants me, tell him to go to hell."

Elvis returned with a dolly. "Is the dresser empty?" he asked.

"It is," she replied. "I'll be up to help in a second."

"I've got it."

Watching the big guy ascend the staircase, Matty asked, "Is he going to bring the furniture down by himself?"

"Looks that way." Bracing herself, Charley dove into the goodbye she'd rehearsed the night before. "Thank you, Matty. For letting me live here. For being my friend. And for letting me cry on your shoulder the last few days."

"You don't have to go," she replied.

Charley nodded. "Yes, I do. When you give up the only thing you've ever dreamed of doing with your life, you don't want to drag the process out." Managing a watery smile, she added, "I have a new adventure ahead, right? Motherhood and all that comes with it."

Matty cupped her cheeks. "This kid is very lucky to have you for a mom."

The simple statement threatened her fragile control. "I'm going to miss you, Matilda Jacobs. Maybe I'll have Grandpa leave a dirty cereal bowl in the sink now and then. It'll be like I never left."

"You're such a brat." The tiny blonde pulled her in for a powerful hug. "Matilda could be a nice middle name," she whispered.

"Yes, it could," Charley mumbled between sniffles. She pulled back and reached for a tissue on the end table. "No more crying. Onward ho, right?"

"If you're of the pirate persuasion, sure."

A quiet thud on the stairs drew their attention as Elvis made his way down backward, slowly dragging the dresser-laden dolly along one step at a time. The shirt beneath the overalls had long ago lost its sleeves, leaving his tattoo-covered biceps in clear view.

"Oh my," Matty breathed.

"No cell phone service," Charley reminded her.

A hand flattened on her roommate's chest. "I could live off the grid."

Charley laughed. "No you couldn't."

Eyes still on the prize, Matty mumbled, "I could for a night. Maybe I should go with you. Help you get settled."

"How many pigs do you have now, Elvis?" Charley asked her helper.

"Six," he answered. "We'll have plenty of bacon for the winter once we get 'em good and fat."

She could almost feel the enthusiasm leave Matty's body as the words, "Well, damn," were whispered with regret.

"Good show tonight, everyone," yelled Fran Templeton. The tour manager had called an after-show meeting for the crew, and since his bandmates weren't speaking to him, Dylan happened to be hanging around backstage, staying out of the way during load-out. "I've got good news and bad news," she said, earning groans from the crowd. "First up, the bad news. The show in Kansas City has been canceled thanks to a water main break under the venue. The performance will be rescheduled at the end of the tour, if the dates work out."

"Well, shit," commented a roadie, verbalizing what everyone else was thinking.

"But now the good news," Fran went on. "As you know, the next show on the schedule is Billings, Montana, on Saturday. We'll head that way tonight, and once we arrive tomorrow evening, you all have four days off."

This news was received with greater enthusiasm, hoots and high-fives echoing off the rafters. Until the obvious question was asked.

"What is there to do in Billings, Montana?"

"It's a big city. Y'all will find something to kill the time." Holding up a hand to silence the responding chatter, Fran added, "If you've got cold weather clothes, you're probably going to need them. Now let's get this show back on the road."

The crew dispersed as Dylan lingered in the wings, sending up a prayer of gratitude for this sudden turn of luck. Within seconds, he'd booked a one-way plane ticket from Springfield, Illinois, back to Nashville, leaving before six the next morning. An airport hotel was locked in next, and then he charged off for the bus to pack a bag as the taxi headed his way.

Charley and Elvis stopped outside Bowling Green for a quick bite to eat. Since she was traveling without a phone, they'd agreed that he'd stop whenever he was ready, though Charley would have been fine to make the two-and-a-half-hour drive without stopping at all. The moment they'd crossed the state line, Charley started to relax.

Fast food wasn't Charley's favorite, and truth be told, Dylan had spoiled her with all the fancy meals he'd bought her during their short time together. Reminding herself that those days were over, she put in her order and settled in across from her childhood friend to eat the burger and fries.

"You want to tell me what's going on?" Elvis asked, emptying a third ketchup packet onto his sandwich paper.

She hadn't shared many details during their short phone conversation Saturday evening. Actually, she hadn't shared any details at all. Mostly because if she did, the big lug chowing down six fries at a time was likely to locate one Dylan Monroe and beat the shit out of him.

"I made some poor choices," Charley hedged. "Now I'm paying for them."

"How bad?" he asked.

Unwilling to lie to her best friend, she said, "I'm eating for two."

Keeping her eyes on her food meant missing Elvis's facial expression, but she heard the expletive loud and clear.

"Who is he?"

"No one important."

They'd had conversations like this before. And like before, Elvis typically won. "Give me a name."

Hoping upon hope that the big guy wasn't up on the latest country releases, she replied, "Dylan Monroe."

"Does he know?"

Charley's chin jerked up. "Of course he knows. Do you think I'd leave town and not tell him?"

Elvis didn't flinch. "Calm your teats, Layton. It's a fair question."

"You've known me for twenty years, *Marigold*. That is not a fair question."

They continued to eat in hostile silence, until Elvis asked, "Do I need to pay him a visit?"

"No."

"A man who leaves a pregnant woman to fend for herself needs to be taught a lesson."

"Breaking his knees isn't going to change anything," she assured him. "And he isn't worth the jail time."

Another six fries went in. "No body. No jail time."

Catching his eyes, she muttered, "That isn't funny."

"Who's laughing?"

Slamming her elbows on the table, Charley held out one pinkie. "Promise me you won't kill him."

Elvis glanced around. Assured no one was watching, he wrapped his pinkie around hers. "Fine, I promise. But he better hope I never lay eyes on him."

In this, she was certain. "There's no chance of that."

Chapter 24

Dylan's phone had blown up somewhere around two in the morning. Right about the time the guys had informed Mitch that he wasn't on the bus.

Somewhere between booking his plane ticket and checking into the hotel, Dylan had a revelation. Once connected to the hotel Wi-Fi, he did a little digging and did what Mitch claimed couldn't be done. In a matter of minutes, all the contacts were back on his phone.

Casey had been right. Mitch Levine was a lying sack of shit.

Unfortunately, it was also after midnight, and if Charley was as pissed as he guessed she might be, waking her from a sound sleep after a week of silence probably wasn't the best way to go. But the minute he stepped off the direct flight at eight fifteen Monday morning, he'd dialed her number. And got the message that Charley's phone was no longer in service.

Maybe pissed was an understatement.

Since she wasn't on the air until ten, he gave the cab driver the station address and urged him to hurry. As usual, the interstate was loaded with stupid drivers, but the mellow guy in the front seat navigated the traffic like a pro. By eight forty-five, Dylan landed on the doorstep of the Eagle 101.5 studios ready to grovel.

Exiting the elevator on the second floor, he dropped his duffel and stormed the reception desk.

"I need to see Charley Layton, please."

"I'm sorry, sir, but Miss Layton no longer works here."

"What?" he exploded, slapping his hands on the counter. "There has to be a mistake."

The receptionist shoved her glasses up on her nose as she rolled backward, putting more distance between them. "There's no mistake. Miss Layton is no longer employed here."

"Did you fire her?"

What could she possibly have done? Charley was the best damn personality the place had, and that included Ruby Barnett.

"No, she quit over the weekend."

There was no way Charley would quit this job. Not unless something was really wrong. Dylan paced to the elevator and back. He'd let the cab driver go, which would mean calling another to get to Charley's apartment. And then he remembered the other half of that apartment was in this building.

"Then I need to talk to Matty," he said. "Matty Jacobs. She still works here, right?"

"Yes, she does." Rolling herself close enough to the desk to dial the phone, the dark-haired woman let Matty know she had a visitor and then hung up, saying, "She'll be right up."

Grateful to finally get some cooperation, Dylan said, "Thank you," and returned to pacing the small lobby space.

"Who is it, Wendy?" Matty asked as she stepped through the connecting door. Upon spotting Dylan, her eyes went wide. "What are you doing here? You're supposed to be on tour."

"I am," he replied. "Where's Charley?"

"Why do you care?" she snapped.

"What do you mean . . ." Dylan shoved the balls of his hands against his sandy eyes. "Matty, I love her. I can explain why I haven't called."

Turning her back on him, the blonde sauntered back through the door. "Too late for that."

On the verge of begging, he yelled, "Jesus Christ, Matty, at least tell me if she's okay. I need to know!"

The blonde spun his way. "Wendy, is the small conference room available?"

The receptionist flipped open a binder. "Yes, it's open."

With an icy glare, Matty locked eyes with Dylan. "Follow me."

Leaving his bag behind, he did as ordered. Not far from the entrance, she turned left into a tiny meeting room. The moment the door clicked shut, she said, "Charley is as fine as she can be in her condition."

"What condition? What happened at the doctor visit? Is she sick?"

Sculpted brows arched. "Don't play stupid, Dylan. I know she told you. I was there."

"Told me what? I haven't talked to Charley since the night before she went to see the doctor."

"She called you on Saturday."

"Saturday?" He'd gotten his phone back that day, but Charley hadn't called him. "I'm telling you, I haven't talked to her in a week."

Matty threw her hands in the air. "She was standing in my kitchen. She called from my cell, because clearly you'd blocked her number."

"I haven't blocked any numbers," he growled. "My phone disappeared Tuesday night during the DC show. I left it on the speaker when I went out to perform, and when I came back, it was gone." Dylan dragged his new phone from his pocket. "Look, I'll show you. There are no calls on Saturday."

Skeptical, she watched over his shoulder as he slid through the screens.

"You must have deleted the call."

Like an unexpected left hook, the truth smacked him in the face. "Matty, what time did Charley call me?"

"I don't know. Ten in the morning?"

"That was eleven in New York. Mitch didn't give me the phone until after noon."

Crossing her arms, she said, "Your manager?"

"Ex-manager," Dylan corrected. "Charley must have talked to him. Did she try to contact me at all on Tuesday, after she left the doctor's office?"

Coming around, Matty dropped into a chair. "She sent you text messages all week. You never responded."

"I never saw those messages," he assured her. "Without my phone, I didn't know her number. Once we were on the road to New York, I had to wait until we got there to get another phone."

Matty rocked the meeting chair. "But what about Friday night? You were with some other girl."

"Denise Halliday is a backup singer for Wes Tillman. She's happily engaged to a woman named Laura."

Finally convinced, Matty rose from her chair. "You really don't know, do you?"

"Know what? Is Charley okay?"

Grabbing a station notepad left in the middle of the table, she pulled a pen from her pocket and wrote something down.

"She's back in Kentucky. The phone number is on my fridge, but I remember the address." Finishing the note, she passed it his way. "It's a two-and-a-half-hour drive. You can be there by lunchtime."

Dylan planted a quick kiss on Matty's cheek. "Thank you."

"Grandpa, I am not going to the press." Charley had made this statement three times since confessing all the day before. "One of us losing a career is more than enough."

"That boy needs to know there are consequences for this sort of thing."

"That boy is a grown man who knows exactly what the consequences are, and he wants nothing to do with them."

"Aw," the old man murmured. "You know what I mean."

Charley placed a kiss on her grandfather's cheek as she passed him by at the table. "I do know what you mean. But I've told you. I refuse to be *that* girl. I'll have a hard enough time explaining the situation to the locals. The last thing I want is my name splashed across the headlines as the woman who got knocked up by a smooth-talking singer on the night she met him."

"The night you met him?" Grandpa railed, and Charley cringed. She'd left that tidbit out until now.

"Me and my big mouth," she mumbled. "I'm not in the mood for a lecture. Karma is punishing me enough for my misdeeds." Immediately, she regretted her choice of words. A baby should never be considered a punishment. "I don't mean that. I mean . . ."

Gramps took her hand in his. "I understand. But you shouldn't have to do this alone."

"Mama did it alone," she pointed out. "I turned out fine."

"Your mama had me and Grandma, and for a while there, you were anything but fine."

A girl who loses her mother at the age of sixteen can go one of two ways. Charley went the wrong one.

Flattening the four hairs atop his head, she said, "That was a minor blip. And I came around soon enough."

"Not soon enough to spare your grandmother and me several sleepless nights."

Hand on her hip, she said, "Is this give-Charley-a-hard-time day? Because I have plenty of unpacking to do."

Grandpa rose from the table. "I'll leave you alone. I've got chores to do anyway. That hay ain't going to cut itself."

"Let Elvis do the heavy lifting," she ordered. "And I'll have lunch ready at eleven thirty. Don't be late."

Dylan thought he'd grown up in the country, but finding Charley's home in Kentucky proved him wrong.

He'd gotten lost twice trying to find Welcome Home Road, which turned out to be a quarter-mile narrow dirt lane canopied by overgrown trees and populated by the occasional cow. The moment Dylan started looking for a place to turn around, the foliage cleared to reveal a one-story farmhouse set high off the ground with a wraparound porch and three dogs lazing on the steps. Except for one crooked shutter, the place appeared to be well maintained.

An ancient Chrysler pickup, two four-wheelers, and Charley's Bronco crowded the gravel patch to the right of the house. Dylan parked his truck in the last remaining spot and marched toward the porch, wishing he'd have stopped for flowers.

Not that Charley was the flowers type, but showing up empty-handed felt lazy. Based on his brief visit with Matty, he knew two things—Charley thought she'd talked to Dylan two days ago, and she believed the crap about him and Denise. Add the lack of contact over the last week, and his initial reception was sure to be on the frosty side.

He didn't blame her, but Dylan would not be leaving this farm until he'd won Charley back. Whether he'd miss the show in Billings to make that happen, he hadn't decided. A lot of people would be thoroughly screwed if he did. But music was a job. Something he'd be lucky to do for the next couple of decades. Charley would be forever if he pulled this off.

None of the dogs so much as flinched as he climbed the stairs. Three quick knocks on the screen door and Dylan stepped back to wait, hoping her grandfather wasn't the shoot-'em-first-ask-questions-later kind of guy. As the seconds ticked by, Dylan shifted left to peer in a window when the door opened. What he turned back to see dropped his jaw. A monolith of epic proportions filled the doorway, clad in dirt-stained overalls, dust-covered boots, and a sweat-stained John Deere cap. Dylan didn't fear many men, but this one knocked him speechless for a good five seconds.

"You lost?" the stranger offered in greeting, eying him up and down, clearly unimpressed.

Finding his tongue, he said, "I need to talk to Charley. Is she here?"

"If you're who I think you are, you've got a lot of nerve for a pansy-ass dipshit."

Squinting, Dylan said, "I'm going to take that as a yes. Could you let her know I'm here, please?"

The big guy stepped through the door with a growl. "Are you Monroe? I need to make sure before I pulverize the wrong guy."

Pushing his luck, Dylan said the first thing that came to mind. "That's a big word, buddy. I'm impressed."

Without warning, a muscled arm shot out, and fingers like a vise grip locked around Dylan's throat. He clenched at the attacking appendage as his oxygen supply was cut off.

"Who is it, Elvis?" Charley said, arriving at the door in time to see Dylan's feet come off the ground. "Dammit, Elvis! You promised you wouldn't hurt him!"

"Nope," he heard the giant say over the ringing in his ears. "Promised I wouldn't kill him. Didn't say nothing about hurting the son of a bitch."

Unappreciative of the insult to his mother, Dylan swung his weight enough to make the buffoon bend his elbow, and with one quick thrust, he drove the ball of his hand into Elvis's nose. The strangle-hold released, air filled Dylan's lungs, and the porch buckled when six and a half feet of angry man hit his knees.

Charley crossed the distance to her protector and used the kitchen towel slung over her shoulder to stop the bleeding.

"Why do men have to be idiots all the time?" she asked no one in particular.

"No," Dylan wheezed, lungs burning and ego bruised. "Don't worry about me. I'm okay."

Leaving Elvis to attend his own injury, she checked Dylan's neck. "That's going to leave a mark."

Incredulous, he stared at her. "You think?"

"Where did you learn to do that nose thing?" she asked.

Dylan leaned on the porch rail. "Fourteen years of tae kwon do. Jesus, Charley. You never said you had a brother the size of a freight train."

"Elvis isn't my brother. He lives on the farm next door." Gentle fingers touched his throat, and Dylan failed to smother the wince. "We grew up together, and he's a little protective of me."

"Yeah. I noticed."

"You broke my nose," Elvis accused, rising to his feet. "You're a dead man."

"No one is dying today," Charley declared. "Elvis, go get some ice for your nose." Turning to Dylan, she said, "What are you doing here?"

Straightening his twisted shirt, he replied, "I came to explain."

"Explain what?"

"Why I went silent a week ago. The truth about those pictures of me and Denise. All of it."

Charley crossed her arms. "So her name is Denise?"

"Yeah, and she's a friend."

"Does she know that?"

"Of course she knows that. And so does her girlfriend."

The arms dropped. "You mean . . ."

"Yes. And I'll tell you everything else, too. But I'm going to need some water first." Dylan wiped his forehead with his sleeve. "Does that dude lift tractors in his spare time?"

She ignored the question and stomped back to the screen door. "Grandpa is in the kitchen, and he isn't much happier with you than Elvis is. I suggest you take a seat in the living room, and I'll be back with your water."

The door slammed shut behind her, leaving Dylan alone on the porch.

Chapter 25

Charley nearly fainted when she saw Dylan on the porch, and not only because his face had gone purple thanks to Elvis's overzealous greeting.

The possibility of him eventually looking her up was always there. She hadn't expected *eventually* to be less than twenty-four hours after she left town. Which reminded her, the man was supposed to be on tour. The next show on the schedule was Kansas City in two days. Last she checked, KC was a long way from Kentucky.

"That bastard broke my nose," Elvis repeated.

"Language," Maynard Layton snapped. "Not in my house, boy."

His tone let Charley know that Grandpa wasn't pleased about their visitor and was taking his annoyance out on poor Elvis.

"You nearly killed him, Elvis. He hit you in self-defense." Pulling a bottle of water from the fridge, she said, "We'll be in the front room. The less you two butt in, the quicker I can get him out of here."

And she had no doubt Dylan would be leaving within the hour. Regardless of his innocence regarding the new love situation, he'd ignored Charley for a week and stayed silent upon learning of his impending fatherhood. Neither of those actions would be so easily excused. Lingering outside the kitchen, she took several deep breaths to quell her nausea. The morning sickness had settled into a pattern—first thing when she woke and again about an hour after every meal. The baby seemed displeased with both an empty stomach and a full one.

Her heart wasn't so easy to calm. Charley hadn't missed the tired eyes or the stubble-covered chin. Dylan's clothes were wrinkled, which never happened, and his words carried the determination he brought to every challenge. To her abject disappointment, she still loved the jerk more than anything. But that didn't mean she'd forgive him.

"Here's your water," she said as she entered the room, keeping her voice as devoid of emotion as possible. The last thing Charley needed was a blubbering cry right now.

"Thank you." Dylan accepted the drink and downed half the bottle as she settled in Granny's old Victorian chair, hoping the older woman's spirit would provide the strength she needed to get through this.

Replacing the cap on the bottle, he set it on a coaster on the oval coffee table. "This is going to sound like a crazy story," he started, "but it's the truth. A week ago tomorrow night, I lost my phone."

A likely story, she thought, but held her tongue.

"I had an argument with Mitch," Dylan said, pacing the small space. "About you and me. That's when I realized his issue wasn't about keeping up appearances for the article. Mitch flat-out didn't want me dating anyone and would keep throwing up road blocks to get his way." Pointing at her, he insisted, "I told him to stay out of my personal life. That you and I were going to be together whether he liked it or not."

"But we aren't together anymore," Charley reminded him.

"Yes, we are." As if searching to find his place, Dylan scratched his hatless head and returned to pacing. "The guys were already heading for the stage while I was talking to Mitch, so I set my phone behind a speaker and went out to do my job. Only when I came back, the phone was gone."

"Gone?" she repeated.

"I told you it sounds crazy. I looked everywhere. Asked the crew, let Fran the tour manager know to keep an eye out for it, but the thing never turned up." Finally taking a seat on the sofa, he added, "I have a feeling it's buried in Mitch's bags somewhere."

Charley leaned her elbows on her knees. "Let me get this straight. You think your manager stole your phone?"

"I'd bet my Gibson on it."

"But why? All you had to do was get a new one."

"Exactly. Which he assured me he'd do, but we pulled out of DC hours later bound for New York City, and he'd booked me solid for the next two days with interviews, radio visits, and previously unscheduled meet and greets." Growing more agitated, Dylan returned to his feet. "By Friday night I was tired of the excuses and said I'd get my own damn phone, but Mitch promised I'd have a new one in my hand the next day."

Which explained why he hadn't returned any of Charley's messages through the week, but not his silence on the phone Saturday morning.

"Why didn't you call me once you had the phone?"

"Because I didn't have my contacts. Mitch claimed the woman at the phone store searched my account and found no data."

Convenient. And totally implausible.

"None of this changes anything," she said, coming to her feet. "You still got your phone back on Saturday in time for me to call and tell you that I'm pregnant. And you said *nothing*. You left me to deal with the situation on my own, believing you'd already moved on to another woman. What excuse do you have for that? Because I can't think of a single one that would make this all okay."

Dylan's ass hit the coffee table. "You're what?"

"You answered the phone, so don't play dumb with me."

"Your condition," he whispered to the floor. "That's what she meant."

Feeling the now familiar tingle behind her eyes, Charley spoke faster. "It's not a condition. It's a baby. And I know you don't want kids, and that's fine. Because me and this baby don't need anything from you." Breaking for the doorway, she willed the tears to wait. "You shouldn't have come here, Dylan. Go back to your tour and your fans and leave me alone."

"Wait!" He cut her off before she reached the hall. "Charley, you have to listen to me. I didn't get that call. Honey, I had no idea we were going to have a baby."

Charley jerked her arm free. "But you answered. I blurted out everything, and you sat there, silent, like it didn't matter at all. Like I didn't matter."

"You do matter. Charley, look at me." Dylan cupped her face in his hands, his gray eyes blurry through the tears. "I believe you that someone answered that call, but I swear that it wasn't me. Matty said you called that morning, but Mitch didn't give me the phone until after twelve o'clock. I'd give anything to have been there for that call. I'd do anything to change the last week, but I can't, baby. I can only make it right from now on. Let me do that."

Her head said to believe him, but her heart said no. This wasn't only about her anymore. Charley's father had walked away without a second thought, and she'd had to grow up with that memory in her head. Knowing he didn't want her. No child of hers would endure that.

"You told me that night in the park that you don't want kids. The mere mention of them nearly sent you running," she snarled. "Don't stand here and tell me that's different now."

Releasing his hold, Dylan slammed his hands into his hair and spun away. "I don't know. I don't know how I feel about a baby. You've had a week to process this. I've had sixty seconds. But dammit, I love you, Charley. So what if it freaks me out? Too damn bad. We're in this together, and I'm not leaving this farm until I know that this is fixed. Until you tell me that you love me, and that you'll come back to

Nashville, and we'll face whatever comes next together. Because I don't want to live without you. Just come back."

Charley blotted her eyes with the back of her hand. "Do you mean all that?"

Dylan pulled her into his arms. "If you aren't scared, you aren't living, right? I can't think of anything scarier than this, darling. But it's a good scary."

Relief washed over her as she burrowed against his chest, grasping his shirt in her hands. "If you ever lose your phone again, I'll sic Elvis on you."

Laughter vibrating through his chest, he replied, "And I'll gladly take the beating."

Dylan may have won back his girl, but her family was a different matter. Elvis stared him down through dinner, through two black eyes and a cotton-stuffed nose. First chance he got, there would be a call of thanks to his parents. They would be happy to hear all that money for tae kwon do lessons had finally paid off.

Charley's grandfather proved harder to read. A man of few words, at least in Dylan's direction, he was polite and welcoming without being friendly. Not unexpected, since a man he didn't know, who happened to get his granddaughter pregnant, had shown up on his doorstep without warning. In the same position, Dylan would likely respond the same way.

And then he realized he could have a daughter of his own this time next year. A helpless little thing fully dependent on him. With a smile, he changed that thought. No daughter of Charley's would ever be helpless.

"What's the grin for?" Mr. Layton asked.

Charley had suggested he call her grandfather Maynard, but Dylan knew he hadn't earned that right yet. He'd been given a dusty room above the garage for the night, and he'd been escorted to his temporary quarters by the older man. Likely preferring not to have his grand-daughter alone with her wayward beau in the vicinity of a bed.

"It's been a good day, sir. Thinking about how lucky I am."

An inaudible grumble served as a reply as he tossed sheets and a blanket on an uncomfortable-looking cot.

"I'm guessing you don't think much of me right now, but I do love your granddaughter."

"So you say."

"I plan to take care of her."

"So I hear."

This was going well.

"She's a special girl."

Deep-green eyes locked with Dylan's. "Son, the fact that you're here instead of off gallivanting on that big tour bus of yours tells me all I need to know. I haven't seen much to be impressed with, but Charley seems to think you're the best thing since the cotton gin, and I trust her judgment. But I'll tell you this. You hurt my girl again and Elvis will be the least of your problems." Waving a finger toward the far window, he went on. "I've got a hundred and sixty acres out there. Lots of nooks and crannies that no one knows about but me. Remember that."

Now he knew where Charley got her gumption.

"Yes, sir." Dylan nodded, believing every unspoken word the man said. Not that he needed a threat to be good to Charley, but since he had no desire to become fertilizer before his time, he acknowledged the unnecessary warning with the proper respect.

Message conveyed, the country gentleman bid him goodnight, leaving Dylan to make the bed himself. After handling the necessaries in the tiny washroom in the corner, he slipped off his boots and lowered him-self to the cot. Layton probably assumed these sleeping arrangements would be uncomfortable for the fancy singing cowboy, but Maynard had clearly never had to sleep on a tour bus before.

Dylan stared at the wooden beams crisscrossing the ceiling for several minutes before his eyes grew heavy. In his mind, a melody bloomed to life, and then lyrics fell into place.

> To the ends of the earth,
> The four corners of the world,
> I'd run through hell and face the fire
> For only one girl.
>
> She's a beauty to behold,
> An angel I don't deserve.
> She's a devil in black lace,
> With all the right curves.

Reaching for his phone to type in the words, Dylan caught the soft sound of a closing door.

"Hello?" he called, and saw a familiar figure reach the top of the stairs. "Well, hello," he repeated, abandoning the phone.

Charley shushed him as he pounded across the floor to meet her. "Grandpa has ears like a bat."

"Good for him."

Sweeping her off her feet, Dylan took her mouth with his, kissing her the way he'd wanted to all afternoon. She melted against him, and his body hardened in response. Tasting. Touching. They made up for lost time, holding each other as if they might never have another chance. For the rest of his days, Dylan would never get enough of this woman.

Pulling away, she buried her fingers in his hair as he let her feet touch the floor. "I don't have much time. I couldn't bear knowing you were up here and not come to say goodnight."

"Stay," he said, nibbling her left earlobe. "I'll have you back in your bed by morning."

"No more sneaking around," she said, and he knew she didn't mean only tonight. "What are you going to tell Mitch?"

"What I should have told him a long time ago. But I don't want to talk about Mitch right now."

Picking her up once more, Dylan carried Charley to the cot and lowered himself down beside her. The ancient piece creaked in displeasure.

"I'm not sure this can hold us both," she mumbled.

"Then let it break. I'll sleep on the floor, so long as you're beside me."

Charley kissed him again, her touch laced with doubts and trust, concerns and absolute faith. She humbled him, aroused him, and scared him half to death. A combination he never thought he'd find.

"Thank you," he said, rubbing a thumb along her cheek.

"For what?" she whispered.

"For loving me. God knows I don't deserve you."

Laying a slender finger against his lips, she closed her eyes. "You deserve better than me, Dylan. But I'll fight any girl who tries to take you."

He tucked her head beneath his chin. "I don't want any other girl. I've already got the best right here."

As she sighed, relaxing in his arms, warm breath danced across his chest, and soon she dozed off. Content to let her sleep, Dylan reached for his phone and quietly finished the song.

Chapter 26

Charley clung tightly to Dylan's hand as they entered the staging area of the Rimrock Arena in Billings, Montana. They'd spent the last three days back in Nashville, moving her things into Dylan's apartment, and moving Casey and Pamela's things into the high-rise condo downtown. The sweet hairdresser had been in awe when she'd laid eyes on her new digs, running to the balcony and tossing her hands in the air like a reenactment from *Titanic*.

Though her morning sickness had begun to fade, Charley's fear of heights had not, so she remained safely inside.

Grandpa had been sorry to see her go after such a short stay, but he'd given them both his blessing, and even let Dylan sleep in the house on the last night. Elvis was breathing better, and after a day of Dylan's help stacking hay bales, in which no one died or cried "uncle," he'd agreed not to hurt the "puny little singer." His words.

Willoughby had been more than willing to give Charley her job back, and Matty had insisted that Elvis crash at her place after driving Charley's furniture back to town. What went on during his visit, Charley didn't want to know. But Elvis stayed an extra two days, much to Grandpa's annoyance, since, as he repeated, the hay wasn't going to cut itself.

The impending confrontation was the last step before the happy couple could focus on the future. The guys in the band, of course, knew that Dylan would arrive in time for the show, but they'd purposely left Mitch in the dark. Until now.

As they entered the large dining room at the end of the corridor, which served as the general backstage area, they heard the stressed-out manager yell into his phone. "I don't know where the hell he is. That's why I'm calling you. Aren't the police supposed to find missing persons?"

"You looking for me?" Dylan drawled, keeping Charley close by his side.

Mitch looked up with relief that turned to fury the moment he spotted his client's companion.

"Are you fucking kidding me? I've been searching high and low for you for four days, and you've been off getting a piece of ass the whole time?"

Dylan's grip tightened. "You don't need to search anymore."

The older man looked around in stunned disbelief. "That shit don't fly, Monroe. You've got obligations. You're on tour, dammit. Where do you get off disappearing like that?"

Charley longed to scream in Dylan's defense, but she'd promised to let him handle the situation his own way.

"The guys knew where I was the whole time. And so did Fran."

Bloodshot eyes narrowed. "And you didn't see any need to tell me?"

"Nope," Dylan said. "No need at all."

"Now you listen here, boy—"

"I'm not your boy," he warned, stepping forward. "And you aren't my manager anymore. Consider this your official notice. You're fired."

"Bullshit," Mitch spat. "I've got a contract that says otherwise."

Jaw clenched, Dylan shook his head. "And I've got a lawyer who says your contract isn't worth shit. Go ahead and fight me. I can afford the fees. Can you?"

One of their tasks upon returning to Nashville had been to do a little research on Mitch Levine. Turned out he was buried in debt. They'd also learned that he'd transferred substantial sums out of Dylan's accounts and into his own. The cheat would learn very soon that charges were pending.

A crowd had gathered to witness the confrontation, and Mitch didn't seem to appreciate the audience. "What are you looking at?"

"Nothing," replied Casey, appearing through the crowd with Pam by his side, Easton and Lance close behind. "Abso-fucking-lutely nothing."

Lip quivering in anger, the old man pointed a finger at Dylan. "This isn't over."

"Yes, it is," Charley cut in. "Now get out of this building. You're not wanted here anymore."

Making one fatal mistake, Mitch lunged her way. "You little bitch—"

He never saw the punch coming. The crowd stood in stunned silence as Charley shook her hand. "That hurt like hell, but it was totally worth it."

Dylan smiled with pride. "That's my girl."

The SOS call from Mitch Levine had been vague at best. The message had come at nine Clay's time. He'd been in the shower after a workout and hadn't listened to the voice mail until nearly ten.

"I don't know where the hell Dylan is," Mitch said. "Shit is about to blow up on this tour. Get your ass out here."

Clay didn't appreciate being told where to carry his ass, but his only artist going AWOL on a tour took precedence. A quick search revealed a not-surprising reality. Flights from Nashville to Billings, Montana, departed two times a day—first thing in the morning, and late afternoon. The first was no longer an option, and the second wouldn't get him there before showtime. Calling in a favor, he'd chartered a private jet to leave before noon.

By the time he entered the Rimrock Arena, he was both relieved and annoyed to find Dylan Monroe standing around with his bandmates.

"I thought you were missing," he said, interrupting what looked to be a celebration.

Dylan shook his head. "Nope. I'm right here."

If this was some kind of a joke, Clay wasn't laughing. "Then why did your manager leave me a message saying you weren't?"

"Right." The singer turned to his friends. "Could you excuse us for a minute?"

"No problem, man," Casey replied, saluting Clay with his beer. "Take all the time you need."

Once they were alone, he waited impatiently for an explanation.

"There's something you should know about Mitch Levine," Dylan said.

"What's that?"

"He's no longer my manager."

An unexpected turn of events.

"Since when?"

"About an hour ago."

Clay crossed his arms. Much had happened while he'd been thirty thousand feet up. "Is there someone else I'll be dealing with?"

Dylan shared a smile that carried no worries. Odd for an artist who'd just fired his representative. "Not yet. But Wes is putting me in touch with his manager. Seems to think we might be a good fit."

Samantha Walters was a powerful name in Nashville. She'd been the driving force behind more than one superstar in the industry, and she was known as a tough negotiator for her clients. Clay had encountered her on only one contract with Foxfire, and by the time they'd hashed out the deal, Samantha's client had received the most generous offer in the label's history.

"That would be quite a score," Clay responded.

"Nothing is a guarantee," the sensible young man replied. "But I'm hopeful."

Knowing without a doubt that Shooting Stars would be offering Dylan another deal, he took the opportunity to broach what he assumed to be a touchy subject.

"I hear you've been writing songs."

Dylan sobered. "From who?"

Clay shook his head. "Doesn't matter. I made some calls and got a copy of your first album. The one that never got released."

"Why?" he asked. "That album is crap."

Ignoring the comment, he said, "Every song on that album is one of yours."

The singer took a long swig from his beer before answering. "Which explains the crap part."

"Dylan, those songs aren't bad. The arrangements are too pop, and the production is way overdone, but that's on the producer, not the songwriter."

"That's not how the label saw it."

Getting to the point, Clay said, "Well, that's how I see it. I say we recut it. Maybe not every song, but the best ones. New arrangements. Better producer. Add in new material, and I believe you could have a gold album on your hands."

As if the offer might be too good to be true, Dylan eyed him with caution. "Are you serious?"

"I don't kid about making records."

"And you want *my* songs?"

"I do." He nodded. "And so do the fans. You're talented, Dylan. You have something to say. Let them hear it."

"All right then," he replied, smile back in place. "Let's do it."

Exactly seven weeks later, a mere two weeks before Christmas, in a heated tent tucked into a corner of Centennial Park, Charlotte Marie Layton became Mrs. Dylan Cavanaugh Monroe in front of twenty of their closest friends and family. The bride wore cowboy boots beneath her simple gown, and the groom couldn't take his eyes off her.

"You know what this means," Dylan whispered as they swayed on the dance floor.

"That I can finally have a piece of that cake?" Charley asked.

She'd been attacking anything sweet for the last month, claiming the baby had a sweet tooth. When Dylan had pointed out that the baby didn't have any teeth yet, she turned surly and refused to kiss him for a painful twenty minutes.

"Almost," he replied. "Now that we've tied the knot, I can officially call you my woman."

Slender brows arched high. "Oh, I don't think so. You married me. You didn't buy me."

"And you married me." Dylan placed a kiss on the tip of her nose. "I'm still in shock about that."

Her laughter would always be music to his ears. "Don't be a nut. I *had* to marry you, remember?"

Dylan pulled back, but not too far. "Are you saying you wouldn't have married me without that bun in the oven?"

Charley sighed. "No. I'm not saying that. You told me once that you fell in love with me that night you met me."

"I did," he confirmed.

"Do you know when I fell in love with you?"

"When I got you in to meet Jack Austin?"

She shook her head. "Uh-uh. When you sang me a song."

"On the night we met?" Dylan asked.

"That's right. So it looks like we fell in love at about the same time."

Remembering the evening well, he pressed his lips against her ear. "Then why did you leave?"

"Because I was scared," she replied, resting her chin on his chest. "You made me want things I'd never wanted before."

"How about now? Are you still scared?"

She drew back to smile into his eyes. "If you aren't scared, you aren't living, right? And I plan to live with you for the rest of my life."

The music faded to an end as he said, "That's good. Because I'm never letting you go."

Someone tapped a microphone, causing feedback that earned a groan from the crowd.

"Sorry about that," Matty said. "Microphones aren't my thing. But I've been told to announce that it's time to cut the cake!"

"Finally!" Charley cried, dragging Dylan to the small round table in the corner.

But before she could grab the knife, he said, "Not yet. There's something I need to say first."

"You're killing me, Monroe."

"You'll like this, Mrs. Monroe." He turned to the crowd. "Gather round everyone. I have a secret to share."

Charley squeezed his hand. "What secret?"

Dylan continued to address their friends and family. "As you all know, my wife and I are expecting a baby in May. And on Monday, we're scheduled to find out what we're having—a boy or a girl. What my wife doesn't know is that I bribed the doc and got the answer early."

"You what?" she snapped, dropping his hand. "That's so unfair!"

"Hold on," he said, tucking her against his side. "I thought it might be fun if we all found out together. The sex was written in an envelope that went straight to the bakery."

"Then you don't know?" Charley asked.

"No," he replied. "I don't." Raising his voice for the crowd, he explained, "The top layer of the cake is either pink or blue. Should we dig in and see what we're getting?"

His bride nearly bounced out of her boots. "Yes! Let me at it."

Matty and Pamela, maid of honor and bridesmaid respectively, teamed up to lower the top tier to the table. With knife in hand, Charley and Dylan sliced through the frosting to find a pretty pink sponge.

"Oh my God." Charley turned to Dylan, nearly stabbing him with the long blade. "We're having a girl. Dylan, we're having a girl!"

Removing the knife from her grip, he beamed at his joyful bride. "Looks like we are."

After jumping up and down several times, she leaped into his arms. "I wanted a girl." A quick kiss landed on his neck. "I hope you don't mind." Pulling back, she looked into his eyes. "Are you upset it isn't a boy? We can have a boy later. But I really wanted a girl."

Dylan was still getting used to the idea of one, let alone more down the line.

"I want a healthy baby and mama, and that's all that matters." Turning to their guests, he said, "Now let's play some music!"

Though a DJ had been hired for most of the night, there was no way Dylan wasn't going to climb onstage at his own reception. Their gear had been set up earlier in the day, and the band had done a sound check before the ceremony. Which meant a quick tuning and the concert began.

Charley even got in on the act, as Wes Tillman pulled her onstage and together they belted out an old Conway Twitty and Loretta Lynn classic. To Dylan's surprise, his bride could carry a tune. He beamed with pride as she cut loose, her fear of the spotlight seemingly cured. Which was a good thing, because he planned to drag her down red carpets for years to come.

As he'd once told a reporter—he was a very lucky man.

Epilogue

Charley Monroe had never been so nervous in all her life. Nor had she ever been so big.

Though eight months pregnant, waddling like a drunken penguin, and unable to endure more than four minutes between potty breaks, she refused to miss her husband's first big awards show. Once Shooting Stars had released "Better Than Before" as a single, including Dylan and Charley's impromptu kiss in the video, the heavens opened and Dylan had his first top-ten hit.

The time apart had not been fun, but he'd completed a six-week, small-venue headlining tour, which had resulted in packed houses from Houston to Hilton Head. And two weeks before the Country Coalition awards, he'd joined the Davis Daniels tour as the second act on the bill. Still an opening gig, but not the opening opener, which was a step up.

Considering Davis Daniels was up for Entertainer of the Year tonight, getting an invite to join his tour had been a huge accomplishment, thanks in no small part to Dylan's new manager, Samantha Walters. She was brilliant and stunningly beautiful, and Charley had liked her from the moment they met. The savvy woman understood the business, supported her new client's family-first policy, and had even sent a beautiful pink bassinet for soon-to-arrive Violet Matilda Monroe.

"Thank goodness your category is the first of the night," Charley whispered to Dylan from their seats in the sixth row. "Violet is dancing 'Cotton-Eyed Joe' on my bladder."

"Maybe she knows something we don't," he replied, squeezing her hand.

This was the only negative to Dylan being nervous. He nearly always crushed her hand in his effort *not* to look nervous. But Charley figured she'd be doing the same to him in four weeks' time when the contractions started rolling in.

When the news had come in January that Dylan had been nominated for Best New Artist, the first thing he'd done had been to kiss his wife. Next, he'd called his bandmates, and then his parents. Once all parties had been notified, he'd settled on the couch with his cell phone, conducting interview after interview with everyone from E! Television to CMT.

And in every one, he thanked his beautiful wife for her love and support.

The memory brought tears to Charley's eyes, which she promptly brushed away. This was not a night for crying. Win or lose, this was a night for celebrating, and though she wouldn't be toasting champagne for many more weeks, Charley would hoot and holler and try to stay awake until the show was over.

"This is so nerve-racking," Pamela whispered beside her. The pretty blonde clung to her fiancé's hand on the other side. "How are you not leaping out of your skin?"

"I'm the size of an aircraft carrier," the expectant mother pointed out. "I'm not leaping anywhere."

Casey shushed them. "Here we go."

Dylan's grip tightened, but his face revealed nothing.

Please let him win, Charley prayed. *Please, please, please.*

"Good luck, buddy," said Clay Benedict, tapping his artist on the shoulder. He and Naomi Mallard were seated behind Dylan and his band, while Samantha Walters had been seated with one of her other artists, who was up for Female Vocalist of the Year.

The artist who'd won Dylan's category the year before announced the nominees, and Dylan had remained stoic as the mobile camera caught him for the big screen. By the time the last nominee was read, Charley had nearly lost feeling in her hand.

"And the winner of Best New Artist is . . ." The envelope was opened. "Dylan Monroe!"

Shock set in first, and then Charley rose to her feet faster than any woman in her condition had a right to.

Dylan wrapped her in his arms and placed a hard kiss on her lips. "We did it, baby. We did it."

"You did it," she said through a joyful sob, hands pressed against his cheeks.

Casey squeezed past Pamela to hug his best friend, Lance and Easton settled for handshakes, and Clay Benedict smacked the winner on the back.

"Congratulations, Monroe. You deserve it."

As Dylan proceeded to the stage to receive his award, Charley clung to Pamela, wiping the tears away as quickly as they came. Though she'd never been a vain woman, the camera hovering two feet to her left meant there would be no ugly crying tonight. Naomi offered a handful of tissues from behind her.

"I can't believe this," Dylan said, award in hand. "Y'all have no idea what this means." The applause faded. "I'm in shock, but I know I need to do this quick. To my parents, who are out there somewhere in this crowd, thank you for always believing in me and encouraging me to chase this crazy dream. To Clay Benedict and my record label, Shooting Stars Records. Samantha Walters, my manager. You are amazing. And to Rock Castle Publishing, with whom I hope to have a long and profitable relationship."

Dylan removed his black hat as the audience laughed.

"Now to the important part." His eyes settled on Charley. "I really do appreciate this award and all the crazy, humbling things that have happened in my short career. But the best thing to happen to me in the last year is meeting my wife. Some of you know her as Charley Layton from Eagle 101.5 here in town, but I know her as the most beautiful woman in the world. The toughest, most interesting person I've ever met. And the mother of my soon-to-be-born daughter."

Lips quivering, he went on.

"Baby, I couldn't have done this without you. You're my rock and the light that keeps me going. On the night we met, you said, 'Sing me a song.' That was the best night of my life, and I intend to keep singing you songs as long as you'll let me." Holding the pretty silver statue in the air, Dylan said, "Thank you so much. I really appreciate this."

Applause filled the room again as Dylan and his presenter were escorted backstage. Twenty minutes later, her husband returned to his seat, award in hand and a stupefied expression on his face.

"Are you okay?" Charley asked with a laugh.

"It hasn't sunk in yet." He settled the statue on the arm between them. "I'm afraid I'm dreaming."

She leaned her head on his shoulder. "No way, honey. You're wide awake."

"Yeah," Dylan mumbled, kissing her hair. "And I'm holding the second-best prize I ever won."

Catching his meaning, Charley hugged his arm tight as she examined the statue. "It really is pretty."

"And heavy." Lifting her chin, he asked, "Did you like my speech? I've been practicing it for a week."

Charley's heart flipped in her chest as a strong foot kicked her in the ribs. "We both liked it," she said, ignoring the pain to lean over and kiss her man.

Acknowledgments

As much as writing is a solitary profession, we never actually create a completed work on our own. Thank you to the team at Montlake Romance, including Alison Dasho, Jessica R. Poore, and the entire Author Relations team, the brilliant minds behind marketing, and the designers who make our books look so good. I also have to send my deepest gratitude to Lauren Plude for helping me whip this story into beautiful shape. And last but never least, to my agent, Nalini Akolekar, and the Spencerhill Agency. You truly are the best.

The following list of amazing and generous women make up the best damn girl squad around: Fran Colley, Marnee Blake, Jessica Ruddick, Kim Law (who let me tag along on her hair appointments just so I could stroll the sidewalks of Music Row), and Maureen Betita. To the Duchesses, Team Awesome, the bloggers who give so much of their time to this genre, and the amazing readers who have changed my life for the better in so many ways. I am more blessed than I could ever properly express.

A few months before starting this book, I moved back to the city of my heart. Nashville is an amazing place, with the amenities of a big city but the heart of a small town. A heart that beats out an endless rhythm of hope and joy as dreamers flock to the bright lights, embracing a cherished musical history and hoping to one day see their own star rise.

As a fellow artist, I understand the drive and the passion. As the former wife of an aspiring musician, I'm also well aware that some dreams don't come true. But they are always worth the effort. I'm grateful that this town took me in more than twenty years ago. And I'm very happy to be back.

Also, that move to Nashville two decades ago brought me the most important person in my life. Thank you, Isabelle, for your endless love and patience and for laughing at my jokes. I grow more proud of you every day.

About the Author

Award-winning author Terri Osburn fell in love with the written word at a young age. Classics like *The Wizard of Oz* and *Little Women* filled her childhood, and the romance genre beckoned during her teen years. In 2007, she put pen to paper to write her own heart-melting love stories, and just five years later, she was named a 2012 finalist for a Romance Writers of America Golden Heart Award. Her debut novel was released a year later. Terri resides in Middle Tennessee with her teenage daughter and a menagerie of high-maintenance pets. To learn more about this international bestselling author, visit her website at www.terriosburn.com.